I COULD NEVER

First Edition

Editing: Jessica Royer Ocken
Proofreading and Formatting: Elaine York, Allusion Publishing
www.allusionpublishing.com
Proofreading: Julia Griffis
Cover Photography: Anders Kavin
Cover Design: Letitia Hasser, RBA Designs

I COULD NEVER

PENELOPE WARD

To my daughter and my godson—
the real-life Scotties

ONE

Carly

"SO YOU DON'T know exactly what you're walking into?" my friend Christina asked.

A deer wandered through the trees in the distance. *You're definitely not in L.A. anymore, Carly.* It hit me for the first time that there could be bears here. New Hampshire was *rural.* I shivered.

"I've only met Scottie a few times," I said, shifting the phone to my other ear. "He seemed really sweet. I'm certain taking care of him will be a challenge, though. I won't know what the heck I'm doing. I've never taken care of anyone in my life, let alone a grown man."

My fiancé, Brad, would've been the one looking after his younger brother himself if he could have. But because he was no longer here, I felt it was my responsibility. Scottie was twenty-three and had severe autism. He was nonverbal and, in many ways, childlike. Brad's father, Wayne, had been Scottie's sole caretaker until he'd passed away after a heart attack last month. And my beloved Brad had died two years ago in a car accident. For the past few weeks, Scottie had been in the temporary care of Wayne's sister, Lorraine, who'd made it clear she wanted nothing to do with looking after Scottie long term.

Christina sighed. "Are you sure about this? It's a huge responsibility."

"It's what Brad would've wanted. There's no way he would've approved of his crazy aunt Lorraine taking care of Scottie. His dad was Scottie's guardian. Since Lorraine is Wayne's next of kin, everyone assumed she'd take on the responsibility. But she's not the right person, and she isn't interested. Wayne probably wasn't too worried—he wasn't even sixty. So there was no plan B besides Lorraine. The first thing she did when I called to check on things was ask if I could come help. She's planning to sleep back at her own house starting tonight, which means I'll be alone with Scottie." I looked over at the house. "Anyway, I have to go. I've been parked in front of the house for two minutes already and need to get inside."

"Okay, well, if you need anything, let me know. I can order stuff and have it shipped to you."

"Thank you. I appreciate that, Christina. But I didn't go to Mars, just New Hampshire." I laughed. "It's only temporary, right? Until I can get him into a group home." Staring off into the adjacent woods, I muttered, "I'll talk to you soon."

"Good luck, Carly."

From the limited research I'd done thus far, I knew the waiting list to get into a supervised adult home could be long, so *temporary* might actually mean years, for all I knew; though I certainly hoped it would be sooner than that.

Exiting my car, I walked over to the front of the small house. I took a deep breath as I readied myself to knock. The wooden log cabin was modest, to say the least. Brad had grown up here in Woodsboro, New Hampshire, a rural New England town. I'd been here with him a few times to visit his dad and brother, but I'd never imagined *I'd* be living here.

After I knocked, Lorraine opened the door almost immediately and let out an exasperated breath. "Oh, thank God!" She moved aside for me to enter. "Do you happen to have one of those hot spots?"

No hello? No how are you?

"Nice to see you, too, Lorraine." I parked my suitcase in a corner and dropped my bag, which made a big thud when it hit the ground.

Scottie was pacing and shaking his tablet around, pointing to the screen.

Lorraine went right on complaining.

"He's been bouncing off the walls because we don't have Internet."

Oh, this is not good. I knew Scottie was totally reliant on his devices. "What's wrong with the Internet?"

"They think it's one of the lines outside. They're not sure how long it will take to fix."

Scottie continued to walk back and forth nervously. With his blond hair and fine features, he reminded me so much of my Brad—the resemblance took my breath away. It was like seeing Brad again, but in the form of an adult child. Brad had been seven years older than

Scottie. Their mom had died of cancer when Brad was eighteen and Scottie was eleven. So life hadn't been easy for this family for a long while. And Scottie's profound autism meant that while he could communicate simply with the aid of devices, he didn't converse or express his feelings verbally. Most of the time, he was in his own world and needed one-on-one care.

I lifted my hand awkwardly to try to get his attention. "Hey, Scottie."

He practically shoved an iPad into my face and pointed to it as if to say, *I don't care who you are, just get this damn thing working.*

"I do have a hot spot," I said. "I'll get it running for you."

Taking out my phone, I scrambled to hook that up. The moment I did, Scottie's screen came alive, and he logged on to whatever site he'd been dying to access. He quickly settled into a spot on the couch.

I turned to Lorraine. "Doesn't take much to please him, huh?"

Rather than respond, she grabbed her coat. "Do you have any questions before I leave, hon?"

She's leaving already? I blinked. "Well, you haven't given me any instructions. I thought we would sit down so you could tell me what he needs, what he likes to eat...stuff like that."

"I made a hair appointment thinking you'd be here a half hour ago, so I do need to rush out for now," she said. "I'm already late, and I don't want to lose my spot. But there's not too much to talk about in terms of what to feed him. Wayne used to make him this one kind of chicken. It was our mother's recipe. It's the only thing Scottie will eat, but it has to be made *very* specifically. I've written down the instructions for you over there on the counter, and I left you with enough for tonight in a Tupperware in the fridge. Made those cutlets a couple days ago. You'll have to make more for tomorrow, though."

I swallowed. I wasn't the greatest cook to begin with, let alone making chicken from scratch for a picky eater. *Lord, help me.* This was going to be a disaster. I'd been counting on the idea of being able to order takeout, at least for the first few days until I got my crap together. *Guess that won't be happening.* "He doesn't eat *anything* else?"

"Only eats that chicken for dinner. And his dessert needs to be lined up just so." She lifted a photo. "I printed this so you can see how it's done and also wrote it down on this sticky."

She handed me the image of a napkin with cookies and other treats arranged in a linear pattern.

"What happens if things aren't lined up correctly?"

"He gets upset, tosses everything on the floor."

"Okay." I gulped. "Well...if the chicken is his dinner, what does he eat during the day?"

"Either more of the same chicken or just crackers and pretzels. His main meal is dinner."

"That doesn't sound very healthy." I frowned. "No vegetables?"

"You could try, but I've never had any luck. He spits them out."

I sighed, turning to where Scottie was sitting on the couch, rocking back and forth as he blasted something on YouTube. At least he was content for the time being.

"Anyway, like I said, I'm late for my appointment. First time I've had a chance to go since I've been staying with Scottie. I'm sure you noticed my roots. You good?"

This woman could not flee the premises fast enough.

"I think so, but can I call you if I have any questions?"

"Of course, sweetheart. Don't hesitate. I'll always be around. I live just a few miles down the road."

I blew out a breath. "Okay."

Before I could say another thing, Lorraine was gone. It felt like a boulder had been placed on my chest.

Feeling lost, I stood in the middle of the house and looked around as jumbled sounds rang out from Scottie's electronics. He must have had three different things playing on as many devices.

The décor in here was dark, from the paneling on the walls to the wrinkled, brown leather furniture. There were only two bedrooms in the one-level, log-cabin-style home. I peeked into one of them and immediately recognized it as Scottie's. There were picture schedules hung up and tons of stickers of cartoon characters I didn't recognize littering the walls, along with one framed picture of Elton John. *Odd.*

I smiled at a photo up on the bureau of Scottie with his brother, Brad. *My Brad.* Looking up at the ceiling, I spoke to my dead fiancé. "I know you would do the same for me. I love you, and I promise to keep him safe until I can find him a good home."

As if someone up above wanted to challenge me on that, I looked through the doorway into the living room and saw Scottie standing on top of the end table by the couch. The table was dainty, and I doubted it could sustain his weight for very long.

I ran out into the living room. "Whoa! You might want to get down from there, buddy!"

He ignored me. Because he didn't talk, I couldn't ask him why he'd decided to do that.

About a minute later, he finally jumped down onto the floor, which caused the entire house to shake. Thankfully, he appeared unscathed. If he'd broken his ankle or something, that would have absolutely sucked. I wiped the sweat off my forehead.

Once Scottie had settled into his seat on the couch again, I went to the kitchen and opened the refrigerator. There wasn't much inside: the Tupperware that contained the chicken and a few large jugs of cranberry juice. I had to assume that was Scottie's favorite drink.

I still had so many questions. Would I take him with me to the grocery store, or was it easier to have groceries delivered? What time did he go to bed? Does he need anything to get to sleep at night? Lorraine was going to be getting a ton of questions from me later, whether she liked it or not.

Somehow, I managed to get through the rest of that afternoon. I mainly sat next to Scottie while he watched his videos or while he played with an app that featured a talking cat that spoke back to you. Since Scottie mainly grunted and hummed into the screen, the cat did the same. I tried to interact with it, but Scottie frowned whenever I joined in—he didn't seem to appreciate my efforts. Pretty sure if he could talk, he'd ask why this dumb bitch had suddenly come to invade his space.

When it was finally time to sit him down to dinner, I tried a few different things to encourage him to leave the couch. Nothing worked until I held up one of the dessert items: an Oreo cookie. He seemed to get the idea and got up to sit at the table in the kitchen.

Scottie immediately picked up one of the pieces of chicken and took a bite. The dessert was lined up just as Lorraine had instructed me to in her note.

Put down one square napkin. At the bottom place two gummy vitamins. Above that, add a cheddar cheese stick. Above that, place four Junior Mints. Then at the very top of the napkin, place two Oreos. His favorite are the double-stuffed.

Thankfully, she'd also left me a shopping list of must-have items.

As Scottie continued to chomp away at the chicken, the doorbell rang.

Hope bloomed in me at the prospect of Lorraine returning. But why would she ring the bell? When I opened, though, my heart skipped a beat as my body filled with dread. Suddenly, this difficult day had gotten a whole lot worse.

What is he doing here?

TWO

Carly

JOSH MATHERS TOWERED over me, smelling like leather, spice, and a hint of cigarettes mixed with the cold, fall air outside.

"What's going on?" I blinked. "Why are you here?"

He walked past me into the living room, rolling a black suitcase behind him. "I came to relieve you."

"Excuse me?"

"I'll be staying with Scottie," he said, without making eye contact. "I was already planning on it. But then I heard you were here and put a rush on things." The jerk finally looked at me with his piercing hazel eyes. "You can go back to La La Land."

I'd only met Brad's best friend a few times. And I sort of despised him, even though I didn't know him very well. But I had a good reason for my disdain. Josh was a player and had been a bad influence on Brad growing up. He was the "wild one" and was always getting the two of them into trouble. I never liked it when Brad went without me to visit Josh in Chicago, either. It wasn't that I didn't trust Brad. I just never knew what his friend might pull while the two of them were inebriated. Josh Mathers was bad news. The idea of entrusting him to take care of Scottie, therefore, seemed ludicrous.

"Relieve me? I just got here today," I said. "But either way, I think it's best for him if I stay."

"I'm sure they taught you a lot in beauty school about how to take care of grown men?"

Placing my hands on my hips, I huffed. "I'm surprised you even remembered what I do for a living. You certainly never made an effort to get to know me when Brad was alive."

"Seriously, Carly?" he snapped back. "You think you're gonna be able to handle him?"

"It's been fine so far." I shrugged.

"You've been here all of what, a couple of hours? It's fine until he has a tantrum and you can't control him." He gave me a onceover. "He's three times your size."

Crossing my arms, I lifted my head high. "Lorraine didn't say she had any issues handling him, and she's no bigger than me."

"She wouldn't have admitted shit to you if it might have discouraged you from coming. She's his guardian on paper, but she's been looking for her ticket out of this responsibility from the moment Wayne died. Did she tell you she had to solicit the neighbor's help last week to get Scottie off the floor?"

I shook my head.

He nodded. "Abe is a friend of my dad's and told him he helped out. Lorraine must've neglected to mention that to you."

"Did she ask *you* to come here?"

"No. Like I said, I've been planning to come back out here to take care of things ever since Wayne's funeral. I just had to tie up some loose ends first."

"Well, you don't need to stay. You obviously have a job and a life back in Chicago."

His eyes narrowed. "And you don't have a life?"

"I decided to put it on hold. My career is a bit more flexible. I work freelance and only take jobs when I want to."

As a contract makeup artist, I often worked on television and movie sets back in California. It was on one such set that I'd met Brad, who'd been a writer on a popular sitcom at the time.

"Well, I primarily work remotely anyway," Josh said. "So it's not a problem for me to be here." He glared at me. "It's what Brad would've wanted."

Moving my shoulders back, I challenged him. "How do you know what Brad would've wanted? Did you discuss this scenario with him? Because last I checked, no one expected Wayne to drop dead at sixty years old."

"We never specifically discussed it, but I mean, come on. You'd only known Brad like what...two years? And maybe met Scottie a few times? Scottie grew up with me around. I'm practically his brother."

"This is not a competition, but since you seem to be making it into one, don't you think if Brad was going to marry me, he would have *also* entrusted me with his brother?"

Josh glared. "Actually, no. He probably knew he could depend on *me* and didn't need to specify anything were something to happen. He knew I'd step in."

I lifted my hands into the air. "Well, I've just uprooted my entire life to move here. Drove all the way across the country. I'm not going anywhere."

Josh glanced at my fingernails. "How exactly do you plan to wipe Scottie's ass with those claws, by the way?"

I looked down at my lavender-colored stiletto nails. In all honesty, I'd never once thought about having to assist Scottie in the bathroom. I suppose it should've dawned on me. But I'd yet to learn everything about what this responsibility entailed. Lorraine had neglected to mention that Scottie wasn't able to fully take care of himself in that area.

Despite inwardly freaking out, I continued to hold my head high. "I'll figure it out." *Fake it till you make it.*

"You likely weren't thinking about that when you asked them to glue those little rhinestones on your nails," he chided. Before I could respond, Josh looked around. "Where *is* Scottie anyway?"

I pointed behind me. "He's eating dinner at the kitchen table."

He looked beyond my shoulders and raised a brow. "You sure about that?"

I turned to find that Scottie had vacated his spot. *Of course!* I was supposed to be keeping a damn eye on him, wasn't I? I hadn't accounted for the unwelcome distraction of Josh Mathers, dickhead extraordinaire.

I ran over to the table.

Half of Scottie's chicken was uneaten, and all of his dessert was gone. But the worst part was that he'd tried to pour himself some cranberry juice—because I'd apparently forgotten to serve it. Now there was juice all over the floor, and the refrigerator door was wide open. First major lesson learned: you can't take your eyes off Scottie for even a few minutes.

"Shit," I muttered.

"You know what? You're right." Josh grinned smugly. "Looks like you have *everything* under control."

I rolled my eyes. This man had been here a matter of minutes, and he'd managed to get so far under my skin, it felt like it was crawling.

There was a humming sound coming from Wayne's bedroom, which was just off the kitchen. Josh followed me in there, and we found Scottie lying calmly on the bed, watching something on his iPad as if he hadn't just destroyed the kitchen.

"Come on, Scottie," I said, reaching out. "You need to wash your hands. I'm sure they're greasy."

He didn't budge.

Josh moved past me and crawled onto the bed. "Let's go, dude," he said sternly. "Time to wash your hands."

When Scottie got a look at Josh, he started to laugh and bounced on the mattress. He was beaming, actually. I couldn't help but smile, even if this meant Josh clearly had one advantage over me: Scottie immediately took to him.

Josh's face lit up. "You missed me, huh?"

Scottie wrapped his arm around Josh's neck, putting him in a chokehold before sniffing the man's lustrous hair.

"Okay, buddy," Josh said. "You got a good sniff of me. That's enough."

"Does he always sniff you like that?"

"He likes my hair. Always has."

I had to admit, it was a nice head of hair—for an asshole. Shiny, thick, and chestnut brown. It was a bit longer than I remembered from the last time I'd seen Josh—at Brad's burial.

Scottie suddenly grabbed Josh by the balls.

My jaw dropped. *Good. I could kiss you right now for that, Scottie.*

"Nope. I need those," Josh coughed out. "Let 'em go."

Covering my mouth, I laughed into my hand. This was definitely the highlight of a long day.

While Scottie did eventually let go of Josh's sack, he re-wrapped his arm around his neck and proceeded to wrestle him until he had Josh pinned. Josh was a big guy, but Scottie was even bigger.

After Josh finally managed to break free, he stood up from the bed, his hair all messed up.

"So much for being a big, strong man who can handle him, huh?" I cracked.

Josh shot me a death stare.

Carly: One.

Josh: Zero.

THREE

Carly

WITH NO HEAT currently on, the house was growing more frigid than the vibe between me and my apparent new roommate. So, Josh ventured out to the store to get wooden pellets for the pellet stove.

While he was handling that, I struggled to give Scottie a bath, which left me looking like I'd won a wet-T-shirt contest. Scottie seemed to think the bathtub was a waterslide. He kept gliding his body from the back of the tub to the front, and each time he did it, a deluge of water hit me and the floor. We won't mention the stiffy he got while I was washing his nether regions, either.

It took a while to get Scottie to calm down enough to go to bed, too. It now made sense why he had a mattress on the floor rather than on a bedframe. He would've broken the bed, considering all the jumping he liked to do.

I exited Scottie's bedroom after getting him settled and plopped down on the couch, exhausted already and feeling overwhelmed. Not only was my first night an epic failure, but it seemed Josh would be here to witness this disaster moving forward. *Is he really staying?* Even though it might be helpful to have a second set of hands, the idea of him being here made me uneasy. Although, maybe he wasn't planning on sleeping here? I decided to corner him to clarify his plans. I could see he'd gotten the pellet stove going, but he was nowhere to be found. Had he left the premises again? *Could I be that lucky?*

A minute later, though, Josh came in from outside, smelling like cigarettes.

I stood and got straight to the point. "So..." I rubbed my hands together. "What's the deal? There's only one bedroom besides Scottie's. So..."

"Yeah." He nodded. "I'll take the couch—until you decide to go back home. Which I still think would be wise, since you're out of your element."

"I told you, I'm not going anywhere."

"Come on, Carly. You're a virtual stranger to him. You don't belong here."

"A virtual stranger is better than a bad influence," I spat.

"You think I'm a bad influence on Scottie? What... am I gonna bring women over and get him drunk? Get your head out of your ass, Miss Righteous. I wouldn't do anything to put him in harm's way." He looked down at my shirt. "You take a bath *with* him or something? Why are you all wet?"

"If you knew as much about him as you claim to, you'd know the answer to that. He thinks the bathtub is a Slip 'N Slide." I sniffed the air. "You reek of cigarettes. I hope you don't think you're gonna be smoking around him."

Josh squinted. "You *do* know Wayne smoked, right?"

"Well, I don't care. No one should be breathing that stuff in."

"I'm trying to quit," he muttered. "I was doing great until coming home. The second I landed in New Hampshire, I just..." He sighed rather than finish his sentence.

"Well, *try to quit* outside—not in this house or around Scottie."

"Did you *not* see that I was just outside?"

"Keep it that way," I scolded.

Josh feigned a smile. "You know where you won't have to worry about my smoking?"

"Where?"

He gritted his teeth. "Back in California."

"You think you're funny?"

"I'm not trying to be." He cocked his head. "Are you saying I am?"

"How do you think Brad would feel about you making a mockery of this situation?"

"I'm making a mockery? You look like you escaped the Titanic. And as for Brad, he was too polite to have told you that you're out of your league. He would be secretly thanking me for attempting to give you a ticket out."

The sound of Scottie screeching from his bedroom interrupted our bickering.

We ran in there to find he'd taken the stuffing out of one of his pillows. Feathers were flying everywhere. Scottie laughed hysterically, as if it was the best thing in the world.

What a mess that's going to be to clean up. "He probably heard us arguing and got upset," I said.

"That shows how much *you* know about him," Josh retorted. "He does shit like this all the time for no damn reason."

This man was getting on my last nerve. The more he annoyed me, the more I was determined to prove him wrong about me being the better caretaker.

"Nothing happens without a trigger," I muttered, disappointed in myself for letting this guy get to me so badly.

Josh and I began silently picking up the feathers. I found a small garbage bag from the kitchen so we'd have somewhere to dump them. Every minute, I swore under my breath at the turn this situation had taken. What bothered me more than anything? Deep down, I really *didn't* think I was capable of handling Scottie alone. I didn't want to admit that. Having another set of hands here was probably a good thing. I just wished they were *any* hands but Josh's.

By the time we were done, it looked like we'd plucked a chicken and tried to hide the evidence. Scottie had calmed down at least and looked like he was about to fall asleep.

Josh drew one of the shades that I'd inadvertently left open. The last thing I wanted was Scottie waking up earlier than necessary because of the sun. I also noticed a static sound machine and turned it on.

After we left the bedroom, Josh and I stood in the living area in front of the flames of the pellet stove. We just looked at each other. As much as I disliked this guy, beggars couldn't be choosers. No one else was going to volunteer to help.

"I hate to admit it," I said, swallowing some humble pie. "But this might be more of a two-person job anyway. I think it would be helpful for us to work together, so we can relieve each other from time to time."

Josh stayed silent. Since he didn't refute my suggestion, I chose to assume that meant he agreed with me.

"Don't you have family in town?" I asked. "You don't have to sleep here. You could come and go."

He raised his forehead. "How's that gonna help you at night if he wakes up and pulls some shit?"

Scratching my temple, I had nothing to say to that.

"I have two brothers and my dad in town," he added. "But I *do* think it's better if I stay here overnight."

"Okay," I conceded. "Where are you gonna do your work during the day? There's obviously no office space."

"That doesn't matter. I can work anywhere. And if there's a meeting, I'll just move my laptop to wherever Scottie isn't. I do have to make a lot of calls, but at least I'll be here if you need me or if you have to go to the store or something."

I knew very little about Josh's career, just that he worked in the corporate world.

"What do you do again?" I asked.

"I'm a recruiter."

"What does that entail?"

"I screen qualified candidates for open positions."

"Ah, so that's why you were so quick to shoot me down for this one."

He shrugged. "You're right. You're not qualified to take care of him alone. But more than anything, I was just trying to give you a break for your own good, Carly."

"I'm up for the challenge." I sighed. "Besides, honestly, everything back in California reminds me of Brad...our life before he died. I need a change of scenery. This is his childhood home, but none of our memories were here." I looked up at him. "I suppose it's the opposite for you, though."

Nodding somberly, he walked away. Clearly Josh had no plans to open up to me.

He walked over and opened the refrigerator. He rubbed the scruff on his chin and soon closed the door. There was nothing to see in there.

"It's empty," I said. "I didn't have a chance to go shopping or order groceries."

He looked over at the clock and scratched his chest. "It's kind of late anyway. I don't have to eat anything tonight. I'll just suck it up until tomorrow."

Tension lingered in the air as we stared at each other. The recessed lighting over him caused a glow in his hazel eyes. Josh was strikingly handsome. There was no way to argue that. His hair alone deserved its own modeling agent. His nose was straight, his lips full, and his chin perfectly angular. Despite his looks, I'd always thought him to be ugly on the inside.

As I took him in, I noticed Josh's eyes had fallen below my neck—and stayed there.

What's happening?

Is he checking me out?

Can't be.

The guy can't stand me.

Before I could ponder that any further, he charged toward me, his hand smacking the top of my chest without warning. Then, I felt the pinch of his fingers against my skin.

"What the fuck?" I screamed, my heart beating out of control.

"Got it." His shoulders rose and fell as he unraveled his fist and opened his long fingers to reveal something unidentifiable in the palm of his hand. "You had a nasty spider crawling on you."

I looked closer, and indeed it was a crushed spider that looked like a daddy long legs.

"Jesus..." I panted. "I didn't know what the hell happened. For a second there, I thought you smacked me for no reason."

He frowned. "Well, that's pretty fucked up."

I looked down at his red handprint on my skin. My traitorous nipples went hard at the sight, which was so twisted I wouldn't even try to analyze it.

I cleared my throat. "I hate spiders. I would've freaked out if I'd known it was crawling on me. So thank you." Brushing my fingertips along the spot, which still burned a little, I added, "Although, I'm surprised you didn't just leave it there for your own pleasure."

He arched a brow, seeming less than amused. "Why would I get pleasure out of that?"

First and foremost, because I had proof he didn't like me. And I'd never understood why. I hadn't done anything to deserve it. I'd also never had the opportunity to *ask him* why he felt that way. This had been a long day for both of us, so maybe I should've stopped myself, but I didn't.

"Why do I think you'd derive pleasure from seeing a spider on me?" I asked, still rubbing the spot he'd smacked. "Because we both know you don't like me. And based on that, I have to say...I'm surprised you're okay with this living arrangement."

His eyes narrowed. "Who said I don't like you?"

"Actually...*you* did." I swallowed, my heartbeat accelerating.

His jaw tightened. "I never said that."

"Not to my face."

"Explain."

I'd held it inside for *so* long. Never even told Brad that I knew—because I was too ashamed and didn't want to start a war between him and his oldest friend. I loved Brad *that* much.

I decided to just spit it out. "I accidentally saw a text you sent Brad when he and I first started dating."

Josh's Adam's apple moved. "Okay..."

"His phone was on the counter while he was in the shower. He'd sent you a photo of us. You responded and said..." I paused, cringing at the memory. "That there was something about my face that bothered you."

He blinked and looked away for a moment. "Well, obviously you weren't meant to see that."

"*Obviously*," I muttered, feeling bitterness at the back of my throat.

"Look..." He sighed. "I didn't know anything about you. If I'd known you and he would end up getting engaged, I might not have—"

"Shared your *true* feelings?" I crossed my arms, although I really wanted to punch him.

"It was a dumb thing to say." He scrubbed a hand over his face. "I didn't mean it literally."

"You didn't mean it literally?" I lowered my voice, realizing I'd just shouted and didn't want to wake up Scottie. "How else can you not like a face...if not *literally*?"

Josh remained silent as he looked down at the floor.

I'd really caught him off guard. *Good.* He deserved it.

"I never told Brad I saw it," I admitted. "As much as I hated you for that text, I didn't want to cause a rift. I knew how much you meant to him—for some godforsaken reason."

Josh finally looked me straight in the eyes. "I should've never said that, and I apologize. Truly. And as much as you don't seem to believe me, that text really meant nothing." He blew out a long breath and softened a bit. "I guess this explains why you were never my biggest fan. Brad told me you didn't like it when he came to visit because you didn't trust me. I figured it was because you thought I was a bad influence. Now I know there was more to it."

"I *did* worry when he was with you."

"You shouldn't have. Brad's a grown man with a mind of his own." He paused. "*Was* a grown man." He shook his head. "I still have a hard time thinking about him in the past tense."

My throat felt heavy. "Well, that's one thing we have in common."

Josh looked down at his shoes and slipped his hands into his pockets. Then he turned toward the living room. “I guess I should find a blanket or something to sleep with.”

“Let me see if there’s something in Wayne’s closet,” I said, still feeling a little bitter.

Josh followed me to the room where I’d be sleeping, just off the kitchen.

When I opened the closet, it was filled from floor to ceiling. All of Wayne’s clothes were still hanging there. It smelled a bit musty, so I made a mental note to clean it out as soon as I had a second to breathe.

“I guess this was Wayne’s solution to the lack of storage space in this house,” I said as I rummaged through. “Just pack everything in here?”

Josh turned on a lamp in the corner of the room. “Brad kept offering to buy him a bigger place, but Wayne never wanted to leave this cabin. This is where he had all his memories with Yvonne, where they started their family.”

“I can understand that.” I turned to face him. “They lost her so young.”

“Yeah.” He shook his head. “That was a terrible fucking time.”

“You and Brad were in high school when she died?”

He nodded somberly.

I knew Josh was the same age as Brad, who would’ve been thirty now if he were alive. At twenty-eight, I was two years younger.

I resumed searching for a blanket and managed to find a small plaid one amidst all the junk in the closet.

"Will this be enough?" I asked as I handed it to him. It seemed like it might only cover half his body.

"It'll work," he said.

I grabbed one of the two pillows on the bed. It was heavier than expected, filled with down.

"Take this, too. I don't need both." I threw it toward him with unintentional force.

He caught it. "You enjoyed throwing that at me, didn't you?"

I winked. "Maybe a little."

FOUR

Carly

A KNOCK WOKE me the following morning. When I emerged from the bedroom, I spotted a shirtless Josh already at the front door. His perfectly carved back, inked with the image of a serpent, blocked my view of whomever was there.

A snake. Appropriate.

I didn't like the man, but there was no denying how damn hot he was.

His deep, morning voice was raspy as he spoke. "Can I help you?"

"I'm Scottie's behavior therapist," I heard a woman say. "I work with him here once or twice a week."

Josh scratched his head of unruly hair. "Oh." He moved aside. "Come in."

I caught the attractive brunette's eyes falling briefly to his chest.

He held his hand out. "I'm Josh. Good to meet you."

"Lauren." She smiled as they shook.

I could have sworn she resisted letting go.

“I didn’t realize Scottie had someone coming to the house.” I interrupted her ogling.

She turned toward me, seeming to notice me standing there for the first time. “Yeah.” She cleared her throat. “It’s a home-based service we provide, funded by the state. I’ve only been working with him for about six months, but he’s been in our adult program for a while.”

“Lorraine neglected to mention that,” I said. “What do you do with him?”

“We read together, do puzzles, sort items, and work on self-care—things like brushing his teeth, dressing, and tying his shoes,” she said. “You must be Carly?”

I nodded. “Yes.”

“His aunt did mention you would be coming to stay with him in place of her. I didn’t realize you were married.”

“Oh.” I looked over at Josh. “He’s not my husband. This is Scottie’s brother Brad’s friend. I was engaged to Brad before he passed away.”

She smiled over at Josh, her eyes lighting up. “I see.”

I bet you do.

The last thing I needed was to be in the middle of a flirt fest—or worse—between Josh and this college student.

She turned back to me. “I’m so sorry about your fiancé. Before Wayne passed, he used to tell me all about him. He was a movie producer, right?”

“He worked in television as a writer, but he’d been promoted to producer before he died, yeah.”

"I'm sorry." She frowned. "So, you're both here to take care of Scottie...together?"

"We're sharing the responsibility right now," Josh said. "Until we can find him a good fit for a permanent home."

Lauren nodded. "That's really cool of you."

"Scottie is still sleeping," I said. "If I'd known you were coming, I would've woken him."

"That's okay. Wayne used to get him up before I arrived, but I don't mind waking him." She looked over at Josh. "If you need anything, let me know. We have a lot of resources at the agency that may be able to help with your search for placement."

It was interesting that she offered to help *him* and not *us*. It was sickening how much of a chick magnet this guy was, given his questionable personality. But then again, Lauren wouldn't know about that yet. Too bad Josh Mathers didn't come with a warning label covering his perfect face.

After she went into Scottie's room, I lowered my voice. "You might want to put on a shirt before I have to clean that girl's drool off the floor."

"I wasn't expecting a guest this morning any more than you were, sunshine." He looked down at my chest. "Clearly."

I closed my eyes. I hadn't put on a bra. Perhaps that would've been a good thing to note before chastising him. Clearing my throat, I covered my chest with my arms. "What time do you start work?"

"At nine."

"Do you drink coffee?" I asked.

"I pretty much guzzle it all day, yeah."

"I checked last night and didn't see any coffee pods. I can go to the store and get some, along with stuff for breakfast, take advantage of her being here with Scottie."

He ran a hand through his thick hair. "Cool. Yeah. I'll jump in the shower while you're out."

I nodded and rushed to my room to put on a bra and some clothes. Brushing my hair, I noted how long it had gotten. I wondered if I'd have an opportunity to get it trimmed while here, or if I'd end up looking like Rapunzel by the time I left Woodsboro.

Before I left, I entered Josh's number into my phone and sent him a quick message so he could add me as a contact in case we needed to text while I was at the market.

The cold air outside hit my face, and it felt so good to get out of the house for a bit. Relief washed over me as I hopped in my car. *Ah, the quiet.* It felt like I'd momentarily returned to my life—the one I'd had before it was turned upside down. It had been less than twenty-four hours, but it felt like years since I'd last sat in this vehicle.

As I took off down the rural road, I called Christina to fill her in on the latest developments.

"Hey! You're still alive," she said as she picked up. "I've been waiting to hear from you."

"I finally have a free moment to breathe."

"How are things over there?"

I broke out in hysterical laughter. I couldn't help it. It felt so good to let it all out. But Christina must have thought I was nuts.

"What the hell is up with you?"

"Oh, Christina." I tapped on my steering wheel. "What a clusterfuck."

"Oh no. Why? What happened?"

"For one… I'm not alone with Scottie. I have an unexpected roommate."

"What? Who?"

"Josh Mathers."

"Josh…" It took her a moment. "Brad's hot-as-hell best friend? That guy? The one who lives in Chicago? The one you can't stand?"

"Yes. One and the same. Apparently, he and I both had the same idea to drop everything and move here temporarily to take care of Scottie."

"Well, if he's there, does that mean you can come home?"

"No." I sighed. "I'm still doing this. But it's also not as simple as I thought. I realized soon after arriving here that this is more than a one-person job. No wonder Lorraine shot out of here like a bat out of hell when I arrived yesterday."

"So, wait… Josh is going to be staying there permanently *with* you and Scottie?"

"For the foreseeable future, yeah."

"Didn't you say the house was small? Where is he sleeping?"

"On the couch. There's only one bedroom besides Scottie's. And it's mine."

"Well, that blows—for him."

"Yeah. Maybe I'll switch off with him, but we haven't gotten that far. I'm still in shock."

She chuckled. "I can understand."

"The worst part is, he acknowledged that he knew I wasn't his biggest fan. And I admitted that I knew he'd never liked me, either. So now there's this tension between us."

I chose not to tell her about Josh's old text. I still had a lot of shame surrounding it, and I'd never told anyone—except Josh.

"Well, sounds like you guys have to learn to like each other if you're gonna be living together." She paused. "Actually, now that I know he's there, maybe *I'll* pay a visit."

"Why?"

"He's single, isn't he?"

"Yeah. But you don't want to get involved with him. I wouldn't let you. He's a player."

"Who says I'm interested in a relationship? The guy is gorgeous."

I rolled my eyes.

"Are you rolling your eyes?"

I laughed.

We talked for several more minutes, until I arrived at the market and found a parking space.

"Anyway, I'd better go. I'm in front of the market and need to get coffee for Mr. Grumpypants before he has to start work."

"That's very nice of you, considering you don't like him."

"Well, I figure he'll be even more annoying without caffeine." I chuckled. "Plus, I sort of need it myself to be able to deal with him."

"Keep me posted," she said.

"You know I will."

After I hung up, I got out and grabbed a cart, nearly crashing into someone on the way in because I was so lost in my head.

As I perused the aisles inside, I decided to be courteous and check in with Josh.

Carly: What kind of coffee do you like?

He texted back almost immediately.

Josh: Any kind is fine.

Carly: So, pumpkin spice, then?

Josh: I'm actually not in the mood to vomit today, so no. Literally anything but that. I hate pumpkin anything.

Carly: That's why I asked. Dark Roast, Blonde Roast?

Josh: Blonde with a hint of nuttiness sounds like your speed.

Seriously? I typed faster.

Carly: Was that really necessary?

Josh: No, but I thought it was funny.

Carly: How nice that you amuse yourself. And just for that, you're getting pumpkin.

Reluctantly, I tossed a container of plain, dark-roast pods into the cart.

Josh: Hey, you know where you should go to get coffee?

Carly: Where?

Josh: The Coffee Bean and Tea Leaf. They have GREAT coffee. Brad took me there when I went out to visit him.

I scratched my head.

Carly: They don't have those here. They're only in California.

Josh: Exactly.

Carly: Now you're getting pumpkin spice with a shot of pumpkin, wiseass.

Josh: Whatever, Pumpkin.

Carly: Also, most of what I buy for the house will be gluten free.

Josh: Great.

Carly: Are you being sarcastic?

Josh: No, I mean things here were so much fun as it was. Gluten free only makes it better.

Carly: Gluten-free pumpkin loaf for you. ;-)

As I continued going up and down the aisles, Josh sent me another text.

Josh: Actually, I forgot to pack deodorant. Do you mind picking some up? I'll reimburse you, of course.

Carly: Any particular kind?

Josh: Anything that's made for a man.

Carly: Extra-spicy manwhore scent?

Josh: That works for me.

Carly: Nontoxic or...

Josh: Are you being serious?

Carly: Yes!

Josh: Toxic. I need it to actually work.

Carly: I use lemons instead of deodorant myself.

Josh: Are you shitting me?

Carly: No. I rub a wedge onto each pit daily.

Josh: That explains why you smell.

Carly: You'd better be joking.

Josh: Maybe I am. Maybe I'm not.

Carly: The lemons work and are completely safe. No aluminum to enter my lymphatic system and kill me twenty years from now.

Josh: All the shit there is to worry about in life and you're concerned about deodorant? You should probably chill out.

Carly: This from someone who willingly sucks in carbon monoxide. I shouldn't have even asked about the deodorant. It's clear you don't give a crap about your health.

Josh: I'll take the toxic shit with extra aluminum, please.

Carly: Toxic deodorant for a toxic guy. Coming up!

Josh: Lemons for a tart. ;-)

Carly: Look at you, so quick on your toes. Why don't you use them to head back to Chicago. LOL

Josh: Kidding. A tart is one thing you're not, actually. A little sour, maybe...but definitely not a tart.

Carly: I'll take your retraction as a compliment.

Josh: See? Even though you called me toxic, I took back tart. Who's the mature one?

Carly: I'll give you that.

Josh: Now you've got me wondering where else you're sticking lemons.

I laughed as I reached for a masculine deodorant that was on sale.

Carly: Up your ass, Mathers. And there goes your mature card. By the way, I've got your toxic deodorant. I'll be here another five minutes or so if you think of anything else.

The tiny dots moved around the screen.

Josh: Actually, can you pick up a carton of ice cream?

Carly: Please don't say any kind. I'll be here all day trying to choose something.

Josh: Pistachio

Carly: Hmm...

Josh: What?

Carly: That's my favorite too.

Josh: Well, looks like we've just found the one thing we have in common besides Brad.

Carly: It's gonna be a long week. Shall I pick up two cartons?

Josh: Yeah. And some alcohol.

FIVE

Carly

LATER THAT AFTERNOON, I went back out to buy extra linens at the nearest Walmart, which was thirty minutes away.

When I returned to the house, I gasped at the sight before me.

Josh was at the kitchen table on a video call while Scottie sat on his lap. Josh had arched his neck to see past Scottie, whose nose was buried in his hair. Meanwhile, Josh had his earpiece in and was talking away as if he didn't have a grown-ass man on his lap.

I wanted to snap a picture, but refrained.

As soon as Josh noticed me, I mouthed, "*I'm sorry.*"

The only reason I'd gone out again was because Lauren had still been here. I'd planned to make it back before she left but had gotten stuck in traffic.

He held his hand up as if to tell me it was okay.

Scottie hopped off of Josh's lap and moved over to the couch. Josh ran his hand over his shirt to smooth out the wrinkles and kept on talking without missing a beat.

When he finally got off his call, I shook my head in amazement. "You handled that like a champ."

"I didn't have much of a choice. Luckily, I'd explained the deal to my colleagues before I came here, so most of them weren't shocked when they saw him come on the screen. They found it pretty endearing. I turned my camera off right after he bombarded me, though."

"You seem to have a calming effect on Scottie."

He cracked a smile. "I might be his favorite, yeah."

"It's definitely not me." I sighed. "Anyway, are you done for the day?"

He took his earpiece out and closed his laptop. "Yep."

"Nice."

He looked down at the bag I was holding. "You get everything you need?"

"Yeah. Some towels, a replacement pillow for Scottie, a bigger blanket for you, and an extra set of sheets. I'm sorry it took so long." I looked around the kitchen, feeling discombobulated. "I have to make his chicken before dinnertime. I know I'm gonna mess it up."

Josh ran his hand through his hair. "Why?"

I put down the bag and grabbed the written recipe Lorraine had left me. "Look at these instructions. The chicken has to be pounded down just right, the oil has to be a certain brand—which thankfully we have in the cupboard because I forgot to buy it earlier—and you have to be careful of the egg-to-flour ratio." I slapped the paper down on the counter. "Otherwise, he won't eat it."

"Piece of cake." Josh rolled up his sleeves. "I can help you."

"Seriously? Do you cook?"

"Does it matter? Neither one of us has ever made this extra-ass chicken before. We'll just follow the directions. It'll be fine."

"Okay." I licked my lips. "Yeah...um, I'll get the oil started. Why don't you wash the chicken and pound the breasts for me." I immediately blushed. That sounded so wrong.

He smirked. "I've been known to give a good pounding in my lifetime."

"That was lame."

"But you're smiling. And you were blushing way before I even said it, so you're the one with the dirty fucking mind, Pumpkin."

"Please don't tell me you're going to call me that?"

"Does it bother you?"

"Yes."

"Then, yes. That's your nickname." He winked. "It's either that or Lemon Pits. You choose."

"I'll take Pumpkin." I rolled my eyes and grabbed the large fry pan from under the counter.

Scottie played on his device in the living room, seemingly oblivious to the fact that Josh and I were probably about to destroy his dinner.

But surprisingly, we developed a groove: Josh washed and pounded the chicken while I dipped each breast in egg, flour, and Italian bread crumbs, then dropped it into the hot oil.

Look at us working together. If we weren't currently the epitome of a domesticated-yet-dysfunctional family, I didn't know what was.

Everything went smoothly until Scottie entered the kitchen with his tablet up to his ear and got a look at what we were up to.

Josh turned to him. "Hey, buddy. We're making your extra-ass chicken. You excited?"

Scottie bounced back and forth on his feet as he observed the flour-covered counter with vested interest. He then left the kitchen and headed straight for my bedroom.

I cringed, hoping I hadn't left anything out that he could get into. Then I remembered the clothes. "Crap. I have some laundry in there that I folded earlier. He's gonna jump on the bed and mess it all up."

"We both have chicken on our hands, so let him be," Josh said. "I'll refold it later."

Just when my nerves about Scottie rummaging through my room calmed down, he reentered the kitchen. The next thing I knew, something flew into my pan of oil. Josh and I jumped back simultaneously.

What the?

I blinked rapidly, glad I hadn't gotten hot oil on me. Scottie had thrown something into the pan before running off.

Josh grabbed the tongs and lifted it out of the sizzling grease before it could disintegrate. "What the fuck is this?" he yelled.

Horrified, I froze.

Josh held it toward me. "It looks like a piece of rubber chicken."

I shook my head. "It's not a piece of chicken."

"What the hell is it then?"

I want to die. "It's one of my silicone breast inserts. He must have gone through my things in there and thought it should be added to our batch." The insert was nude-colored and looked exactly like a chicken breast.

Josh's expression morphed from shock to pure amusement. His shoulders shook as he set the insert down on a paper towel. He leaned against the counter. "It does look like fucking chicken." He held onto his stomach as he barely got the words out through his laughter. "He was just trying to help."

The laughter spread like wildfire, erupting in me as well. We were both practically crying.

I wiped my eyes. "I'm gonna have to get a lock for that door."

Scottie scurried back into the kitchen.

"Scottie, no going in my room!" I told him.

"Yeah. That's gonna work," Josh declared sarcastically. "You can go into any room you want, buddy. Tell her to calm her chicken tits."

I elbowed him. "Very funny."

"You're right. My humor is kind of...*flat*."

Grabbing a dishtowel, I whipped it at him.

"Chicken Tits!" He snorted as he swung the rag over his shoulder. "That's even better than Lemon Pits!"

• • •

The silicone-tit incident seemed to be a turning point in our dysfunctional situation, because by some miracle, later that evening, the three of us managed to sit down to a fairly nice and normal dinner. There was no arguing. No Scottie tantrums. *No Josh and Carly tantrums, either.*

Even though gluten could make me sick, I was too lazy to make a separate meal, so I sucked it up for one night and ate the same chicken as everyone else. We'd made a big enough batch to go round *and* last Scottie for a few days after. I'd also put together a salad and roasted sweet potatoes in the oven for Josh and me.

I spoke with my mouth full. "These cutlets are pretty good. It's no wonder he likes them."

"Really? All I taste is silicone." Josh winked as he chewed. "I must have gotten the bad one."

I gestured with my fork. "Not sure I'll ever be able to live that down."

He chuckled. "You know who would've loved that whole thing?"

I stopped chewing and whispered, "Brad."

Josh seemed lost in thought for a moment. "He would've figured out a way to write it into one of his scripts, you know? He was always on the lookout for material. Any time something crazy happened when we were out together, he'd call me later and say 'guess what made it into the show?'"

"Did you ever watch the show?"

"Not all the time. But I've seen maybe half the episodes," he said.

"Did you see the one where the character, Maddie, sends a raunchy text to her doctor by accident?"

"Yeah. I remember that one."

I pointed to myself. "This girl right here."

"Oh, damn." He chuckled.

"Yup. Brad thought it was funny, even if I was mortified."

Josh sighed. "Well, he would've found the silicone-chicken incident just as funny."

My chest tightened. "Yep. He would've died laughing." I realized what I'd just said. "Ugh." *Died.* Laughing.

We sat in silence, watching Scottie devour the last of his chicken.

"I can see now that it would've been really challenging going at this alone." I wiped my mouth and sucked up my pride. "I'm glad you're here."

Josh hesitated but nodded, seeming a bit taken aback by the olive branch I'd extended. He crumpled his napkin and tossed it aside. "I don't know how Wayne did it every day, to be honest."

"I guess love gives you strength. Scottie was all he had left."

"And now Scottie has no one." Josh shook his head slowly. "Life is so fucking unfair. I've struggled a lot with anger these past couple of years. I hoped it would get easier, but it really hasn't."

"I thought I was the only one."

Josh's voice was barely audible. "I would've given anything for it to be me and not him."

I fought my tears. "Well, that's a testament to your friendship."

Scottie interrupted our somber moment when he jumped up from his seat. I took him over to the sink and helped him wash his hands before he disappeared into his bedroom.

"He really loved you, you know."

I'd started cleaning up, but Josh's words stopped me in my tracks. I turned around to face him. "Yeah. I do know. But thank you for saying that."

Josh leaned back in his chair. "I didn't want to believe he'd bitten the dust with you. I tested him a lot in the beginning—threw temptation in his face when he came out to visit. But none of it mattered. Eventually, I saw how committed he was. And I envied him for finding that kind of connection with someone."

"That might be the most mature thing you've ever said, Mathers."

"Don't get your hopes up, Pumpkin. It's not a trend. I just got caught in your sappy soup for a moment."

I grinned. "Well, you can't find something like what Brad and I had if you're not open to it."

"Yeah." He sighed. "I never really have been. Too busy having fun out there, I guess." He stood and began clearing the rest of the table.

As I loaded the dishwasher, I was again surprised by him.

"Have you dated anyone since...you know?"

"No." I shook my head. "I know it's been two years, but I haven't felt ready."

He wiped the counter. "I think he'd want you to move on."

"I know he would. But it has to feel right, and it just hasn't yet. Maybe once I get through this...sabbatical here."

He nodded. "Speaking of which, we should probably get on with the process of putting Scottie on a waiting list for a home. I don't think either one of us wants to be here in Woodsboro any longer than we have to. The therapist, Lauren, gave me her number and said she'd help set up a meeting with the agency she works for, if we want."

"Interesting how she gave you *her* number and not the direct line for the agency."

He smirked. "Yeah. I didn't miss that, either."

I didn't know if it was all the talk about Brad, or the fact that I was feeling oddly guilty about enjoying being around Josh tonight, but I suddenly needed some space.

"Why don't you do what you need to do tonight?" I told him. "I got this cleanup."

"I should help with the dishes," he insisted.

"There's not much left. You had a long day at work and then helped me cook."

He raised a brow. "You sure?"

"Yup."

He slapped the dishtowel against the counter. "I'd actually love to take a shower so I don't have to do it in the morning."

"Go for it."

Josh washed his hands before heading over to his suitcase in the corner of the living room. He took out some clothes and carried them to the bathroom.

Left alone in the kitchen, a wave of emotion hit me. Josh had given me a little peek into his softer side tonight. Talking about Brad had really brought it out. Interesting, but no surprise. Brad always brought out the best in people; he certainly always brought out the best in me. He made me feel cherished after every other male who'd come and gone in my life had let me down. I really missed him tonight.

A few minutes later, I was putting detergent into the dishwasher when I heard what sounded like Josh yelling from down the hall.

"No! Let go of my dick!"

I shut the dishwasher door and rushed over to see what was going on. The bathroom door was open. Through the frosted glass of the shower, I could see the silhouettes of *two* naked bodies. Scottie's clothes were on the floor next to Josh's.

"Why did he go in there?" I cried, stifling my laughter.

"Fuck if I know! Weren't you watching him?"

"He was quiet in his room. I thought things were under control while I was finishing up the dishes."

"One second I had my eyes closed, rubbing shampoo into my hair. The next thing I knew, the door slid open and he was standing in front of me, yanking on my crank."

I cracked up harder, unable to hide it now.

"When you're done laughing, do you mind taking him out of here and drying him off? I'm naked, so I can't exactly leave right now." He slid the door open just enough to let Scottie out. "Go on, Scottie."

"Come on, Scottie. Leave Uncle Josh alone," I said, trying not to stare at Josh's body through the glass. "We'll give you a bath after."

Finally able to get him out, I dried Scottie off and led him back into his bedroom to get dressed. *Maybe he prefers showers?*

When Josh finally came back out into the living room, he wore a black T-shirt and gray sweatpants that were a bit tapered at the bottom. He smelled amazing, like soap and cologne. I tried not to admire how attractive he was, the way the shirt hugged his chest, the way his wet hair fell over his forehead. His big feet. The bulge straining through those fitted pants. Noticing such things had happened more times than I wanted to admit, and I hated myself for it. I chalked it up to the fact that I was a lonely, dried-up person right now who hadn't had sex in more than two years and couldn't help what my body reacted to.

I cleared my throat. "I'm sorry about that whole thing."

Josh ran a hand through his hair. "Not like you could've anticipated he would do that, I guess."

"How did Wayne handle showering? I hadn't even thought about all of the trouble Scottie could get into while unattended."

Josh knelt to rummage through his suitcase. "Wayne must have taken damn quick showers."

"Yeah. Or wait..." I snapped my fingers. "I just thought of something."

He looked up. "What?"

"Maybe he showered *with* Scottie, so he didn't have to worry about that. That's why Scottie jumped in the shower with you. He thought he was *supposed* to."

Josh ran his teeth along his bottom lip. "Actually, that makes a lot of sense."

"I know. So much we have to learn, huh?"

"Yeah." He sighed as he stood and massaged his lower back. "One day at a time."

"What's wrong?" I asked.

"Eh, that couch isn't the most comfortable. Fucked up my back a little."

"Why don't we switch off?" I suggested. "You sleep in the bed tonight."

"No. I don't want you having the same problem. No one should be sleeping on this couch. I'll go to the store tomorrow and find one of those inflatable air mattresses. We don't have room for much else around here."

"That'll be a pain in the ass having to blow it up every night, won't it?"

"That's the least of my worries these days, Pumpkin."

I chuckled. "I guess."

He looked down at a DVD I was holding. "What's that?"

"I found a box of DVDs in Wayne's room. Most of them aren't labeled. Any idea what they are?"

"No." He pointed over to the television. "But there's a DVD player right there. Pop that one in."

I slipped the DVD into the machine and pressed play before sitting on the sofa next to Josh. After some initial interference on the screen, a home movie of the boys when they were younger came on. Brad must have been about eight, and Scottie was a baby who'd just started to walk. Their mom, Yvonne, sat on the ground, playing with them. She was so beautiful, with short blonde hair and large eyes. She kind of reminded me of a younger version of Carol Brady from *The Brady Bunch*. You could hear Wayne in the background, complimenting her. Yvonne blushed at one point. I'd never actually seen footage of her before—never realized how much Brad and Scottie looked like her, either.

"This house looks the same now as it did then, doesn't it?" I said.

"Yeah, you ain't kidding."

Josh and I continued to peer into this heartwarming family moment. Scottie looked like he'd made more eye contact as a baby. It made me wonder how his autism came about, and whether he was born with it or something changed inside of him one day.

The camera returned to Yvonne again. Her face reddened every time Wayne focused on her. She didn't seem to love being the center of attention.

"I remember Yvonne like it was yesterday," Josh said, mesmerized. "She was basically a mom to me."

I turned my attention away from the screen for a moment. "Your mothers must have been friends?"

His expression was stone cold. "I didn't have a mother."

My stomach sank. "Your mother passed?"

"No. But I don't really want to talk about it." He turned to me with a look of warning. "Okay?"

"Okay," I whispered.

Josh stood and disappeared into the kitchen. I sat there in a daze, continuing to watch the video. It seemed the man I'd once thought was heartless had a heck of a lot of feelings bottled up. There was likely *a lot* I didn't know about Josh.

SIX

Josh

"HOW LONG DO you think it will take to get him into a group home?" my brother Michael asked as he handed me a beer.

"Well, I'm sure as hell not just dropping him off at any old place. It needs to be the right fit. So I honestly don't know."

Michael was married to his high school girlfriend, Vanessa, and lived about two miles away from Wayne's. My other brother was single and also lived in town.

I'd stopped over at Michael's to get supplies I needed to fix a few things back at the house.

He cracked open a bottle of Blue Moon. "You're gonna live in that little house indefinitely? Why don't you just sleep here? We have a guest room."

"Carly won't be able to handle it if something goes down in the middle of the night. He's too damn big."

"How did the aunt handle it?"

"Lorraine apparently called Abe next door when things got out of hand. But that's not fair to him."

Michael popped a pretzel into his mouth. "You never liked this Carly girl, right?"

It seemed stupid now to think that I'd ever had negative feelings toward Carly. Most of that was based on my impression of her feelings toward *me*. Now that I knew she'd seen that stupid comment I'd texted Brad—one I hadn't even remembered until she mentioned it—I couldn't blame her for holding a grudge. She'd had every right to think I was a prick. But lately, she was growing on me.

"I thought I didn't like her back when Brad first started dating her. But after living with her for the past week, I realize I never really knew her. At the time, I felt like Brad was rushing into things—you know, getting engaged to the first piece of hot-blonde ass he fell for out in California."

"Hot-blonde ass, huh?" He laughed from behind his bottle. "What do you think of her now?"

"She's alright." I took a long sip of my beer. "I still don't know her all that well. But you have to respect anyone who'd willingly come to take care of a grown man she barely knows."

He smirked. "*And* you think she's hot..."

My eyes narrowed. "What does that matter?"

"I don't know. Maybe the two of you should...you know...try to make the *best* of it while you're stuck in the same house?"

His suggestion irked me. "What the hell are you insinuating?"

Michael shrugged.

My brother is nuts. "If you're implying what I think you are, you're whacked. I'd never go there with Brad's girl." I lightly punched his arm. "You crazy?"

"Since when do you have morals, brother?"

His question offended me. Sure, I hadn't been good at relationships and had cheated on my fair share of girlfriends back in high school. Might have even stolen a girl from a friend or two back in the day. But Brad? Brad was different. Brad was *family*.

I slammed my bottle down. "There are some lines you don't cross. Messing around with your brother from another mother's fiancée is one of them."

Michael examined my face. "I know what you're thinking, Josh. But it wouldn't be the same situation as what Uncle Stone did to Dad with Mom."

An old, familiar feeling of rage stirred within me. Just as I'd always done at the mention of my mother's betrayal, I exited the conversation so I didn't have to deal with it.

My chair skidded across the floor as I got up. "Thanks for the beer. I'd better get going."

• • •

On the way home, I texted Carly.

Josh: Anything you need while I'm out?

The dots moved around for a while before her response came.

Carly: I need you not to kill me when you get back.

What the?

Josh: I wasn't planning on it. Is there a reason I'd want to?

Carly: Possibly.

Josh: Tell me what it is.

Carly: It's better if you see it, rather than explaining over text.

Josh: Great. Okay. I'll be home in a few.

I'd thought things at the house were crazy as they were, but apparently, I had no clue how much worse they could get. I worried her text had something to do with Scottie, but no. When I walked through the door at Wayne's, he was sitting on the couch as usual, rocking back and forth to his music.

Then a gigantic dog with its tongue hanging out came running toward me.

"Why is there a goldendoodle in this house?" I demanded as it got up on its hind legs to greet me.

"Oh, is that the breed? I couldn't think of the name of it."

"Answer my question, Carly. Why the fuck is there a dog here?"

She grinned awkwardly. "Honestly… I don't know."

"Okay. You're gonna need to explain a little better than that."

"I went out to check the mail, and he was just standing there by the mailbox staring at me. He looked lost and has no collar. Then he followed me inside, and I gave him some tuna fish."

"Tuna fish?"

"It's the only thing we have in the house that's safe for dogs, according to the Internet." She sat down at the kitchen table, and the rusty-brown-haired dog put his front legs on her lap. She massaged behind his ears. "I have to call the police or something."

"Or *something*? You haven't called them yet?"

"Not yet." She buried her nose in his fur.

"How long has he been here?"

"About an hour."

Inhaling slowly to calm myself, I tried to reason with her. "Okay, the last thing we need in this goddamn house is a dog, Carly. I don't need to tell you that. There's barely enough room for the three of us. We have to contact them *now*."

She flashed a guilty smile. "I'll get on that."

She moved into the kitchen as the dog and I followed her.

I pulled out a chair and sat down. "You don't look like you're in any rush."

She ran her hands along the dog's fur. "He's so cute and fluffy."

"And stolen..." I corrected.

Carly batted her lashes. "Don't be mad."

Fuck.

I don't know what snapped in me in that moment, but an image of fucking her flashed through my mind. *Where the hell did that come from?*

Carly thought I was mad at her. And apparently, I wanted to back her up against the counter and fuck her instead. That realization was extremely troubling. I'd much rather be mad at her. Why I'd gone from annoyed to egregiously horny in a millisecond was beyond me. It must've been the damn stress of being here catching up with me.

Sure, Carly was hot. There was no denying that. But to have that kind of vivid image pop up—and to have *liked* it? All because she batted her lashes at me? Ticket straight to hell.

The dog jumped up on my lap and proceeded to lick me.

"Jesus..." I muttered, scrunching my face and pursing my lips shut, trying not to let him French kiss me the way he seemed to want to. "His breath smells like he went down on a fucking tuna fish."

Carly burst into laughter. "He likes you."

Scottie came up behind me soon after and took a big whiff of my hair as Tuna Breath continued to lick my face.

"You're very popular around here, Josh," she teased.

"Everyone likes me in this house—except you, Pumpkin."

She laughed. "I'll like you if you don't complain about the dog for the rest of the night."

"The rest of the night? It needs to be gone before then!"

She laughed harder as the dog continued to attack my face with its tuna tongue.

I rolled my eyes and dug my nails into the dog's fur. "I should've stayed at my brother's."

• • •

That evening, as expected, the damn dog was still with us, sitting by my feet like I'd been his master for twenty years. He was collecting scraps of the supper Carly had prepared. At least she'd called the police—I'd made sure to watch as she did—but they hadn't received any reports of a missing animal yet. Come to think of it, I had no proof there was actually someone on the other line of that phone call she placed. I'd have to trust her on that.

Scottie had eaten his chicken earlier and was already in bed for the night. Carly and I had opted for this unusually late dinner after he went to sleep. At least this way we could eat in peace without having to worry about what he was up to.

We'd just finished the last of Carly's gluten-free pasta. I had to admit, Carly could cook, even if she claimed not to have much experience.

I wiped my mouth. "This was really good—even without the gluten."

"Anything's better than fried silicone breast insert, right?" she cracked.

"That's true." I chuckled. "Before coming here, I can't remember the last time anyone made me a home-cooked meal. So that part's been nice."

"Is that the only nice part?"

"It's not as miserable with you as I thought it would be," I admitted.

"Oh, Josh. Do you ever know how to charm a girl." She batted her eyes like a cartoon.

I shrugged. "What can I say? I'm a charming kind of guy."

After I got up to put my plate in the dishwasher, I opened one of the drawers to get a dishtowel for the pans but found dozens of small notepads instead. They all had the same thing printed on the top: ***A Thank You from The Trappist Monks of St. Francis.***

I lifted one out. "What the heck are all these?"

"I saw those, too. I guess Wayne must've given them a lot of donations over the years."

"Jesus." I laughed. "No pun intended."

"We could write something down every minute of every day and not make a dent in those notepads. I thought about clearing them out to make room in the drawer, but I don't want to just throw them away. Wayne obviously earned those. So we should use them."

"I guess, yeah," I said, tossing it back in the drawer.

She sighed as she stood up and brought her plate over to the sink. "How was the visit with your brother earlier? I never asked."

"Good. It was nice to see him. It'd been a while."

"He has kids, right?"

"He and his wife have a girl and a boy. Maya is eleven, and Max is nine. They were in school, so I haven't seen them since I got back."

"You said you have another brother?"

"Yeah. He's single and also lives in town, not far from my dad."

"Your dad lives alone?"

"Yup."

I got the feeling she was itching for me to say more about my family—namely what happened with my mother. But I was in no mood to get into it. So I changed the subject by turning the tables on her.

"What about your family? Where are they?"

"It's just my mother. She lives in Oregon with my stepfather."

"No siblings?"

"No."

"Whereabouts in Oregon?"

"Bend. That's where I grew up."

"Isn't that where the last Blockbuster video store was located?"

"Yup." She laughed. "Very good."

"What about your dad?"

Carly hesitated a moment. "He left when I was ten. Moved to Arizona. Remarried a widow and basically became a father to her kids instead."

Wow.

I swallowed. "I'm sorry."

"It's okay. I've gotten used to the idea of him not being in my life. Not everyone stays a permanent part of your life, you know? I've learned that the hard way, I guess."

I let her words sink in. "That's a lesson I've also learned. Some losses are much tougher than others, though." I leaned against the counter, gathering my thoughts. It seemed only fair to open up a little in return. "The other night...I cut our conversation short when you asked me about my mother. I'm sorry. I didn't want to talk about it because it's still tough for me."

She nodded but stayed silent.

"She left our house when I was eleven—moved a couple hours away and I didn't see her much. Still don't, really, after all these years."

Carly's mouth curved downward. It looked like she felt sorry for me, which I fucking hated. It reminded me of how I'd felt as a child at events where every kid had their mom with them except me. I never wanted people to feel sorry for me, mostly because I never wanted to bring attention to the fact that my mother had chosen not to be in the picture. It would've been different if she were dead and had no choice. But to me, there was no greater shame than your parent consciously deciding that life was better without you.

"She just didn't want to be a mother?" Carly finally asked.

It was even more complicated and messed up than that.

"My mother had an affair with my father's brother. She's still with him today. My dad kicked her out, and she didn't exactly put up a fight to stay in our lives. We keep in touch occasionally, on a superficial level, but we're not close. She's selfish and has never made an effort to make things better." I paused. "I also think she stays away because she knows how painful it is for my dad to see her with my uncle Stone. But she's refused to leave him. She chose him over us. That's the very short version of the story."

"Wow. Okay." She nodded sympathetically. "Everything makes more sense now. I know you said Yvonne was like a second mother to you."

"Not a second mother, my *only* mother." I looked down. "While she was alive."

"I'm sorry. Brad never mentioned your family situation."

"He was probably conditioned to not talk about it because that's how I trained him." I looked up at her. "When you told me about your dad leaving, though, I felt like I had to say something."

"Between my father and your mother..." She shook her head. "I guess we found a third thing we have in common."

"You've been counting?"

"Well, there are so few..." She winked. "Not that hard to keep track."

"What are the other two again?" I arched my brow. "It ain't a love of pumpkin."

Carly counted on her fingers. "One was missing Brad. Two was pistachio ice cream."

"Ah. Yes," I muttered. "One won't ever change."

She looked like she was gonna say something else, but I'd had enough of talking about sad shit for now.

"Well, dinner was delicious. Thank you again."

"That sauce was Brad's favorite. One of the few things I can cook well."

Cue the damn sadness again. A pang of guilt hit me. Brad should've been the one to enjoy this delicious meal with her. It felt wrong to derive any pleasure at all from this. The moment felt stolen. Just like the damn dog staring up at me with googly eyes. *Stolen.*

Suddenly the guilt became too much to bear. It was late, but I needed some air and to get out of this house for a bit. I'd need to take her car. We'd decided that since only one of us ever left at a time, it wouldn't be necessary for me to rent one.

Taking my phone out, I pretended to check the time. "I actually have to go out for a bit. Scottie's already sleeping and should be good for a while. Is it okay if I take your car?"

"Of course." She tilted her head. "Where to?"

"I'm meeting someone I met online for a drink," I lied. "I'll be back in a couple of hours, though."

"This late?"

"Yeah."

Her expression fell. "Ah. Okay...no rush. Have a good time."

As I got into the car and drove off, I had no clue where I was headed. All I knew was that being back in Woodsboro made me feel things I didn't want to feel—things I hadn't felt in a while—about my mother and about Brad. I'd come home for Christmas over the years, but those trips were always a quick stay at Michael's house and then right back to Chicago. In and out. But now, being in Brad's old house without him made me feel like an imposter. Not to mention, the daily reminder that three out of the four people in the Longo family were now gone was a hard pill to swallow.

Needing a way to drown it all out for a bit, I just blasted the music and drove, with no destination in sight.

SEVEN

Carly

IT WAS PRETTY remarkable how well Josh and I had learned to manage things in just a couple of weeks. That's not to say we always got along; bickering seemed to be one of our favorite pastimes. But we were on a schedule and in a groove. I looked after Scottie as best I could while Josh worked during the day. Then he'd take over while I ran errands or got dinner ready in the evenings. It wasn't always seamless, but the house and Scottie were both still in one piece, so I considered that winning.

The goldendoodle I'd affectionately named Bubba was still with us as well. There were no leads as to where he'd come from, and much to Josh's chagrin, it looked like the dog would continue living with us.

Josh continued to sleep every night on the air mattress he'd bought. Despite my many offers to take turns with the bedroom, he refused.

I decided to take advantage of Lauren, Scottie's therapist, being at the house one afternoon and booked an appointment to get my roots touched up. Although I had naturally dark blonde hair, back in L.A., I had always gotten lighter-blonde highlights.

Nadine's Nest was certainly unlike the glamorous salon I went to back home. There were only two chairs in the whole place, and instead of photos of hair models on the walls, there were a few posters of 70's icons like Elvis and Cher. The owner of the salon, Nadine, ran it with her daughter Bianca. As Bianca did my foil highlights, I ended up telling her the entire story of how I'd ended up in Woodsboro.

"So you don't have all that much time today, then," she said as she painted some of my strands.

"I told Josh I'd be back by four."

She paused. "Josh is the guy who's helping you take care of your fiancé's brother?"

"Yes."

"What's his last name?"

"Mathers."

"Oh..." She smirked. "Small world around here. I know Josh Mathers."

Of course, you do. "Why did you make that face?"

"He dated my sister in high school." She folded a piece of foil. "They graduated the same year. We have a nickname for him."

"What is it?"

"The dick."

Yep. I rolled my eyes. "Not very original."

"Well, he had a big dick and he *is* a big dick. So it's fitting."

My skin heated. "Okay. I didn't need to know that."

"He cheated on Nicole, actually. But that was a long time ago. I'm sure he's changed by now."

I'm not so sure. "So you must've known my fiancé, Brad Longo, too?"

"Ah, yes. He was a sweet guy. I was so sorry to hear he passed. I didn't make the connection when you mentioned the brother with autism, but now this all makes sense. You were *Brad's* fiancée. Wow." She stopped working for a moment to look at me. "Again, I'm really sorry for your loss."

I hated when people said that. It always brought me back to the week Brad died and the awful state of denial I'd been in, one I probably hadn't fully exited even now.

"Thank you."

She examined my face in the mirror. "How are you doing?"

My chest felt heavy. "Most days I just live in denial and try to occupy myself with work or responsibilities. Of course, there's no such thing as traditional work while I'm here. I'm taking a sabbatical from that."

"What is it that you do?"

"I'm a makeup artist."

Her face lit up. "Seriously?"

"Yes. I work freelance out in L.A. Mostly television and movie projects."

"This is going to sound totally random, but any chance I could convince you to do wedding makeup on Saturdays while you're out here? I know that's not as exciting as television, but I could really use the help. It's so hard to find someone reliable who knows what they're doing."

"Not sure. Depends on if it's worth my time."

"It would be five-hundred dollars for just a few hours of work in the morning. Most of the weddings are in the afternoon, so you'd for sure be done by one or two."

It'd be nice to have a little extra spending cash. "Let me talk to Josh and see if he'd be willing to look after Scottie on Saturday mornings. I can get back to you."

She smiled. "Cool."

After the appointment, I had an hour to spare before I'd told Josh I'd be back.

Carly: Any reason I have to rush back? I'm thinking of getting my nails done, if they can fit me in.

Josh: No rush. Take your time.

Carly: Is Lauren still there?

Josh: Yeah.

She was likely using my absence to sink her teeth into Josh without my prying eyes.

Carly: Cool. Also, when I get home, we need to talk. I have some nudes.

Josh: Very interesting. I thought you were a bit prudish for that.

Carly: Huh?

Josh: Are you using DICK-tation, by any chance?

I scrolled up to see what I'd written. *Ugh!*

Carly: Not nudes. News! I was using voice to text.

Josh: Damn. Nudes sounded intriguing.

• • •

When I returned to the house after my appointment, an interesting scene was playing out on the couch. Not only was Scottie sitting on Josh's lap during a Zoom call, the dog was humping Josh's leg.

As I covered my mouth in laughter, Josh gave me the finger.

When I went into the kitchen, I found a piece of paper on the counter from one of Wayne's notepads. Josh had written something on it and used a lemon as a paperweight.

A Thank You from The Trappist Monks of St. Francis:
I almost used this lemon for my iced tea. But then I realized it was the last one and I didn't want you to stink tomorrow. So maybe add lemons to the next grocery run.

I rolled my eyes and laughed, but chose not to acknowledge the note until Josh got out of his virtual work meeting.

After he disconnected from the call—and escaped from the couch—he came into the kitchen.

"Well, that scene was a sight for sore eyes," I chided.

He sighed. "I have to just keep my camera off permanently. Should probably shut the damn blinds, too. Anyone peeking into this house would get quite the show."

I lifted the note he'd left me. "Thanks for the unnecessary manner in which you told me we needed lemons, by the way."

"Anytime. Figured we should start using up those notepads."

When the dog strolled in, I bent to pet him. "Bubba, you were enjoying yourself a little too much." I rubbed his ears. "You little horn dog."

Josh arched a brow. "You told him I was easy, didn't you?"

I laughed. "Yup."

"Have you followed up with the police again, or are you secretly hoping they never get back to us?"

The latter. "Last I heard they had no leads, but I'll follow up with them again."

"Sure you will." Josh's mouth spread into a smile. "Your hair looks nice, by the way."

His smile and unexpected compliment warmed me all over. What was going on with me? I must be damn lonely if I was reacting to *Josh* like that. He hadn't done anything but smile and tell me my hair looked nice, and I was turning into a pile of mush. A genuine smile and a compliment aimed at me were rare things from him, though.

"Thank you," I finally said, clearing my throat. "I ran into an old friend of yours today."

"Who?"

"My hairdresser. Her name is Bianca DiLoreto. You dated her sister in high school."

"Oh." He scratched his chin. "Nicole's sister. Hardly a friend, but yeah, okay."

"Anyway, she offered me a job doing makeup for weddings on Saturday mornings. That was my news."

"Your *nudes*." He winked.

"Right." I chuckled. "Anyway, I didn't want to accept without checking in with you since you'd have to stay with Scottie while I'm out."

He didn't hesitate. "That's no problem at all."

"Really?"

"Did you think I'd have an issue with that? It'd be good for you to get out. And why not make some extra cash for yourself?"

"Thank you." I nodded. "I agree."

"It's good for your sanity, too."

Hmm... It surprised me that a man I'd originally worried would make me *insane* was concerned for my sanity. I must've stared at his ridiculously perfect face for too long as I pondered that.

"What?" he asked.

"I keep waiting for the other shoe to drop with you," I admitted.

"What the hell are you talking about?"

"You've been patient, fairly respectful aside from busting my balls, and generally nice to me. There's not much to hate as of late."

"Are you *looking* for reasons to hate me?"

"Not at all. This process is much easier if we're getting along."

"Maybe you drew the wrong conclusions about me from the get-go. Did you ever think of that?"

"Maybe I did...about certain things. Although, the truth is, we've been living together for a couple of weeks now and getting along just fine. But at the same time, I still don't feel like I know you. Who we are when we're living in this situation and who we are outside of here are probably two different things."

"Getting to know each other isn't a requirement of the job, Carly. But I don't have anything to hide. You can ask me whatever you want."

Ask him whatever I want. That was an invitation I couldn't refuse. I took a deep breath and unleashed the question that had been eating at me for years.

"What was it about my face that bugged you?"

Josh's eyes widened, then fell to the ground. "You went right for the jugular there, I see."

My blood was pumping. "You think I'm ugly or something? Is that why you said it?"

"No," he replied immediately. "Absolutely not."

"That's not something people typically say—that someone's face bugs them."

"You shouldn't have taken it personally."

"How does one not take that personally? It's my fucking face!" I yelled.

"It didn't mean anything, Carly, as hard as that may be to believe. I was just being a shithead. I liked to give Brad grief about a lot of things. He'd just started dating you, and I made a dumb comment. There's not much more to it than that."

"You still haven't answered my question, though. That was a very specific insult. There was a reason you thought to say it. You just don't want to admit it." I felt my cheeks burn in frustration. "So much for this conversation."

His ears were red as he finally looked me in the eyes. "You want me to lie and say it was because I thought you were ugly just to give you an answer?"

I put my hands on my hips. "I can't change my face, you know."

"Jesus, Carly. It wasn't about your face at all."

Chills ran down my spine as he moved closer.

"It wasn't about my face? Then why the hell did you mention my face? Now you're confusing me."

Josh expelled a long breath and looked up at the ceiling. "When Brad showed me your picture, you reminded me of someone I didn't want to be reminded of. That's the only reason I said what I did."

I narrowed my eyes. "Who?"

You could hear a pin drop before he finally spoke.

"You reminded me of my mother in that picture."

I blinked. "Your mother?"

"You don't even look that much like her, but there was something about your expression in that photo—your face. That's why I said it. I never even explained that to Brad. He just thought I was being a dick, I'm sure. *He* never asked me why I'd said it."

My mouth dropped. "Well, that's a bit...fucked up."

He crossed his arms. "You think?"

I didn't know what to say. *I'd reminded him of his mother?* The one who'd cheated on his dad with his uncle. The one who abandoned him. At least his comment made a little more sense now. Not knowing what he'd meant had bothered me for far too long.

"Well, thank you for your honesty."

"I couldn't have you go on thinking there was something wrong with your face," he said. "That would've been more fucked up than I am."

"You're not fucked up because you have trauma from your mom. And you don't have to tell me anything more. You answered my question. We can drop the subject."

He exhaled and started to pace. "There's not much to tell. Our mother decided a long time ago that her life was better off without her husband and kids. Being back in Woodsboro is never easy for me, but especially now that Brad is gone. This place, and the Longos, were always my distraction from my home life. I always felt wanted here."

"Your dad didn't handle things well, I take it?"

He stopped pacing and turned to face me. "He did the best he could, but he was always depressed. He's better now. But back then my brothers and I had to fend for ourselves for the most part, while also looking out for him. That's why I was always over here. It was my escape, my way of handling it—by pretending to be part of another family. Then after Yvonne died, that was a whole different kind of loss. It was worse than my mother leaving, to be honest."

"Every corner of this house must have a memory for you, huh?"

He looked around and whispered, "Yep."

When his eyes found mine again, I asked, "Do I still remind you of her?"

Josh shook his head. "No. It was just a weird first impression based on one snapshot. You don't look like her, and you're nothing like her, trust me. You care more about that damn dog than my mother ever cared about us. And you're great with Scottie, even if half the time you don't know what you're doing. You try your best."

I laughed. "Are you saying I deserve a booby prize for my efforts?"

Josh gave me the side eye. "What the fuck is a booby prize?"

"You've never heard of that?"

"No, it sounds interesting though." He snapped his fingers. "Wait, was that silicone tit we fried your booby prize?"

I snorted. "I thought you were smarter. A booby prize is not actually about *boobs*, Mathers."

"Sorry. I only know one kind of booby—very well, I might add."

"It's a term for the prize given to the last-place finisher. Like a consolation prize. Booby prize."

"Ah. Well, then yeah, you definitely deserve a booby prize." He winked. "A for effort, though."

"Well, thank you." I tucked a piece of my hair behind my ear. "I know you're trying, too. We would tie for the booby prize around here."

We just looked at each other for a few moments. "It's my turn to ask you something," he said.

"Uh-oh." My pulse raced. "Okay."

"How come you freaked out whenever Brad would come to visit me in Chicago? Was it just about that text, or was it something more?"

"I didn't trust you at all," I explained. "He always said you'd gotten him into trouble growing up, and I worried that would extend into adulthood. He told me about all the women you dated, how he never thought you'd settle down."

"How bad do you think I am?" Josh chuckled. "I'll admit, I liked to party. And I like women. But I never tried to steer him wrong once I realized how committed he was. In the end, I respected his feelings for you."

"I believe you now. But that wasn't easy to see then."

Josh leaned against the counter. "Honestly? Living on the edge has gotten a little old for me, especially since Brad died. Maybe it's depression, but nothing gets my rocks off anymore. Nothing stimulates me." His eyes bore into mine. "I wish I could find something that did."

I felt my face heat. "How was that date you had the other night?"

"Oh." Josh looked away. "It...didn't work out."

"Shame." I sighed. "Maybe it's not so much that nothing gets your rocks off, but more the fact that you're getting older, wanting different things."

He shrugged. "I don't know what I want. That's always been my problem, but especially now that everything in life seems trivial." He glanced down at my fingernails and grinned. "You cut your claws."

"You were right. I couldn't wipe his ass with them."

Josh broke out into laughter. "The things you never thought you'd have to worry about, huh?"

"Actually, speaking of things *you* never thought you'd have to worry about... I have a favor to ask."

"What?"

"Would you consider letting Scottie shower with you from now on—planned, of course? Me bathing him isn't working out. He doesn't like to sit still, and I get water all over me. I think it would go smoother if he was able to stand in the shower with someone. He clearly prefers that, and I suspect that's what he was used to. Obviously, it's not appropriate for me to shower with him."

"I'm sure I speak for him when I say I think he would *love* that." Josh grinned mischievously.

I could feel myself blushing. "Yeah, well, *I* wouldn't..."

"You'd rather me get my crank yanked."

"Basically, yeah."

Josh glared at me, then sighed. "Okay. I'll take him in with me. But I need, like, ten minutes to myself in there first. Then I'll holler and you can bring him in. Sound good?"

"Yeah. Of course."

My imagination ran wild about what Josh might need those ten minutes alone in the shower for. Brad always used to jerk off in the shower. Given this living situation and the lack of privacy, I assumed the shower had to be where Josh pleasured himself. I felt an unwanted tingle between my legs at the thought, once again a reminder that I needed to cool off. For some reason, I found that visual so freaking hot—found *him* so freaking hot—which was quite disturbing. It was grossly inappropriate to think sexual thoughts about Brad's best friend. But I'd found myself more and more aware lately of just how long it'd been since I'd been touched by a man. If Josh were anyone else, I might've taken advantage of our living situation. But since that would *never* happen, I had to control these sexual thoughts.

• • •

After dinner that night, Josh helped me with the dishes before he sat with Scottie while I took a shower.

"Bathroom's free," I announced as I emerged, fully dressed, with the ends of my hair dripping down my shirt.

"Any idea why he listens to Elton John songs played backwards?" Josh asked.

I ran a hand through my wet strands. "He has this app that records songs and plays them in reverse. It's crazy all the shit he knows how to do, even if he won't talk to us." I sighed. "But he definitely loves Elton John."

"It took me a bit to figure out that he was listening to 'Can You Feel the Love Tonight?'" Josh stood. "Anyway, I'm actually gonna work out before I shower him, if you don't mind."

"I didn't realize we had a home gym," I teased.

"I'm just gonna do what I can in the space we have. I need to do something. I belong to a gym back home. I'm starting to feel disgusting."

That was comical, considering he *looked* far from disgusting. The man was physical perfection, and his body was rock solid. But I supposed when you were used to working out and had to stop, you felt out of commission.

"Why don't you join a gym in Woodsboro?" I suggested.

"The closest one is like thirty minutes away, but I might have to, depending on how long we're here. For now, I'll just improvise."

He was right. Neither of us knew how long we'd be stuck in Woodsboro, so we needed to set up routines here. I made a mental note to follow up on the process for getting Scottie on a waiting list this week. Josh had made some calls, but thus far no one had gotten back to him. We'd been so busy adjusting to life here, we hadn't had a chance to be very proactive with that yet.

Scottie retreated to his room, and I busied myself in the kitchen while Josh began his workout. He started with crunches, then moved to push-ups. Since the kitchen opened to the living area, I had a front-row seat to his exercise routine. So did Bubba, who had situated himself in the corner of the living room. Could've sworn the dog was drooling. *I can't blame you, Bubba.*

When Josh eventually began lifting the end table up and down, using it as a weight, I really became transfixed. The shape of his muscles changed, depending on the movement. The ripples of his stomach became even more defined when he strained. A thin line of hair led down to the V at the bottom of his abdomen. And then there was the glistening sheen of sweat over his flawless skin... His tanned body was like a work of art behind hypothetical velvet ropes I'd never have the right to cross. And we won't talk about the subtle grunting noises that made it very easy to imagine what he might sound like having sex.

When he'd finished, Josh grabbed a towel to wipe the sweat off his body. My tongue buzzed as my mouth fell slightly open, the muscles between my legs awakening even more. I might've appreciated that sight a little too much.

"Can I help you?"

His question snapped me out of my trance, but it took a few seconds to register why he'd asked me that. He'd caught me staring. My stomach dropped.

"Nope," I said as I shook my head and pretended to be busy in the kitchen.

Motherfucker.

After that, I disappeared into my bedroom and didn't speak to him for the rest of the night.

EIGHT

Carly

A FEW DAYS later, I still hadn't gotten over that terribly awkward staring moment the other night. As embarrassing as it was, I decided to tell Christina during our catch-up call while driving home from my first official makeup gig at the salon.

She was grasping at straws, trying to make me feel better about it. "When he said 'Can I help you?' maybe he was just asking if you needed anything?"

That was laughable. "I wish." I shook my head. "No. It was definitely his way of chastising me for staring. Josh is a cocky fucking bastard."

"So what if he was teasing you?"

"So what? It's mortifying, that's what."

"I still think you could be misinterpreting why he said that."

"No. I think the dick side of him that I'd thought had gone into hibernation came back out. He's full of himself. He knows he's good-looking. He caught me staring, and he decided to call me out on it. Just when I was starting to think he was nice."

"Have you said anything to him?"

"Neither of us has mentioned it again. I've just pretended like it didn't happen, pretended to let it roll off of me. I made small talk with him the next morning. And the past few days have been business as usual."

"Well, then it's already blown over."

"For *him*, maybe. Not for me. I still feel dumb for staring at him like that, and even dumber for letting my guard down long enough to get caught."

"You're only human." She paused. "You need to get out of that house. Have you made any friends there you could go out with?"

"Well, I did makeup this morning for a wedding and got to talking to one of the bridesmaids—Lisa. She says we should go out for a drink or dinner some night. She's also new in town. So I think I'm gonna take her up on it."

"Perfect. Make that sooner rather than later, please." She sighed. "For the record, I don't blame you for ogling Josh. I can only imagine what a sight he was all sweaty."

"You're not helping."

"The man just looks like he knows how to fuck, doesn't he?"

"Goodbye, Christina!" I hung up.

But yeah, he does.

• • •

I thought I'd reached the peak of embarrassment the other night, but I was wrong.

Josh sat at the table, casually having coffee as I walked into the house after my drive home from the salon. The smell of cigarettes emanated from him. He hadn't smelled like that since the first day he arrived.

"Where's Scottie?" I asked.

"In his room," he answered without making eye contact.

I stated the obvious. "You smell like smoke."

"Must be the firewood." He brought his mug to his mouth.

"Bullshit. The pellet stove doesn't emit any fumes."

"Yeah. I caved and had one. Big deal." He pointed toward the door. "I did it outside, though, while keeping an eye on Scottie through the window."

"You'd been doing so well. What happened?"

He still wasn't looking at me, and instead stared straight ahead. "Just human, I guess."

Then something in front of him on the table caught my attention: pieces of ripped pages piled atop...*my journal.*

A rush of adrenaline shot through me. "Why do you have that?"

"It's apparently your diary."

"I'm quite aware of that." My heart began to pound. "You were snooping in my room?"

He shot daggers at me. "Think, Carly. Of the two guys in this house, who is the one more likely to have been ransacking your room?"

"You were supposed to be watching him while I was at the salon," I yelled.

"God forbid I take a piss in peace. Is it not bad enough that I'm showering with him now? Getting my balls tugged?"

I wanted to laugh, but this moment was far from funny.

"Scottie ripped those pages out?"

"The notebook is bright orange, like his iPad cover. Probably caught his attention. The drawer next to your bed was open, so he must have gone in there. I assume that's where you kept it. Admittedly, I'd been letting him hang out in your room, but you sometimes do, too. I went to check on him, make sure he wasn't doing anything bad, and found those pages strewn about." A vein popped in his neck.

Josh was angry. *Why?* I should've been the angry one.

"Did you read it?"

"I only happened to see what was on the pages he ripped. I didn't read anything else once I figured out what the hell it was."

This is bad. Starting to sweat, I asked, "But *how much* did you see?"

He stood up from his seat and slowly approached me. With each step he took toward me, I took one back. When we could go no farther, he placed his arms on either side of me, leaning his hands against the wall. And I forgot how to breathe.

Fear. Arousal. Embarrassment. You name it, I was feeling it right now. Every emotion hit me at once.

His breath grazed my face. "How much did I actually see?" He paused. "Enough to know you think I'm an evil pig."

Ugh. No. Now his anger made sense.

When he backed away, I walked over to the ripped pages on the table and sifted through them.

"It's the last one, for reference," he noted.

I read what I'd written the other night.

I'm mortified right now. I was staring at Josh while he was working out, and he caught me. The evil pig called me out on it! But worse, what kind of woman checks out her dead fiancé's best friend? I must need to get laid in the worst way. It's not about Josh. I know that. He's a very attractive man, but it's not about him. I'm just lonely. And I think it's suddenly hitting me. But I feel so damn guilty.

I stared down at the paper, unable to look him in the eyes.

"You feel guilty for finding me attractive?"

My first inclination was to deny that I found him attractive, but I'd freaking written it down. There was no way to take it back.

I finally looked up. "Of course, I feel guilty. It's wrong."

"There's nothing wrong about physical attraction. It's natural and automatic." He dragged his hand through his hair. "But what *is* wrong...is the way I shamed you for looking at me. I was just messing with you." His eyes seared into mine. "I *liked* the way you were looking at me, in fact. So I'm a little fucked up, too, see? I also liked calling you out on it and teasing you, so maybe I am a bit of a dick—and a pig, as you say." He sighed. "I'm sorry if I embarrassed you. And you're not the only one who feels guilty lately." He shook his head. "Most days I feel guilty just for being fucking alive."

"That's why you smoked—because you saw what I wrote. It upset you."

"Maybe," he said as he returned to his seat. "It made me realize how much of a horrible person you think I am. But I was upset at myself before I even saw what you wrote—because you've been acting weird toward me, even if you thought you were pretending nothing was wrong."

So much for my acting potential. "Despite what I wrote in that journal in the heat of my embarrassment, I don't think you're horrible. Nor do I think you're an evil pig. But you *do* have your moments. We both have them lately." I blew out a long breath, feeling on edge. "If I smoked, I might have one right now, too." I pulled up a chair and sat across from him. "I've been locked inside this house for far too long. Which reminds me, I'm going to make plans to go out one night soon with this woman I met today—for a girls' night."

"Look at you, getting a life." He smirked.

"Trying to."

He nodded. "I'm happy to watch Scottie while you go out...as soon as I get back."

"Back?" My eyes widened. "Where are you going?"

"I was gonna tell you when you got home today. I have to go back to Chicago for a couple of days."

My muscles tightened. "Oh...did something happen?"

"I have to meet with a brand-new client. My job is ninety-percent remote, but occasionally I'm required to go in person. It should only be for a few days. I'll be back before next weekend. And then you can go out."

"Okay...well, thanks for letting me know."

It was funny to think there'd been a time when I thought I could do this all alone. Now I didn't know how I was gonna make it through a few days without Josh. I could never admit that to him, though.

"You'll be okay," he said. "Worse comes to worst, if something happens, Abe is right next door."

Waving my hand, I feigned confidence. "Yeah. I'll be absolutely fine. No worries."

Josh and I said nothing else about the diary entry that night. But I wasn't going to be able to let go of that easily. It would likely come out to haunt me when Mr. Hyde decided to make an appearance again someday.

• • •

The following morning, Josh had already left for the airport by the time I woke up. Scottie was still sleeping, and the house was eerily quiet. Is this what it would've been like had Josh never showed up that first day? At one time, that's what I'd wanted—to be left alone here to take care of Scottie, to make my mistakes without an audience. But now I absolutely hated it. He'd only just left, and I was already counting the minutes until Josh returned from Chicago.

When I went to grab a mug, I noticed a note on the counter.

A Thank You from The Trappist Monks of St. Francis:
Is it weird that one of my favorite foods is bacon? You know, considering I'm a pig and all. Does that make me a cannibal? Just kidding, Carly. (Seriously.) See you in a few days.

When I opened the drawer to get a coffee pod, there was another note.

A Thank You from The Trappist Monks of St. Francis:
You told Bubba what a dick I've been, didn't you? He left me a surprise in the kitchen this morning, and I stepped in it. He's never done that. You trained him well, Pumpkin. Just kidding again. Not about the dog crap, though. Unfortunately, that actually happened.

As I prepared my coffee, I smiled through my yawn. But when I opened the fridge for the cream, I found another note taped to the carton.

This one nearly made my heart stop.

A Thank You from The Trappist Monks of St. Francis:
Your face is beautiful. I'm sorry for ever making you doubt that.

NINE

Josh

AFTER ANOTHER BUSY day at the office, I headed to the Piccadilly Pub in downtown Chicago with some work friends. My mind kept wandering to Woodsboro, though, and namely what was going on back home with Carly.

The night before I flew out here, I'd heard the sound of something eerie coming from her room after she went to bed. It was Brad. His voice. At first, I'd thought I was hallucinating. But then I realized Carly was playing one of his old voicemails over and over. I'd placed my ear against her door to listen and nearly broke down. It had hit me in the gut, and I'd thought of little else since.

She and I'd had a pretty intense exchange over the diary, too. The way her breath had hitched when I'd backed her against the wall wasn't lost on me. So, yeah, I supposed there were multiple reasons I hadn't been able to stop thinking about that night.

I wondered how she was holding up after the past couple of days with Scottie alone. I sent her a text from the pub.

Josh: Everything going okay over there?

She responded right away.

Carly: Well, I just showered with Scottie. So there's that.

Oh shit.

Josh: Um...how the hell did you manage that?

Carly: He's gotten so used to showering with you that I couldn't get him in there unless I went with him. I put on my bikini.

Fuck. The visual that gave me.

Josh: Way to improvise, Pumpkin.

Carly: At least I have a solution in case you don't come back.

Josh: If you plan to start wearing that bikini around the house, I'll definitely be back.

I immediately regretted that. It was way too flirtatious, even if I was just joking. The alcohol was making me ballsy.

Josh: Kidding, of course. But was that your way of checking to make sure I'm coming back?

Carly: I can't imagine you'd want to after getting a taste of freedom again.

That was the fucked-up thing. I *did* miss being at the house with Carly and Scottie—and the damn dog, too. That was starting to feel like home, while this—being out in a cold bar—felt foreign. This feeling of missing someplace was definitely new to me.

Josh: I'll be back tomorrow.

Carly: Cool.

Josh: Then you can have your night out on the town. Although, just a warning, Woodsboro isn't all that exciting.

Carly: Just being out will be exciting. I'll text my new friend Lisa to confirm. It will probably be Saturday night.

Josh: Yeah. Whenever.

Carly: How is it being back in Chicago?

Josh: A little strange. But I'm enjoying my bed.

Carly: I bet!

Josh: How's the dog?

Carly: Still here.

Josh: Damn, I was hoping he'd be gone by the time I came back. ;-)

Carly: You don't mean that.

Josh: You're right. I don't. I'm getting used to having him around. Never thought I'd say that.

Carly: He misses you.

Josh: He misses my leg.

Carly: LOL

Josh: Only action I'm getting lately. So maybe I should just appreciate it.

The three dots moved around for an unusually long time.

Carly: No action out in Chicago? I'm surprised.

Josh: What do you think, I step off the plane and have a woman at the ready?

Carly: Maybe that's how I imagined your life.

Josh: I've had my share of fun over the years. But it's not as wild now as you imagine.

Carly: You did say things changed after Brad died. You lost interest or something?

My head spun a little. I'd already had one too many, but I typed the words anyway.

Josh: Everything changed after Brad died, Pumpkin. Everything.

Carly: I know.

Josh: I've also started to realize that the fun I always thought I was having was probably just my way of masking other issues. But that's a discussion for another day.

Carly: You're way more human than I thought, Mathers.

Josh: What was I before, a primate?

Josh: Wait… a pig? ;-)

Carly: No, LOL. But it's nice to know there's someone out there who understands what I've been going through.

My chest tightened.

Josh: This is too deep of a conversation to be having in the middle of a crowded bar. I'm also a little drunk, so I should probably stop texting before I start telling you secrets or some shit.

Carly: You're not driving, are you?

Josh: No. Calling a ride.

Carly: Okay, good. Be careful.

Josh: Yes, Mom.

Carly: That's a little disturbing, you know, after what you told me about my photo reminding you of her.

Shit.

Josh: I didn't mean it like that.

Carly: Okay. ☺

Josh: Tell Scottie I said hi.

Carly: I will.

"You texting a woman?" my friend asked.

I flinched. "No. Why do you think that?"

"You were smiling. So I just assumed."

I put my phone face down, a bit disappointed in myself. "I was?"

"Yeah."

Jordan was my work buddy and closest friend in Chicago. I'd yet to tell him about Carly being in Woodsboro with me and our living situation. He thought I was taking care of Scottie on my own, which was the original plan.

"I was just checking in on things back in Woodsboro," I said.

"I can't believe you're staying out there."

I took a sip of my drink. "It's not that bad."

"Really? You were dreading going..."

"I was. But it's been okay."

"Who's with the dude now while you're here? His aunt?"

I didn't want to get into it. "It's a bit of a long story."

He pushed. "I got time."

"Brad's fiancée is with him, actually. She's been living with us and helping me."

"Whoa." His eyes practically bugged out of his head. "How did that happen?"

"We both had the same idea and both thought we were the right person for the job. We showed up around the same time and told the other to leave. Neither one of us budged. Then we both realized how difficult it was and decided to stay and help each other."

Jordan was still processing. "Wait...you've been *living* with her?"

"Yes." I took another sip of my drink.

"This is the girl you never liked, right?"

My throat felt bitter. "I never really knew her."

"What about now?"

I moved my straw around in the ice. "I think she's... great, to be honest. We have our moments when we bicker, but I sort of enjoy them. Makes the time go by faster."

"That's some crazy shit. You've been holding out on me."

"It's really not that crazy. It's just the way things worked out."

"The way you were smiling when you were texting her... You sure there's nothing going on there?"

Feeling a rush of nervous energy, I shook my head. "No, of course not. It's not like that."

"I wouldn't judge you if there were something happening, you know."

"There's not," I snapped.

"You're not attracted to her?"

"That's irrelevant. I couldn't do that to Brad even if I were."

"Brad's not here anymore, Josh."

The slap of his statement hurt my chest.

"He is." I pointed to my heart. "He's here." I pointed to my head. "And here. So, no."

I felt myself sweating. The thoughts I'd had since I caught Carly ogling me had run rampant in my mind over the past few days. So had the guilt. It was bad enough I'd woken up drenched and hard last night after a vivid dream where I was angry-fucking her from behind while pulling on her long, blonde hair. I knew I wouldn't act on my impulses, but the thoughts were there—a perfect example of why I'd volunteered to come out here, though I technically didn't have to. I could have gotten out of it. But I needed a breather from the tension.

"I can respect your feelings on Brad," Jordan said. "But just curious—I mean, if you're cohabitating with her, and there's some mutual attraction there, it's gotta be tough. Living in the middle of the woods with a hot woman? You can't tell me the line doesn't blur a little."

If I knew Jordan, he was going to keep pushing until he got everything out of me. So I decided to make his job easier.

"We had one awkward thing happen that was entirely my fault." I crunched on some ice.

"What happened?"

I explained the diary incident and what prompted it.

"She must think you're the biggest dick." He laughed.

I chuckled. "She's thought that for a long time. So nothing new. I guess I only confirmed it."

"She doesn't want to want you..." He smirked. "But she does."

"Carly doesn't *want* me. Believe me. She just thinks I'm attractive. That doesn't mean anything."

"Sure. Tell yourself that." He snickered. "I can't imagine how tense things must've been after that."

"It was pretty much right before I came out here. I think we both needed a break, which is why this trip came at the perfect time. Even if it's only for a few days."

"Well, then..." He placed his hand on my shoulder. "We should make the most of your time back here. Let's go to the club."

Jordan would use any excuse to keep the party going. The Ivy Club was his go-to place for a nightcap. I already felt like I'd had one too many, but...

"Yeah. Sure. Why not? It's my last night."

Once we got to the club, I continued to feel out of sorts as I nursed another drink and pretended to be interested in this woman who'd started a conversation with me. But I knew I'd be going home alone tonight. And that was fine.

On the car ride back, I noticed I'd missed another text from Carly.

Carly: Goodnight, Josh.

I felt bad that she probably thought I'd chosen to ignore it. But I didn't want to wake her by texting back in the middle of the night.

I stared at the phone for several seconds, thinking about the fact that she'd bothered to text me goodnight. Goodnight texts were not something I got from anyone on a regular basis. Sending someone a text before bed implied that you were one of the last things they were thinking about. It made me feel...undeserving. But also good—warm inside in a way I wasn't used to. I knew we couldn't be more than friends, yet I basked in that feeling for a moment. As uneasy as this situation made me, I couldn't wait to get back to Woodsboro.

TEN

Josh

CARLY PRACTICALLY JUMPED off the couch when I entered the house the following evening.

"Josh!" She ran to greet me. "You're back early."

"Yeah." I dropped my travel bag on the floor. "Things at work wrapped up sooner than anticipated, so I caught an earlier flight."

She had a huge smile on her face. "I'm not happy you're here to relieve me or anything."

"Not at all." I winked and bent to pet the dog, who'd been circling around me for attention. "Hey, Bubba. Your boytoy is back."

Then I moved to the couch and sat down, wrapping my arm around Scottie. He hadn't had much of a reaction when I walked in.

"You miss me, buddy?"

An automated voice from Scottie's iPad said, *"I want to take a bath."* He'd pressed the bath icon on his picture-board app.

Carly laughed. "I think he misses your naked man-showers."

"Oh, I'd bet he's going to miss your bikini ones more."

Carly blushed and tucked a piece of her hair behind her ear. "I'm making gluten-free pasta and that sauce you like. Are you hungry?"

Fuck. Was I ever hungry. Her question reminded me of the dream I'd had last night about fucking her while she called me an evil pig and pulled my hair. And of course, that only confirmed the fact that I *was* an evil pig to be having that kind of fantasy about Brad's woman. I felt like a dirt bag.

I cleared my throat. "I'm starving, actually. Thank you. I've had nothing but peanut-butter sandwiches and alcohol the past few days."

"Sounds...nourishing." She chuckled.

I stared at her for a moment. Carly had sauce on her white shirt and her hair was all over the place, but she still looked stunningly beautiful—somehow even more beautiful than before I left. For a moment, I imagined a world where I'd just come home to this woman, lifted her up onto the counter, and kissed the hell out of her. A world, of course, where she hadn't also been the love of my best friend's life.

Get these fucking thoughts out of your head, Josh.

There was one sure-fire way I knew to switch gears with my thoughts—bringing up Brad.

"You were listening to Brad the other night...before I left." I gulped.

Carly stilled. "How did you know?"

"I heard his voice coming from your room."

Her cheeks reddened. "It was a voicemail."

"I know. I figured that out." I scratched the dog's ears. "Do you do that a lot?"

"Sometimes it brings me comfort. He always had my back. And hearing his voice reminds me of what it felt like to be loved. I feel very fortunate to have those voicemails."

"I don't have any voicemails from him saved. Not sure why. We always texted, I guess. But it was nice to hear him again."

She walked over and grabbed my sleeve. "You can listen to them whenever you want."

I smiled sadly. "Thank you."

Carly looked like she was about to cry. She cleared her throat. "So, how was the trip?"

"Good. But like I told you before, it felt a little weird being back there—like I was a fish out of water in my own life."

"I'm sure I'd feel the same way if I were in California right now."

"It was strange to have all this free time on my hands—even with work. I wasn't responsible for anyone else. I didn't know what to do with myself."

"I can imagine."

"I sort of missed being back here," I admitted.

She tilted her head. "Really..."

"Yeah. Really," I said.

"Well, this is an exciting place," she teased.

A loud knock interrupted our conversation.

When I opened the door, there was a police officer standing there.

My hands tensed. "Can I help you?"

"I'm looking for Carly Garber?"

What the hell?

"That's me," she said from behind.

"Officer Allan Spencer from the Woodsboro Police. It seems we've finally located the owner of the dog you've been keeping here."

Oh shit.

"What?" Carly's expression fell. "Are you sure?"

"Yes. Seems he belongs to a local woman with dementia. Name's Heidi Donahue. She lives on Wilson Road. She took him for a walk in the middle of the night and couldn't remember what happened. Her daughter's been looking for him ever since. Ms. Donahue apparently hadn't told her the dog was gone until recently, thus the delay." He showed us a photo.

Carly took the picture from him and examined it. "Wow. Okay. Yeah. That's definitely Bubba." She looked up at the officer. "What's his actual name? Do you know?"

"Hank."

I stifled laughter. "Hank?"

Carly looked over at me. I couldn't tell if she was about to laugh or cry. "Hank," she whispered.

"I'm sorry, Carly," I murmured.

"You have to take him back now?" she asked the officer.

"I'm sorry, ma'am, but yes."

Carly went over to the couch where Bubba was sitting. She buried her face in his fur. "You have to go home, Bub—Hank. I didn't know that was your name. I'm sorry."

"I'll let you say your goodbyes," the officer said. "I'll be right outside."

Tears filled Carly's eyes as she wrapped her arms around the dog. Was it too much to ask of the damn universe to let this woman keep the one thing that seemed to make her happiest? Not that we should've been harboring a missing dog, but Carly worked hard around here to make *us* happy. She deserved the joy that dog had brought her in the short time he'd been here. Hadn't she fucking lost enough in her life? Now she had to say goodbye to him, too.

It's official. Being here is turning me into a fucking sap.

She sniffled. "Say goodbye, Scottie. Bubba has to go."

Scottie rocked back and forth, seemingly oblivious to the situation. He held his iPad to his ear and blasted some music. It was probably a good thing not to care one way or the other under sad circumstances. I envied him sometimes.

I sat down on the couch on the other side of the dog. "Bye, Bubba." Massaging behind his ears, I added, "I'll miss your extra-special leg rubs."

The dog leaned in to lick my nose. His breath smelled like biscuits.

"You take him outside, Josh," Carly said, getting up suddenly.

I stood. "You sure?"

"Yeah." She paced while wiping her eyes. "I can't say goodbye again."

I nodded. "Okay."

After I handed Bubba to the officer outside, I watched as he put the dog into the back of the car. Bubba—Hank—stared at me from the window. He looked helpless. The freaking dog was making my eyes water now. *Damn it.* I waved at him and watched as the car took off down the road. Being back in Woodsboro was turning me into a pussy.

When I walked back into the house, Carly was on the couch next to Scottie, looking morose.

She stood, and I walked over, putting my arms around her and bringing her close.

I spoke into her hair. "I'm sorry."

My chest constricted as I fought the feeling holding her elicited in me. I hadn't thought it through. It'd just felt like the natural thing to do. But the way my body reacted only confirmed my worst fears.

She looked up at me. "I can't believe he's gone."

I moved back. "We'll always have good memories of Bubba-Hank. I mean, what the hell would we have done with him when we had to leave?"

"I was planning on taking him back to California with me," she said.

Damn, she was fucking sweet. I should've known. "You were a good dog mama, Pumpkin." I smiled. "Why don't you get a dog when you get back?"

"I probably will." Taking a deep breath in, Carly looked up at me. "You don't smell like smoke. I just realized that."

"I resisted the entire time I was away."

She smiled. "Good."

My eyes fell to her lips, and I forced them back up. *You have no fucking right to this, Josh. Get your god-damn eyes off her.*

She cleared her throat. "We should eat."

"Yeah." I nodded. "Let's do it."

We sat Scottie down with his chicken and perfectly aligned dessert and joined him at the table. Carly served us two heaping plates of gluten-free pasta with sauce while I poured two glasses of red wine.

After we finished dinner, I picked up our empty plates before she had a chance to and brought them over to the sink.

"Did you shower yet today?" I asked her.

"Why?" She raised her eyebrows. "Do I smell?"

"No." I chuckled. "I was just wondering if you wanted to take one in peace."

"Actually, I did hold off in the hopes that I could do it alone tonight."

"Why don't you go relax and take a long one. He and I'll go in after."

"That sounds divine." Her eyes rolled back.

My dick twitched. *Fuck.* The way she did that with her eyes... *Make it stop.*

"Go." I shooed her away. *Please go.* "I've got the cleanup."

She beamed. "You sure?"

"Yep."

After Carly disappeared into the bathroom, I noticed that she'd jotted something down on a notepad next to the sink.

A Thank You from The Trappist Monks of St. Francis:
Proud of you for not smoking.

Grinning, I walked over to Scottie who was still sitting at the table. "You must've enjoyed those bikini showers when I was gone, huh, you devil? Probably wishing I'd go away again, aren't you?" I shook my head. "Brad would have both of our heads if he knew about some of the stuff going on around here lately."

Scottie squealed, as if in agreement, though I was pretty sure he was reacting to his cookie.

About the time I'd filled the dishwasher, cleaned the pans by hand, and wiped down the countertops, Carly emerged from the bathroom.

I slung the dishtowel over my shoulder. "That was fast."

"It was really nice. Thank you." She ran a hand through her wet hair. "Are you still good to watch him tomorrow night?"

I'd nearly forgotten about her plans to go out with that new friend of hers. "Absolutely. Do you know where you're going?"

She cocked her head. "The Bar?"

Great. That place was a meat market. I nodded. "I know it well. There aren't that many options in Woodsboro. But they have good live music."

"And that's the actual name—The Bar?"

"Yeah. Real original, right?"

It would take all of five minutes for Carly to get hit on in that place.

"You should go out too...one night this coming week or whenever," she suggested.

"Maybe. I haven't hung out with my brothers in a while."

"I would imagine going out in Woodsboro is a lot different for you than it is for me," she said. "It must be weird running into all these people you used to know way back when..."

I nodded. "That's one of the reasons I haven't yet. I'm in no rush."

"I can understand that." She sighed. "If I run into someone I know at the store, I turn the other way instead of going toward them."

"That's what you wished you could've done when I showed up here that first day, I bet."

"God, yeah."

I laughed.

After I took Scottie into the bathroom with me for shower time, I helped him get dressed before changing into my evening clothes. I'd definitely be missing my bed in Chicago tonight.

When Scottie and I returned to the living room, Carly was sitting on the couch with her feet up. Her dainty toes were painted red. My eyes might have lingered on them a little too long.

"Did you watch any more of the DVDs while I was away?" I asked.

"No. I waited for you." She sat up. "You want to watch one now?"

"Sure." I took a seat next to Scottie, who promptly began playing on his iPad.

Carly popped another DVD into the player. It was a video from when Brad was home for Christmas. It looked to be about five years old, if I had to guess—so probably right before he'd met Carly. Someone was shooting footage of Wayne and Brad watching Scottie open his Christmas presents.

To my surprise, Scottie got up from his seat on the couch and walked over to the television. He must've recognized Wayne's voice. I'd thought he wasn't paying attention, but I was wrong. He placed both palms flat against the screen and gently pressed his cheek to the glass.

Carly and I both stilled. We were speechless. There was so much inside of Scottie that begged to come out. So much we didn't know about what he could comprehend. Watching him connect with what was on the screen was both sad and beautiful. I didn't know whether he believed they were coming back, or perhaps he thought they were literally inside the television. Either way, it was pretty damn heartbreaking.

Carly moved to the spot next to me with tears in her eyes. "He doesn't understand why they left. He doesn't understand death." She let out a shaky breath. "Josh, what if he thinks they abandoned him?"

Fuck. My eyes were starting to water now. I reached my hand out, and she took it.

"There's nothing more important than this—us being here for him right now," she said.

My voice was strained. "I know."

When the DVD finished, Scottie returned to the couch and resumed playing on his device like nothing had happened.

But Carly and I didn't get over it so easily. We sat in silence for a long while before I said, "I don't know about you, but I could really use some pistachio ice cream right now."

"Between this and losing Bubba-Hank..." She shot up, shaking her head. "I'll get some bowls."

"Bring the whole tub," I hollered after her.

ELEVEN

Carly

ON SATURDAY, WE'D finally arranged for Scottie's therapist, Lauren, to take us to her agency's group home in town. Lorraine had agreed to watch Scottie for a few hours while we were out, and I was feeling good. We were making real progress. If we ended up liking the place, we would take steps to get Scottie on the waiting list. There weren't a lot of options in and around Woodsboro, really only two potential places, and we planned to visit both of them. We'd discussed that the biggest requirement for Scottie's eventual home was that it needed to be local, so Lorraine could be nearby if anything ever happened.

After we arrived, Lauren introduced us to Julie Wilks, the house manager of the place. Julie then took us around, room by room. She explained that all of the tenants had their own bedrooms, and they had twenty-four-hour staff onsite.

She gestured to a large, central room with a television mounted on the wall. "This is the main living space.

Although most of the time the guys who live here prefer staying in their own rooms, we have them congregate together for a couple of hours each night."

"Do most of the men who live here have autism?" I asked.

"Right now we have six tenants, and five of them have autism."

"I see."

Josh scratched his chin. "How many people are on staff?"

"There are three people on duty at any given time, around the clock, in different shifts."

"What's the average wait time to get into a room here?" he asked.

"That's tough to say. We generally only ever have openings if one of the tenants becomes problematic and has to be moved, or if someone's family moves out of state, warranting their child being transferred to another home somewhere else."

My blood ran cold. "So this could literally take years..."

"It could." She shrugged. "But you never know."

Josh and I looked at each other, eyes wide.

Julie then took us out back. Overall, the place seemed well-kept and nice enough. The property was pretty secure, with a fenced-in yard and triple locks on the outside doors. There would definitely be more space here for Scottie than at home. There was only one problem: it *wasn't* home. And I had no idea how he'd react to living in a brand-new environment for the first time in his life.

"I have a question," I said as we reentered the building. "Our guy has some very specific dietary restrictions. For example, there's only one kind of homemade chicken he's willing to eat for dinner. Would there be anyone here who could make it for him, if we gave them instructions?"

She laughed and shook her head. "Oh no. I'm sorry. The cook has enough of a challenge finding something to suit everyone's needs as it is. There's no way he could make an extra meal for just one person. Scottie would have to eat whatever was offered to him."

Josh's forehead crinkled. "What if he didn't?"

"I suppose he'd eat eventually, when he got hungry enough."

"Excuse us for a moment..." Josh said as he took me aside. He lowered his voice. "This isn't gonna work... for a few reasons."

I nodded. "I know. The chicken thing, and they said they have a strict lights-out policy with no electronics after a certain time at night. Scottie needs his devices."

Josh ran a hand through his hair. "I just worry we won't have a choice. All these places might operate the same way."

After a moment, Julie and Lauren joined us in the hallway.

"Is everything okay?" Julie asked.

"Let me ask you this..." I turned to her. "If we could get someone to make Scottie's special chicken and bring it here, would that be okay?"

She paused. "I don't see why not. We do have family members drop off food from time to time."

I let out a sigh of relief. "Okay. At least that's an option."

We would certainly have to talk to Lorraine about that, since she would be the only person local to make it once Josh and I moved back to our respective cities. Heck, I'd make it and ship it on dry ice, if I had to.

With our tour concluded, Julie showed us back to the front door.

"Well, thank you for your time. We really appreciate the tour."

"It's been my pleasure." She smiled. "My recommendation is to get on the waiting list as soon as possible. We might have an opening come sooner than you were expecting."

"We'll consider that," Josh said. "Thank you."

As we stood on the sidewalk in front of the place, Lauren looked between us. "What did you think?"

"It's an option," I said, looking back over at the brick house. "I don't know if anything is going to feel exactly right. No place is going to be his home."

"He'll get used to it," she assured us. "They all do."

Pffft. Easy for you to say. Visiting this place made *me* feel overwhelmed.

Josh must have noticed my expression as I stared out toward the street.

He placed his hand on my arm. "You okay?"

"Yeah," I muttered. "Thanks for bringing us here," I told Lauren.

"No problem. If you need any help with the waiting-list paperwork, let me know."

"I have the application." I nodded. "Thank you."

Josh and I had begun walking to my car when Lauren's voice came from behind.

"Hey, Josh? Could I talk to you for a second before you leave?"

I froze. *What's this about?*

He turned and walked back toward her. "Sure. What's up?"

I continued toward my vehicle. After all, she hadn't called for *me*. And I suspected I knew why, given the way she'd been flirting with Josh today.

Swallowing the lump in my throat, I stood by the car, waiting for him.

When their quick conversation ended, Josh jogged back toward me. "Want me to drive?" he asked.

I handed him the keys. "Sure."

Entering through the passenger side, I refrained from asking him anything about his conversation. And he didn't offer anything as we pulled away in silence.

About five minutes into our ride home, the curiosity was killing me.

I caved. "So, what did Lauren want to talk to you about?"

He looked over with a smirk. "Were you intentionally trying not to ask?"

"Were you *intentionally* trying to bug me by not saying anything?"

"Maybe." He chuckled and waited several seconds. "She asked me if I wanted to go out some night this week."

I knew it. "Wow." My temperature rose. "Pretty ballsy."

"She's definitely confident."

I blew a breath up into my hair. "What did you say?" My heart sped up in anticipation.

"I told her this week wasn't great for me, but maybe another time."

"So you lied. What's wrong with this week?"

"Actually, this week isn't good for me. I just got back from Chicago, and I'm not in the mood to psych myself up for a date."

"So you *would* consider dating her..." I said bitterly.

He shrugged. "She's cute, yeah. There's no off-the-charts chemistry or anything, but I wouldn't rule it out."

"Isn't that a conflict of interest, though? Because she works with Scottie?"

"I suppose it could be. Not sure who would be policing that." He glanced over again. "Unless it were you."

"Why would I do that?" I huffed.

"Then I guess there's no problem..."

"Right," I muttered, annoyed that my blood was boiling right now. I wouldn't allow myself to analyze my reaction, though. I needed to change the subject before he had a chance to sense that I was feeling discombobulated. "So, if you had to grade that house, what would you give it?" I asked.

"C-plus before she said Lorraine could drop off the chicken. B-minus after. You?"

"I would say about a B-minus, too. We should definitely look at the other place in town. Although, I guess if they're both acceptable, it will come down to which one has the first opening."

After we returned home, Lorraine went back to her place. Scottie seemed pretty calm; that might not have been the case if he'd known what Josh and I had been up to today.

For the rest of the day, the tension that had started with Lauren asking Josh out only seemed to escalate—because of me.

Josh ran out to the store to buy a few things we needed, and I couldn't seem to hide my bitchy mood when he texted me a simple question.

Josh: They're all out of your gluten-free muff. Do you want regular?

Carly: Muffins, you mean?

Josh: Yeah, of course. You usually get my sense of humor.

Carly: It's no wonder you have muff on the mind today.

Josh: What's that supposed to mean?

Carly: You should probably buy condoms, too, muffmaster.

Josh: Someone is a little miffed at the prospect of my getting muff?

Carly: Why would I be miffed?

Josh: I don't know. You tell me. You've been weird all afternoon, ever since that thing with Lauren.

Carly: I'm not miffed at your muff. Get over yourself. My mood has nothing to do with that.

Josh: Okay. Whatever. But you didn't answer my muffin question.

Carly: What was it?

Josh: Whether you wanted me to get the regular kind since they don't have gluten free.

Carly: Oh. No. Don't bother.

Josh: No muff for you. Got it.

Throwing my phone aside, I stewed for a while before I had to start getting ready to meet Lisa.

As I changed and did my hair and makeup, I continued to find myself incredibly annoyed that Lauren had asked Josh out, and even more annoyed at myself for being unable to hide that it upset me. Nothing like good old jealousy to bring inappropriate feelings to the surface. There was only one solution, and that was to get a freaking life outside of this house, which was exactly what I planned to do tonight.

TWELVE

Carly

THE BAR WAS a pretty happening spot, with live music, plenty of greasy-food options on the menu, and rustic wood décor. The windows provided a view of the traffic on nearby Highway 106. It was loud and packed when we arrived. Fortunately, we found a table.

Lisa spoke over the ambient noise. "This is actually much more crowded than the last time I was here."

I played with my straw. "Oh, I didn't realize you'd been before."

"Only once, but yeah."

Lisa told me she'd just recently relocated to Woodsboro from Minneapolis to be closer to her sister, who'd moved here with her fiancé a few years earlier. While initially Lisa had looked at the move as an adventure, she was finding life here quite boring thus far. It definitely wasn't the best place to be if you were single.

She was nice enough, and I should have been thrilled to have an evening out, but my mind wandered throughout our conversation. I'd love to be able to tell you I was mulling over legitimate concerns, like where Scottie would end up or how far I'd be able to stretch my limited income and still have a social life. But no. I was still stewing over the fact that Lauren had asked Josh out and he was considering going. I kept trying to tell myself it bothered me because she was Scottie's therapist, but I knew better. That uncomfortable ache in my chest was jealousy. I hadn't experienced that since I was a teenager. Why now? Why was I jealous over a man I could never be with?

"He's kind of cute..." Lisa interrupted my thoughts.

"Who?"

She angled her head toward the bar. "That guy over there."

I turned around to find a dark-haired man sitting alone on one of the stools. He wore jeans, a plaid shirt with rolled-up sleeves, and clunky construction boots.

"I guess."

A few minutes later, I turned around to look over again and found that another dark-haired guy had joined him. They looked to be in their late twenties or early thirties.

"I think I just saw them looking over here," Lisa whispered, her eyes sparkling.

I chose to ignore that, since I wasn't in the mood for anything more than a casual night out with a friend. But her expectations seemed a bit different.

Luckily, our food arrived as a distraction, and Lisa and I chatted while we shared a plate of nachos with our drinks.

But before we'd finished, the two men from the bar walked over.

"Are these seats taken?" one of them asked.

"Not at all." Lisa grinned flirtatiously.

They then helped themselves to the other two seats at our table.

"How are you ladies doing tonight?" one of them asked.

"Not bad, you?" I answered.

Lisa gave me a knowing look. She was quite excited about this turn of events.

The one with the construction boots, whom Lisa had said was cute, had seated himself next to me. He held out his hand. "I'm Neil."

I took it. "Nice to meet you. I'm Carly."

"Are you married?" he asked.

"No."

"Boyfriend?"

Forcing a grin, I repeated, "No."

"Okay. I just didn't want to be inappropriate."

"I appreciate you asking."

We got to talking, and I began to warm up to the whole situation. It turned out, Neil had grown up in Woodsboro and managed a construction company. We made easy conversation while his friend, Rob, chatted up Lisa.

Neil was handsome with classic features. I wouldn't put him in the same category of hotness as Brad and Josh, but looks were only part of the equation. He seemed to have a pleasant, down-to-earth personality and most importantly, kind eyes.

But despite the fact that I was enjoying his company, I felt uncomfortable giving him too much personal information. So I kept my current situation a bit generic, only divulging that I was in town helping a friend with a personal issue, and I would only be here temporarily.

The guys bought us another round of drinks and a couple more appetizers. Our impromptu party of four continued over the next hour.

My phone chimed a little after 10 PM. It was a text from Josh, so I excused myself to the bathroom so I didn't seem rude while texting him back.

Josh: I swore I wouldn't bother you unless I absolutely had to, but I can't for the life of me find Scottie's underwear. He's been freeballing it for the past hour.

I laughed as I typed.

Carly: I did a whole load of laundry this morning. Everything is folded in a basket that's hidden in my bedroom closet. I didn't want him to get into the clothes like he sometimes does. You know how he likes to throw everything around.

A minute later he responded.

Josh: Ah! It's like a gold mine of underwear in here. Thanks.

Carly: You'll have to sift through it to find his.

Josh: I assume the black thong ain't it. ;-)

Carly: No. That's mine.

Josh: Well, it WAS yours. Now it's mine.

Before I could figure out how to respond to that, he wrote back.

Josh: Just kidding. But why did I imagine that Miss Organic Lemon Pits wore granny panties?

My eyes widened. *Ew!*

Carly: Well, the thong is organic cotton, so…

Josh: Ah! I knew there had to be something weird about it. So, even your ass eats organic? Picky little thing, it is.

Carly: OMG! You're nuts.

Josh: My nuts are gluten free.

Carly: Josh! LMAO

Josh: Sorry, I have the sillies. Must be going crazy from listening to an hour straight of "Bennie and the Jets" backwards. I'm about to choke myself to death with your thong.

Carly: You can put it down now.

Josh: You mean take it out of my pocket?

Carly: That'd be great.

Josh: Maybe you'll meet someone at The Bar who'll get to enjoy your organic cotton thong.

I hesitated.

Carly: I have met someone here actually. He's nice.

Josh didn't respond after that. So I assumed he wasn't going to. But about five minutes after I returned to the table, my phone pinged again. I looked down casually to read the text.

Josh: Well, that's good. I had no doubt it wouldn't take long.

My thoughts were stuck on his message until I reminded myself to refocus my attention on the people at my table.

As we were readying to leave, Neil asked for my number. "I'd love to see you again," he said with a smile.

I couldn't think of a reason to say no. I knew I needed this distraction badly. "Sure. That would be great."

He handed me his phone, and I entered my number.

"Cool," he said as I gave it back. "I'll call you this week, and maybe we can arrange something for next weekend, if you're not too busy?"

"I don't have any plans, so that should work," I told him, though I'd have to clear it with Josh.

"Wonderful." He leaned in and gave me a hug that ended in a gentle squeeze. "It was great meeting you, Carly."

I respected the fact that he didn't try to kiss me. That would've been way too soon. "You, too, Neil."

Lisa hugged her prospect goodbye as well, and we watched from in front of the bar as the guys each got into their respective trucks. Lisa's brother-in-law had offered to be our designated driver tonight and was due to arrive any second.

Lisa looked up at the night sky and sighed. "Holy crap. Can you imagine if we both just met our future husbands tonight?"

Is she serious? That made me want to vomit. "Whoa." I laughed. "I think that might be a little far-fetched to even ponder. You like Rob that much already?"

"Honestly? Yeah," she said. "What's not to like? He's adorable and has a great job as an engineer. But I agree, my optimism might be a bit overboard."

"Just a little." I winked. "But I'm happy you liked him."

"Neil is really cute, and he seemed super nice, too."

"Yeah. I'd have to see him again to know for sure how I feel. I don't think you can really know someone after only one meeting."

Although, I remembered explicitly knowing Brad was the one from the first night I met him. But that kind of instant connection wouldn't likely repeat for me. Maybe that's why I was so hesitant to declare Neil a catch. Was it comparison to Brad? Or worse, did my hesitation have to do with the weird-as-hell feelings I seemed to be having for Josh lately?

THIRTEEN

Josh

I DIDN'T WANT her to come home and see me awake, as if I was waiting for her. But I couldn't sleep for shit.

My phone rang, and I thought it might be Carly, but it was my brother Neil. I owed him a phone call.

"Hey, dude," I answered. "What's up?"

"I didn't wake you, did I?"

"No. Not at all. And I've been meaning to call you since I got back, but things have been busy."

"I know. Michael told me. Scottie's a real handful, huh?"

"He sure is."

"How are things going with Brad's ex being there?"

"We're getting along. It is what it is."

"What's her name again?"

"Carly."

The phone went silent. For a moment I thought we'd been disconnected.

"Did you say Carly?" he finally asked.

"Yeah. Why?"

"What does she look like?"

"Why?"

"Just answer me," he said.

"Blonde...medium height...really pretty."

It was radio silence again on the other end of the line.

"I think I met her tonight," he said.

My eyes widened. "You met Carly?"

"Yeah. At The Bar. I'm supposed to go out with her next weekend." He exhaled. "Holy shit. I was on cloud nine and needed to talk to someone about her. That's why I called you."

Fuck.

Fuck.

Fuck.

"How the hell did you not know who she was?" I didn't mean for that to come out so harshly. I softened my tone. "Didn't she tell you what she was doing in town? You didn't put two and two together?"

"She told me she was helping a friend. I could tell she was holding back, but I thought maybe she was being cautious. And I couldn't remember Brad's fiancée's name, so I didn't make the connection."

"You never mentioned my name as your brother?"

"No." He heaved a sigh. "I told her I grew up in Woodsboro but never mentioned my family or anything."

"Well, shit," I muttered.

"Small fucking world, huh?"

"Yeah. For real." I swallowed. "She agreed to go out with you?"

"You sound surprised."

"It was just a question, Neil."

"Yeah. Like I said, next weekend potentially. Is there a reason I shouldn't go out with her?"

I wracked my brain for something I could say, but I had no legitimate reason. "No. I mean, she's a great girl," I answered.

"Didn't you not like Brad's fiancée? I'm a little confused."

You're not the only one. "Yeah, I thought I didn't. But I really had no basis for it. I never got to know her until this trip."

"Should I text her right now and tell her who I am?"

"She'll be here soon. I'll tell her."

"Let me know how she reacts once you do."

"Yeah, man. Okay."

After we hung up, I sat on the edge of the couch and held my head in my hands. This was not a scenario I had anticipated—though it wasn't far-fetched at all considering how small Woodsboro was. This damn situation with Carly and me was complicated enough, though, without her dating my brother. But I had no right to interfere. Carly deserved a good guy.

Hearing Neil say how much he liked her—so much that he had to call me—was bittersweet. I knew what I felt was jealousy, but there was no better human than my brother Neil. He was the opposite of me in every way. He never cheated on his girlfriends, was always respectful, and was the most dedicated to our father of all of us. He also seemed the least scarred by our mother's abandonment. While it would be completely inappropriate for me to make a move on Carly, there was no reason Neil had to feel guilty. He hadn't been Brad's best friend. There was no conflict of interest. He wouldn't go to hell for dating her, like I would have.

When the door opened, I stood up from the couch. *So much for not being obvious about waiting for her to walk in.*

Carly put her purse on an end table. "Hey. I'm surprised you're still up."

"Yeah, well, I'm up half the night on that shitass mattress anyway." I raked my hand through my hair and tried to seem nonchalant. "How was The Bar?"

"It was really good, actually." She plopped down on the couch and sighed. "I was surprised how good the food was. I wouldn't have expected that in a dive-bar atmosphere."

"Yeah, the food's always been good there."

I waited for her to say something else, but she didn't. Carly simply closed her eyes and leaned her head back against the couch. She kicked off her shoes, revealing those red-painted toes that always turned me on in some twisted way.

"You seem pooped, party girl."

"It's definitely way past my bedtime." She yawned.

"So...tell me about this guy you met." I fidgeted with my hands.

She opened her eyes and looked over at me. "I mean, the jury is still out. He seemed nice. But I don't really know him."

"He *is* a nice guy. And you can trust him."

Her eyes widened. "What are you talking about?"

"I'm talking about Neil."

Her mouth fell open as she sat up straight. "Did you set me up or something?"

I had to chuckle at that. "Yeah, because I had all this time to orchestrate setting you up while I went on a scavenger hunt for Scottie's goddamn underpants." I laughed again. "Relax. I had nothing to do with it."

Her face turned crimson. "Then how do you know his name?"

"Well, my brother called me on his way home to tell me about his night out."

"Your brother saw me there?"

"No, Carly." *Holy shit. She doesn't get it.*

Then she covered her mouth.

Bingo. The realization finally hit.

"Oh my God. Neil *is* your brother?"

"He sure is."

She continued to put two and two together. "This is the single one..."

"Yes. Thankfully. Otherwise, I'd be headed over there tonight to strangle him."

She leaned her head into her hands. "My first night out and I freaking meet your brother? How small is this damn town?"

"Pretty fucking small."

Carly stood up and started to pace. "Okay, this is super awkward, Josh."

I agreed, but I attempted to deny it. "It doesn't have to be."

"I guess not?" She sighed. "I don't know."

"Do you like him?" I braced myself for her answer.

"Like I said, I barely know him."

"Neil wouldn't hurt a fly. He's the best person I know. So you have no reason not to trust him."

"Well, thank you for the testimonial, although I have to wonder if it's a bit biased."

"I don't care that he's my brother. If he were a prick, I'd warn you to stay away from him."

"A prick like you?" she teased.

"Well...yeah."

"I'm kidding."

"No, you're not." I laughed.

Her face turned serious. "I don't think you're a prick anymore, Josh. I *was* kidding." She looked at me for a moment as an awkwardness hung in the air.

I cleared my throat. "Well, I suppose if you're going out with Neil next weekend, you'll need me to watch Scottie."

"If you don't mind. I'll return the favor, of course."

"Actually, I was gonna take Lauren up on her offer next weekend, but if you have a date with Neil, I'll reschedule."

Carly's mouth opened and closed a few times. "Oh...I didn't realize you were definitely going out with her."

It's news to me too. "Yeah, why not? Got nothing to lose. Not like I have much else going on out here."

Her neck grew red and blotchy. "Well, if things don't work out, you'll still have to see her. I suppose that would be one downside."

"I'll just have to deal, right?"

"Yeah...I mean, if you don't mind the awkwardness," she said, her cheeks pink.

"Nothing really fazes me."

"Okay, then, Mr. Heartless." She looked down at her toes for a second. "Anyway, if you want to go out next weekend, it's your turn, so I can tell Neil the weekend after."

"We can figure something out between Friday and Saturday. Doesn't have to be an either-or situation."

She nodded and yawned again. "Well, I'm exhausted. I'd better go to sleep. Before I know it, we'll have to get up with Scottie."

"Yeah. It's late. Goodnight."

"Goodnight, Josh." She headed into her bedroom.

That night, I tossed and turned, and for once it wasn't the air mattress keeping me up.

FOURTEEN

Josh

ON FRIDAY NIGHT, I'd arranged a date with Lauren, and Carly had made plans with Neil for Saturday.

Carly had been especially quiet all of Friday afternoon. I could tell my going out with Lauren made her uncomfortable. But being the dick I was, that was part of the point, wasn't it? I'd had no plans to reach out to Lauren until I found out about Neil and Carly. Then I needed the distraction. Carly going out with my brother had gotten under my skin. But it wasn't just about that. I sensed that Carly was starting to have feelings for me. Was it my imagination? I couldn't be sure. But if my suspicions were true, I needed to nip that in the bud.

Friday evening, I opted to meet Lauren at the restaurant, even though she'd offered to pick me up. I borrowed Carly's car to drive over there to spare her having to see Lauren. I knew that would have been awkward. While there was definitely an ulterior motive to this "date," it wasn't to upset Carly.

When I arrived at the one Mexican restaurant in Woodsboro, Lauren was already there. I waved at her as I came in, feeling more hungry than interested in making small talk. I concluded pretty early on that I wasn't feeling it for her, though it would've been conveniently fantastic to have that kind of connection. I was a picky motherfucker as it was, but lately it had been even worse. Essentially, from the moment I sat down at the table, I knew this wasn't going anywhere.

But I did stay to eat. I shoveled some fajita into my mouth and chewed a moment before I spoke. "So you must have a passion for human services to work in the field you do..."

Lauren put her fork down and wiped the corner of her mouth. "Can I be honest? I love my clients. But working with the special-needs population isn't something I want to do forever. It's very taxing emotionally, and physically sometimes."

While I appreciated the honesty, her answer surprised me.

I dipped a chip in some salsa. "You have a good handle on Scottie and always seem so energetic. I just assumed you loved what you did."

"I do love Scottie, and the other people I work with, but not necessarily my job as a whole. It's a lot of work and long hours for very little pay." She cleared her throat and changed the subject. "Tell me more about what you do."

I spent the next several minutes boring even myself as I rehashed the basics of my job while plotting my early-exit strategy tonight. Lauren was attractive enough, and I was pretty certain she would've been a sure bet tonight, based on the way she was looking at me. But even the idea of meaningless, no-strings sex didn't interest me. I was either broken, or I had a much bigger problem—and I wasn't going there. I knew one thing, though: I needed an excuse not to go back to Lauren's place tonight.

Sure enough, when we'd finished our meals, she straight-up asked me if I was interested in coming back to her apartment. So I had to come out with it.

"Lauren, I think you're an amazing girl," I told her, setting my margarita down. "And I enjoyed getting to know you better tonight. But the more I think about it, the more I think it's better if you and I remain friends, given your working relationship with Scottie."

That was a lie. A cop-out. But so was this entire date.

Her face fell as she ran her hand through her long, brown hair. "Why did you even agree to this date if that's how you feel?"

I'd thought I'd be better at faking it. "I guess I only realized that conflict tonight."

I hoped my bogus excuse was better than just admitting I wasn't feeling it. But the disappointment in her eyes told me she might've read between the lines anyway.

The rest of the evening was awkward as fuck, to say the least.

• • •

The following night, my "date" with Lauren was a long-forgotten memory. As I sat in the living room, watching TV next to Scottie on the couch, my eyes kept wandering over to Carly's room. Through the open door, I could see her getting ready for her night out with Neil.

She hadn't asked me about my time with Lauren, and I was grateful. I didn't want to lie to her, and for now it was my preference that she assumed it had gone better than it had. I didn't need Carly suspecting I was invested in the least in what was going on between her and my brother.

I couldn't help but notice how damn beautiful she looked tonight, though. She wore a short pink dress and had pinned a matching flower in her hair. It was like a burst of spring in dark, cold Woodsboro. But it didn't matter what she wore; she was always damn beautiful. Her blonde hair had gotten longer over these past weeks, and her perfectly placed curves were the ultimate temptation—*thank you, pistachio ice cream.* I had to constantly remind myself that I had no business having these thoughts about Brad's girl. Her going out with Neil was probably a blessing. Now I had double the reasons to stay away from her. This situation would definitely seal the deal.

In spite of all that, I got up and walked over to stand in her doorway.

"Where are you guys going?" I asked.

She put down her makeup brush. "Some place called Vincenzo's?"

"Ah yeah, one of the nicer restaurants in Woodsboro."

Carly turned to me and opened her arms. "Do you think I'm dressed well enough?"

I gave her a onceover, trying not to let my eyes linger too long on her body. "Yeah. You look great. It's a nice place, but not super fancy or anything."

She faced the mirror again and started to apply eye makeup. "You never told me how your date with Lauren went last night."

Well, that reprieve didn't last long.

"Yeah, uh..." I slipped my hands into my pockets. "It was okay."

"Just okay?"

"Yep."

She closed her tube of mascara. "Okay, I can tell you don't want to get into it. Which is fine. You don't owe me any explanation."

She probably thought I was being aloof because I'd fucked Lauren and didn't want to admit it. Carly seemed to have the impression that I was a manwhore. But having her make that assumption about last night didn't sit right with me.

"Nothing happened, if that's what you're wondering."

She blotted her lips. "I'm surprised. With the way she looks at you—throws herself at you—I would've assumed she had you at her apartment before they could even serve dessert."

I stepped into her room. "I'm not that easy, you know. I had the opportunity. I just didn't take it."

Her eyes went wide. "You turned her down?"

"I don't believe in leading someone on if I'm not sure about things. It's not like she's just anyone. She works in this house. So I need to handle it carefully."

Carly resumed looking in the mirror. "Well, that's very mature of you, Mathers. I did wonder since you came home earlier than I expected."

"I thought you were asleep when I came in. I didn't realize you were paying close attention," I teased.

"There are lots of creaks in this house. It's hard not to wake up when someone so much as moves. I wasn't waiting around or anything, if that's what you think."

I nodded. "And I won't be waiting for you tonight. So don't worry about that. Neil wouldn't hurt a fly, so I have no reason for concern."

Carly fluffed her hair. "You'd be up waiting and worried otherwise? If it were someone else?"

Shit. "Well, yeah. I don't trust people. I'd be wary of you meeting anyone new while you're out here, if I didn't know them." I raised my chin. "I mean... Brad would want me to look out for you."

"So this is about Brad?" She turned to me. "You would worry out of a sense of obligation to him?"

"Not exactly. I consider you a friend now. I'd be looking out for you either way."

"My face doesn't bug you anymore?" she taunted.

My stomach tightened. "No, Carly." I glared at her. "It doesn't."

"That's good to know."

I hung my head for a moment. "I guess I'll never live that one down."

"Probably not." She winked.

"Maybe I deserve it."

Her heels clicked as she moved toward me. "Don't be so hard on yourself. I'm just kidding. I'm over it, truly. Especially after you explained the reason behind it." She paused and sniffed the air. Her expression shifted.

Crap. Busted.

"You smoked."

"I had a quick one a few minutes ago."

"Why, Josh?" She frowned. "You were doing so well."

Now I definitely had to lie. I couldn't admit that her date with my brother was freaking me out. I couldn't admit that the date last night had been a total sham, mostly for her benefit. And I certainly couldn't admit that her lips were begging me to kiss them right now, which made me *really* need another cigarette.

"I just fell off the wagon. It happens."

"Well, you can always get back on, right?"

I sighed. "That's what I do."

She paused and seemed to be examining my face. "Are you okay with this? Me going out with your brother?"

Her question made me sweat. *Fuck. She can see right through me.* "Why would you ask that? Of course, I am. Do I seem like I'm not?"

"Not really. But I can see how it might be a little awkward for you. Because we live together, you know? First, you're living with your best friend's fiancée, and now you're living with some girl your brother is dating?"

"You're not *some girl*. And if going out with Neil makes you happy, then even if it's a little awkward, I need to suck it up."

She chewed on her lip. "Can I be honest about something?" she asked.

"Sure."

"The Lauren thing..."

I tensed. "What about it?"

"I *was* miffed about your muff." She laughed nervously. "What I mean is, it bothered me when she asked you out and when you were out with her last night." She looked away and hugged her arms. "At first I thought it was because of the conflict of interest—because she's Scottie's therapist—but I'm not so sure." Carly's eyes met mine. "I think that's more just what I *wanted* to believe."

"What else would it be?" My question was barely audible. In my gut I *knew* the answer.

"I think I'm..." She hesitated.

My heart raced. "What?"

"I think I'm getting attached to you or something... and confused, maybe?"

Her words mirrored my own feelings, yet I said nothing as she stood there, turning redder by the second.

"Don't get me wrong, I know that you and I... We could never...you know. Because of Brad. But I think this whole living-together thing... It's messed with my head a little. And anyone new coming into the mix would shake things up. I guess I was being kind of selfish." She exhaled. "So I'm sorry."

Now would've been a great time to tell her she wasn't alone, that I'd been having *all* those same feelings and then some. But admitting the truth still felt like betraying Brad. Say I fessed up to having feelings for her. Then what? I couldn't do a damn thing about it. So

I chose to keep it all to myself. I needed to continue to do that until this living arrangement came to an end—whenever that would be. While Carly and I had an appointment to visit the other group home in town soon, we still had no clue how long getting Scottie a placement would take.

"I understand, Carly. We've both been through a lot. We're still going through a lot."

She nodded, looking down at her feet. "Sometimes I think you're the only one who truly knows how I'm feeling—why the past two years have been a blur."

Her words penetrated my soul, reminding me just how alone I'd felt, until her.

"Have you ever seen a therapist?" I asked.

"No, but I probably should."

"I've considered it," I admitted.

"Really?"

"Yeah. Not just because of the grief, but because of the guilt."

She tilted her head. "Guilt about what specifically?"

Many things. "You know I was supposed to go to Tahoe with him that weekend, right?"

Her eyes widened. "No. I didn't."

"Yeah. He'd asked me to join him and his work friends on that trip, and I'd even booked a ticket. But I canceled at the last minute because I was up for a promotion at work and found out I needed to put together this presentation to sell myself. I decided going away that weekend was going to be too stressful. I told him I'd go the next time." I shut my eyes.

"So you think if you'd been with him, maybe the accident wouldn't have happened..."

"Of course. I'm certain it wouldn't have. I might have been driving, or one little change in the itinerary could have prevented the whole thing."

She put her hand on my arm. "I'm sorry, Josh. I had no idea. I wasn't supposed to be with him because it was a guy's trip. But I've certainly had thoughts like, what if I *had* been—would he still be here? Or what if I'd asked him not to go? Stuff like that."

I shook my head. "Anyway, it's pointless to think about. You can't change the past."

"No, you can't. But it's important to talk about the things that haunt you. Letting them out is the only chance in hell we have at getting over them."

"There's no getting over it," I corrected. "Just getting *around* it."

"That's true, yeah," she whispered.

I forced myself to take a couple of steps back. "Well, I've managed to ruin the mood for you tonight."

"You didn't. I appreciate knowing I'm not alone."

"Okay. Enough sad talk, though. Go have fun. But don't be surprised if you come home to find the pistachio ice cream gone."

She smiled. "Go for it. I'll pick up some more this week." She moved closer and poked her index finger into my chest. "Better that than smoking."

"I agree." I grinned. "Actually, Scottie and I have big plans tonight. So that'll keep me distracted."

"Oh yeah?" She raised her brow. "Do tell."

"Well, first we're gonna listen to Elton John backwards. That should eat up a good hour or so."

"Fun..."

"Then we're gonna heat up some chicken from the fresh batch you made last night, and I'm gonna make this honey-mustard sauce and go all out."

"That sounds pretty tasty."

"Then, for our manshower, I'm gonna blast his other favorite, The Wiggles, on the Bluetooth speaker."

"He's gonna love that." She giggled. "What else?"

"After all that excitement, I suppose I'll hope he sleeps well so I can properly demolish that pistachio ice cream in peace."

"Sounds like a good way to top off the night."

Actually, a good way to top off the night would've been having her here, too. I cursed myself silently. I had to stop having these damn thoughts.

"Are you taking your car, or is he picking you up?" I asked.

"I told him I preferred to meet him. I like the ability to go home whenever I want."

"Makes sense."

Carly looked at the clock. "Actually, I'm running a bit late."

"That's my fault. I'll get out of your hair."

"I'm glad you came to talk to me, Josh."

Stop being so fucking nice to me. You're not helping.

She walked out into the living room where Scottie was sitting on the couch. "Be good for Uncle Josh," she said, kissing his cheek.

He ignored her and kept playing on his iPad.

She put on her coat and slung her bag over her shoulder. "Well, I'll see you later. If anything comes up, just text."

"The only way I'm gonna bug you is if the house burns down, and thankfully I won't be cooking anything, so we should be good."

"Okay." She laughed. "Bye."

The door closed behind her, and I stared at it for a few moments as I listened to the sound of her car starting. I felt hollow as I ventured into the kitchen and found a note she'd left on the counter.

A Thank You from The Trappist Monks of St. Francis:
I left you a little surprise in the refrigerator.

Perking up, I opened the fridge. On the shelf was a small baking pan covered in foil. There was another note attached to the top.

A Thank You from The Trappist Monks of St. Francis:
I made your new favorite this afternoon, pumpkin bread! Don't knock it till you try it, Mathers.

A smile spread across my face as I peeled back the foil, grabbed a fork, and took a bite.

It was surprisingly good—not too sweet, very moist, and she'd even added chocolate chips. Lately I was starting to like *a lot* of things I'd never anticipated I would.

After a few mouthfuls, I put the pumpkin bread back into the refrigerator and joined Scottie in the living room, where he was still playing on his iPad.

"It's just you and me tonight, dude."

He grabbed me by the hair, pulling me toward him to take a good whiff as a montage of commercials from the eighties played on his device. That was another one of his things: vintage jingles.

"You know, I think you might have the right idea. Living this simple life—no women, no complications. Just good chicken, music, and sleep. Repeat." I slapped him playfully on the knee. "Not a bad life, dude."

He looked me in the eyes for a few seconds. That was always rare. Like a gift, really—not only because those looks were few and far between, but because through his familiar eyes, I got to visit with Brad again. For a quick moment in time, my best friend would come alive through Scottie.

"God, you look so much like Brad. Maybe that's him coming through to remind me exactly why I shouldn't care about what Carly is doing right now."

As Scottie turned his attention back to his jingles, I continued to talk to him.

"I wonder how much you can understand sometimes. Something tells me it's a hell of a lot more than we think. There's so much I should probably explain to you about life, but maybe it's better if you don't know. Sometimes ignorance is bliss, too." I stared up at the ceiling. "I'll give you an example. I wish I didn't know Carly was on a date with Neil right now. Not knowing that would be freaking fabulous."

Scottie and I had a grand old time that evening. Focusing all of my attention on him was a great distraction. Rather than just going through the motions like

I typically did, I took time to study him, enjoying each moment, and trying to engage with his sometimes bizarre nuances as best I could.

We had dinner together, took our shower, and I even let him hold the blow dryer over my hair, which he seemed to get a huge kick out of. Everything was going awesome until I got the bright idea to pump up my air mattress *before* Scottie had gone to bed. Normally I did it after he was asleep, but I decided to risk it. Then I went to use the bathroom only to come back and find the bed deflated. Scottie must have thought it was a giant balloon and had popped a big hole in it.

Great. I could probably figure out a way to patch it, but right now I didn't have the materials. I'd be sleeping on the hard-ass couch again tonight.

I shook my head. "I can't even get mad at you, Scottie, because it's my own damn fault."

He rocked back and forth on the couch.

Scottie usually hit the sack around 10 PM, so when the clock struck ten, I situated him in his bed with all of his devices. Then I hung out with him there for a bit.

After he started to doze off, I left him alone and shut his door. My plan was to break out that container of pistachio ice cream. Maybe pile it atop some pumpkin bread.

Just as I headed for the freezer, though, I heard the front door open.

FIFTEEN

Carly

"WHY ARE YOU back so soon?" Josh asked.

"It's not that early. I've been gone a few hours."

"I know. I just thought you'd be out longer."

I threw my purse onto an end table. "How did tonight go?"

"Shouldn't I be asking you that?"

Taking off my coat, I said, "Tell me how Scottie was first."

"Well, we had a blast. He's already out like a light, but not before ripping a hole in my air mattress."

Looking over at the corner of the room, I noticed the lifeless rubber laying on the floor. "Oh no! How did that happen?"

"Fuck if I know. That's what I get for trying to be efficient. I blew it up early, then left the room and came back to it all deflated. Never found the weapon."

"Shit. I'm sorry." I covered my mouth. "I shouldn't laugh, but it's kind of funny."

Josh shrugged. "It's no biggie. I'll try to patch it tomorrow or just get a new one. It was my fault for blowing it up before he went to sleep. That's like asking for trouble." He sighed. "Did you have a nice time?"

"It was very nice. And you were so right about your brother. He's a sweetheart." I pursed my lips, unsure how much I wanted to divulge. I didn't want anything getting back to Neil. But I also wasn't in the mood to sugarcoat anything.

Apparently, Josh could see it on my face, though. "You look like there's a *but* in there somewhere," he said.

"Like I said, we had a very nice time." I hesitated. "I don't know if it was a lack of physical chemistry or whether I'm just not ready, but—"

He held his palms out. "You don't need to explain."

"I know I don't *need* to explain," I said. "But I want to. I'm sure he's going to say something to you."

"You can trust that I won't tell him anything you don't want me to."

"Your brother is a true catch. Our conversation was honest and engaging. He's family-oriented and everything a woman could want, as near as I can tell. There was not one single thing wrong with our date. But yet... it still felt like something was missing. Sometimes you can't put your finger on it."

Josh nodded. "I hear you."

His short response made me wonder if he was holding back.

"Do you think I'm being too picky?"

"No, and you shouldn't care what I think, either. You have to follow your heart. Neil's a big boy. I'm sure he could sense it if you weren't totally feeling it."

"All I could think during dinner was that this man was going to make someone very happy someday."

"It's just not gonna be you..."

I stared down at my nails. "I don't think so, no."

"How did you leave things with him?"

"He asked if I would be interested in going out again, and I told him I didn't want to lead him on and I didn't feel ready for anything more. I apologized for wasting his time tonight, and he was so gracious about it." I shook my head. "Maybe I'm just broken, Josh. Because there is not one single thing wrong with your brother. I just—"

"You can't choose who you're attracted to or who you have chemistry with. That's the bottom line, Carly."

"I know. I just feel crummy for wasting his time."

Josh snapped his fingers. "I have a solution for that."

"Oh yeah?"

"It's green with nuts—and colder than your attitude toward my brother tonight."

"Josh!" I kicked the air, pretending it was him.

"I'm kidding, Pumpkin. Relax."

Why do I love it when he calls me that now? I followed him into the kitchen and leaned against the counter as he opened the carton of ice cream.

"I'm surprised you didn't demolish that already," I said.

"Well, Scottie had other plans for me tonight, so you're in luck."

Josh prepared two heaping bowls. He handed me one, and I sighed in ecstasy after I took the first bite.

"This was exactly what I needed," I said with my mouth full.

Josh spooned up a big bite. "My brother didn't buy you dessert?"

"I wasn't hungry for it at the time, but suddenly I'm starving." My heart lurched. That could be a metaphor for the physical attraction I felt toward Josh right now, instead of his brother. I should just go straight to hell at this point.

"I guess we both batted a thousand with our dates this weekend," he said, shoveling ice cream into his mouth. "Better luck next time, I guess."

"You should take the bed tonight," I told him, licking the back of my spoon. "Seriously. I don't mind sleeping on the couch."

"I can't do that to you."

I wiped ice cream from the corner of my mouth and tried to garner the courage to say what I was thinking. "So then just sleep in the bed..." I murmured. "It's big enough. I won't even notice you there."

He scratched his chin scruff. "I'm trying to figure out if that's an insult or not."

"It's not!" I chuckled. "But for Christ's sake, we've been through so much these past several weeks. We're both adults. We can share a bed."

"I don't know." He looked away, but seemed to be considering it. "We'll see..."

Was his hesitation because he knew I was attracted to him? *Oh no, does he think I'm trying to suggest something?* Everything in me said it was a bad idea to clarify my intentions—or lack thereof—but I had to explain myself further, or I wouldn't be able to sleep tonight.

"I don't want you to think I'm hoping for any funny business..." *Ugh.* That didn't come out right.

His eyes widened. "*Funny* business?"

"Yeah, you know..."

"No, I don't. Define funny business." He snorted. "Is that like booby prize?"

"Josh..."

His expression turned serious. "I know. You're just being sweet in offering."

"I guess I'm paranoid because of the whole diary thing. You read what I wrote about finding you attractive."

"Much to your chagrin, you find the pig attractive," he taunted with a nod.

"I don't want you to think I'm hoping for something, or that I would ever go there. I know that would be wrong, and I have no intention of—"

"Jesus. Quit while you're ahead, Carly. I know you weren't insinuating anything, okay? That's not why I hesitated. It's just the principle of it, you know? Even though in the end it's just a bed, lying next to you is still...lying next to you. And I guess I feel weird doing that when...he can't."

Okay, so this is about Brad. "I get it," I muttered. I needed to just go to bed and escape the awkwardness I had created. "Well, I think I'm gonna turn in. I'd love to take a shower, but I'm afraid to wake Scottie."

"He's a pretty heavy sleeper. I think you'll be good."

"Okay. I'll be quick."

Once in the shower, I lathered shampoo in my hair, berating myself again for suggesting Josh share the bed with me tonight. How could he *not* think that was out of line? A part of me just wanted someone to sleep next to, that feeling of heaviness in the bed, of security. But I still needed my head checked for thinking it was a good idea with Josh.

Despite what I'd said about taking a quick shower, I took my sweet time under the water, hesitant to face Josh again. Eventually, I forced myself out and got dressed.

He was on the couch, surfing the net on his phone when I emerged from the bathroom. Bouncing his legs rapidly, he didn't look like he was ready to go to sleep anytime soon. I went straight to my room without saying anything to him. That seemed safest.

About fifteen minutes into lying down, I was still ruminating when I heard him at the door.

His voice was low. "Is the offer still open?"

I stilled, then turned to face him. "Yeah."

"That fucking couch is like a rock. I tried for a few minutes and gave up."

"There's plenty of room here." I slid over.

Josh put his pillow in place, fluffed it a few times, and lay down. I immediately turned away from him, because that felt like the right thing to do.

Things were quiet for a minute.

"Do you always sleep at the very edge of the bed like that?" His voice cut through the darkness. "If I so much as cough, you're gonna go tumbling."

I *was* practically dangling over the side. "I was just trying to give you some space."

"How big do you think I am? There's more than a foot and a half between us. You can afford to sleep like a normal person."

"Yeah." I moved back toward him a bit. "Okay. You're right."

"This bed is freaking comfortable," he said. "You've been living the good life."

His phone chimed.

"Shit," he muttered.

"Who is it?"

"It's Neil. He's just checking in—probably feeling me out for info on your reaction to the date. I'll respond to him in the morning."

I turned toward him and leaned up on my elbow. "You should respond now. Otherwise, he'll think something bad."

"Okay, yeah. I'll just tell him I'm in bed with you," he deadpanned.

"You don't think that'll go over too well?" I joked.

"Pretty sure it won't." He chuckled.

"Yeah, maybe wait."

As I turned my back to him again, I could feel him rustling around in the sheets and adjusting his pillow.

"Damn..." He groaned. "Now that I know how comfortable this bed is, you might have a tough time getting rid of me."

A long moment of silence passed. Then he whispered, "Thank you for the pumpkin bread."

"Did you like it?" I asked, putting my hands under my cheek.

"It was really good, yeah. I think you might be converting me."

He let out a loud yawn, and I settled back in. I was almost asleep when he spoke again.

"I never asked you why you started doing makeup. How did you get into that?"

"That's kind of a random question," I murmured.

"Yeah, well, that's how I roll when I'm wired."

I smiled, my back still facing him. "I used to love to put on my mother's makeup growing up. I kept practicing into my teenage years and realized it was something I was pretty darn good at. So, rather than force myself to do something I wasn't interested in after college—I'd majored in liberal arts—I went to cosmetology school and became even better at it. Mostly I love making people feel more confident about themselves."

"Although, out in Hollywood you've got a pretty good baseline to work with, I'd imagine?"

"Yeah, but I don't only work on celebrities. I also volunteer. I've done makeup for homeless shelters, too—women looking to rejoin the workforce."

"That's cool. See? I didn't know that about you. Glad I asked about this."

"The things you learn when you start asking random questions at one in the morning, huh?"

"That's right..." He exhaled and seemed to be thinking for a moment. "You're a good person, Carly."

My heart fluttered. "How do you know that?"

"You wouldn't be here if you weren't."

"I guess that makes you a good person, too."

"I wouldn't go that far." He chuckled. "Anyway, with Wayne's mattress as my witness, I hereby, in this moment, officially take back anything negative I've ever said about you."

"Oh... Besides my face, there are *more* things I don't know about?"

"Doesn't matter. They'd all be lies."

"Well, then I take back calling you an evil pig."

"You might want to hold on to that one. I can't say it's entirely inaccurate."

"I don't believe that."

"That's because you can't see inside my head lately, Pumpkin."

Wait, whaaaat? Were those offending thoughts about me or something else?

Josh stopped babbling after that, and eventually his breathing turned rhythmic. Listening to it soothed me. But even though there was a good amount of space between us, I realized I could sense the heat of his body behind me.

And now I found myself a bit wired. I retraced my steps through the events of the day. I felt terrible for wasting Neil's time, and even worse for how much I'd wanted to come back home and see Josh. Now, with him on the other side of my bed, I felt even more guilty for relishing this feeling of warmth and safety.

• • •

The following morning, I learned a hard lesson. Sometimes even when you have the best intentions and try to do everything right, life still fucks with you.

Despite the fact that I had intentionally fallen asleep facing away, and with plenty of space between me and Josh, when I woke up, I was not only facing him, but my nose was only a few inches from his. I could feel his breath on my skin as he slept. I could practically taste him, and I had no desire to move back. This was the only way I could experience being this close to him.

So instead of moving away, I took the opportunity to stare at him in peace, to appreciate how handsome he was—the way his brown hair fell over his forehead, the ruggedness of his jawline, his masculine scent. This quiet observation was peaceful indeed—until his eyes shot open.

I flinched, jerking back. *Who the hell wakes up like that?* Don't your eyes usually blink open gradually or something? His flashed open in one shot.

"Hey..." His voice was groggy. "Did I scare you?"

"No, uh..." I licked my lips. "I was just waiting for you to wake up."

"You were watching me while I slept?"

"Yeah. I guess I was."

Josh nodded and slowly got up from the bed.

I'd been expecting ridicule, or at the very least a response.

But he said nothing.

I watched his muscles move as he stretched, his T-shirt rising just enough for the sexy serpent inked on his back to taunt me.

He left the bedroom and turned toward the kitchen.

I lingered in bed so I wouldn't have to face him for a while. After a few minutes, I could hear him getting Scottie up. The water started up in the bathroom, so he must've decided to do their manshower now.

I eventually dragged my butt out of bed, much later than usual.

Scottie and Josh were sitting in the living room, both with wet hair. Scottie was doing something on his iPad while Josh worked on his laptop.

"Morning." I waved. "You showered early..."

"Yeah, Scottie woke up with a little surprise."

"Ah."

Scottie didn't often have accidents at night, but occasionally it happened.

I walked over to make myself some coffee and spotted a note Josh had left me.

> ***A Thank You from The Trappist Monks of St. Francis:***
> *"Somebody's Watching Me" by Rockwell came on while I was showering with Scottie. Coincidence? ;-)*

SIXTEEN

Josh

LAST NIGHT WAS undoubtedly the best sleep I'd had in ages—even better than those nights back in Chicago in my own bed. Despite the guilt I felt for sleeping next to Carly, I couldn't help looking forward to doing it again tonight.

When I'd finally messaged Neil back this morning, he'd asked if I wanted to get brunch. Carly had offered to watch Scottie, so I'd agreed. I figured it would be easier to address any questions he had about Carly in person. Plus, I hadn't even seen him since I'd gotten to Woodsboro, so this was long overdue.

Neil had already chosen a corner seat at the Old Mill Diner when I arrived. He lifted his hand and smiled as he spotted me. An unsettled feeling developed in the pit of my stomach. I knew what it was: the now-familiar guilt I'd felt too many times to count.

"Hey." I sat down.

"Hey, man. It's good to see you."

"How are you doing?" I asked.

He stared down into his cup. "I've been better."

The waitress set a mug in front of me and poured me some coffee. I nodded in thanks.

"What happened last night?" I asked Neil, playing a little dumb.

"She didn't tell you?"

I hesitated. "She said she had a good time..."

He chuckled. "But..."

I remained vague. "Well, she told me how she ended the night."

"Yeah. She wasn't feeling it. Or at least that's what I took from her saying she didn't want to go out again." Neil shook a sugar packet. "It sucks. I really liked her." He stirred his coffee. "But that's okay. It is what it is. Her loss."

I nodded. "You absolutely deserve a woman who appreciates you, my man. I always say, you're the best catch there is."

He stared out the window. "Maybe I need to move out of Woodsboro. My options here are limited."

"You'd be surprised, brother. The grass isn't always greener. Not sure I ever really appreciated Woodsboro until this most recent trip home."

"Interesting. I always thought you hated it here."

"I did."

"What changed?"

"I'm not sure." I shook my head. "Maybe I'm just more mature now and can appreciate all the things I used to take for granted—like breakfast with my little brother." I winked.

Neil and I were only a year apart. He was twenty-nine to my thirty, while Michael was two years older than me.

He took a sip of his coffee. "I'm not buying it."

"Why?"

"I got a vibe last night." He stared into my eyes. "And I want you to be honest."

"A vibe about what?" I gulped the coffee too fast and nearly burned my throat.

"You and Carly..."

Now I nearly choked on it. "There's nothing going on there," I insisted. "If that's what you're getting at."

"Are you sure? I won't be mad if it's true. I'd understand."

"Nothing's going on," I repeated. "Why would you think that?"

"It was the way she lit up when she talked about you. It made me wonder if her disinterest was less about me and more about you."

I laughed, my guilt surging. "I don't know what you're talking about."

"Okay, now I *know* you're lying."

"Why?"

"Your eye just twitched. That always used to happen when you fed me bullshit when we were kids."

Is it hot in this damn place or is it just me? Grinding my teeth, I said, "Maybe I'm just uncomfortable because you're making assumptions about me and my best friend's girl."

"Josh, if you can't be honest with me, who the fuck can you be honest with? You mean to tell me you've been living with Carly, and nothing has happened all this time?"

I looked him straight in the eyes. "Nothing has happened. Not even when we slept in the same bed last night."

His eyes were like saucers. The words had escaped me before I could think better of it.

"Ooooohkay. Hold up." Neil rubbed his temples. "Say what? Last night? After she came home from her date with me?"

"Yes, but it had nothing to do with that. Scottie busted my air mattress, and the couch is like a rock. So she insisted I sleep in the bed. She was on her side, and I was on mine. No...funny business." I chuckled at my use of that Carly-ism.

He raised a brow. "Funny business?"

"Yeah." I wiped my forehead. "If something was going to happen, it surely would have been under those circumstances. But there's nothing, so..." I bounced my legs anxiously.

"You think sleeping next to your dead buddy's girl equates to *nothing* going on? You're kidding yourself. Maybe nothing happened last night, but it's bound to eventually." He shook his head. "I knew something was up."

"You're wrong, Neil. If something was *up* between her and me, I never would've said you should go out with her. I don't share."

He leaned back in his seat and crossed his arms. "I think you were hoping I'd take away your burden—

which is the fact that you've got the hots for Brad's fiancée, and you don't know what the hell to do about it."

I rolled my eyes. "You're making up stories now."

"Hey, boys."

Our heads turned in unison. My father had just arrived.

"Hey." I stood to hug him. "I didn't realize you were coming."

"Neil invited me."

"I'm glad. I should've thought of that."

My father sat down across from me next to Neil. He looked between us. "Boy, it's rare that I ever see you two together. Mr. Big City finally gracing us with his presence."

"I'm sorry, Dad. I know I've been a shitty son."

He frowned. "Who said that? I'm only kidding. I'm damn proud of you—especially for what brought you back to town. Brad is lucky to have a friend like you, looking out for things when he can't be here."

Neil snorted.

Jackass. I glared at him.

"What the hell is so funny?" my father asked.

Dad knew I'd been sharing the house with Carly for the past month. I figured I'd beat Neil to the punch so I could at least put a semi-accurate spin on it.

"Neil seems to think I have a thing for Brad's fiancée."

"Oh." He tilted his head. "Is there any truth to that?"

"Not in a serious sense."

Dad squinted. "What the hell does that mean?"

"I find her attractive—as any warm-blooded man would. And I think she's a great person. But actually going there is another thing entirely."

Neil interrupted, "See? That's more honesty than you gave me. The truth is starting to come out." He turned to my father. "I went on a date with her last night, Dad."

Dad blinked in confusion. "Say what?"

"Yeah, she let me down easy. But you should've seen the way her face lit up when she was talking about how good Josh is with Scottie. It's no wonder she had no interest in me."

The waitress came back by and placed a mug in front of my dad.

"Coffee?" she asked.

He nodded. "What else is there to live for? Thank you." Then he turned to Neil. "I'm confused. How did you end up on a date with her?"

"I met her the week before at The Bar and didn't know who she was. She also had no clue I was Josh's brother." He pointed to me. "After I figured it all out, this one still encouraged me to go out with her. So I did and immediately felt like a third wheel."

"He's blowing it out of proportion," I insisted.

"Is he?" Dad chuckled. "Or are you just in denial because you're afraid of what it would mean if you had feelings for her?"

He'd touched a nerve there.

"Okay..." I looked between the two of them. "The obvious dilemma aside, Brad was a great, stand-up guy. Just like Neil—and you, Dad. Me, on the other hand?

Carly deserves better, someone who doesn't have a shitty track record with women. All that and yes, Brad would be rolling in his grave if I ever made a move on her."

"How can you know that?" my father asked.

"That's understood. There are millions of women in the world, and I have to go for his?" I exhaled. "Come on."

Neil poked my dad with his elbow and announced, "They slept in the same bed last night..."

I gritted my teeth. "You had to add that?"

"Sorry," he mumbled.

"No, you're not," I seethed.

"What the hell?" Dad blurted. "I thought you said there was nothing going on."

"I wish I was recording this." Neil laughed. "Dad's reactions are too much fun."

"My air mattress broke, and I had nowhere else to sleep," I explained. "It was innocent."

"What was innocent?" a voice asked.

I turned to find my brother Michael, who'd shown up fashionably late. Evidently Neil had invited him to join us, too.

"I just told Dad that Josh slept in the same bed as Brad's fiancée last night."

Michael gaped as he sat down next to me. "I knew it. I told you something was gonna happen. That whole thing is a ticking time bomb."

Neil turned to him. "You knew about this?"

"Okay, seriously." I threw my napkin on the table. "You're *all* whacked. Nothing happened! My damn air mattress had a hole in it, so she offered to let me sleep in the bed with her. It's a very big bed with plenty of room for both of us."

"Maybe nothing happened from your perspective," my dad said. "But you should think about whether she has feelings for you. And if you think she does, you might reconsider the idea of sleeping in her bed again. If you're serious about not wanting to make a move on Brad's girl, you shouldn't lead her on."

"I wasn't leading her on..." I defended. "I was trying to get some damn sleep on a bed that didn't feel like a rock. Period."

I didn't know shit about Carly's true feelings for me, aside from the fact that she found me attractive and no longer hated my guts. Then again, she had been staring at me this morning when I woke up. Bottom line, what Dad said resonated with me. There was no good reason to be sleeping next to Carly, no matter how damn nice it might've felt—because of the *mattress*.

"You know what?" I blew out an exasperated breath. "You're exactly right. I'll go get another air bed as soon as I leave here. That'll solve the issue." I sipped my coffee. "Now, maybe you goons will get off my back."

"Exactly how long are you gonna be living with her?" Dad asked.

"Neither of us knows. It could be days, weeks, or years. That's the nature of the waiting-list scenario. But we're getting him on the waiting list for both group homes in town. We just have to visit the second one to make sure it's okay. The house manager there's been out sick, so we haven't been able to get in to see it yet."

"Did you know I went on a date with Carly last night, Michael?" Neil smirked.

Here we go again.

Michael's jaw dropped. "No freaking way. What am I missing? How did that happen?"

As Neil recounted the story yet again, I got lost in my head. I was glad I'd come to this brunch, because talking it out and seeing their reactions helped me realize what an asinine decision sleeping in Carly's bed last night had been.

Now I needed to undo the damage.

• • •

When I entered the house that afternoon, Carly was dancing with Scottie in the living room. He had classical music—Canon in D Major—blasting from his iPad, and the two of them were rocking back and forth in each other's arms.

Neither one noticed me walk in, so I set my new air bed down carefully and took a moment to watch. It was beautiful. It was unusual for Scottie to interact with either of us that way.

Carly finally noticed me and stepped back. "Oh, hey." Her hand moved to her chest. "Didn't see you come in."

"I didn't mean to intrude..."

"We were just dancing."

"I could see that." I smiled.

"It was Scottie's idea. He grabbed me by the hand and led the way. It was the weirdest thing. I don't really understand, but I'm not sure I care *why* he did it. It was awesome."

I ruffled Scottie's hair. "You're so freaking spontaneous and complicated."

The moment was definitely over, as Scottie walked away from me to go sit on the couch.

"I feel bad now for interrupting."

"That's okay," she said. "How was brunch with Neil?"

"It was good. My other brother Michael and my dad showed up, too. Always nice to catch up with them."

"So..." Carly bounced on her toes. "Did you talk to Neil about me?"

"You might have come up one or two times, yeah."

Or a thousand fucking times.

She cringed. "Does he think I'm a total bitch?"

"Not at all, Carly."

"Good. I was worried about that." She looked toward the door, where I'd dropped the box I brought home. "I see you bought a new air mattress?"

"Yeah. I figured that was better than hogging your bed."

"I really didn't mind."

Attempting to get the picture across without being blunt, I met her eyes. "I think this is a better long-term solution."

She nodded and looked down. "Whatever you want."

If I didn't know better, I'd think she was disappointed. I didn't want her to think I didn't *like* sleeping next to her, so I tried to make a joke. "It's just that the inflatable mattress is so damn enticing. The way the entire thing flattens to the ground every time I so much as move? The rubbery feeling against my skin? You can't beat that."

"You do you, Josh." She smiled, but it didn't reach her eyes.

I worried I'd offended her. "I appreciate you sharing with me last night, though."

She nodded and turned away.

• • •

Things might have seemed like business as usual that evening through dinner and Scottie's bedtime routine, but I knew better. Carly was quieter than normal, an odd tension still lingering in the air. But I told myself that her being offended over the bed situation was better than me losing control, fucking up, and doing something I could never take back.

After Carly took her shower, she headed for her room without saying goodnight. That was completely unlike her.

I stopped her just before she closed the door behind her. "Hey, Carly..."

She froze and turned to face me. "Yeah?"

"You sure you're okay? You've been quiet most of today. And you usually say goodnight before you go to bed."

Carly played dumb. "If I'm quiet, it's not intentional."

Bullshit. "This doesn't have to do with me choosing not to sleep in there again, does it?"

Her face turned pink. "No, of course not. Why would you think that?"

"Swear on Bubba-Hank."

"What?"

"Swear on our former dog."

Her eyes widened, and she gave me a horrified look. "I'll do no such thing."

She then turned around and escaped into her room, slamming the door shut.

I didn't know which was worse: the fact that I'd used Bubba-Hank's life as a pawn to get Carly to tell the truth, or the fact that she was indeed mad at me.

SEVENTEEN

Carly

AS I WAS preparing my coffee the next morning, I noticed a note on the counter.

> ***A Thank You from The Trappist Monks of St. Francis:***
> *Roses are red.*
> *Violets are blue.*
> *I dreamed I was choking on a lemon.*
> *And thought of you...*

I looked over at Josh. He smiled from behind his coffee mug.

"Did you really dream that?" I asked.

"Strangely, I did."

I pressed start on the coffeemaker. "Maybe it was symbolism."

"Symbolism?"

"You were feeling guilty after you used Bubba-Hank to trick me last night. You knew I would *never* swear on his life."

"I guess I know how to get anything out of you, huh? That's a pretty powerful tool."

Of course, my behavior yesterday had everything to do with Josh choosing not to share the bed with me again. My staring had freaked him out—I knew it. I'd analyzed that to the gills yesterday but vowed to move on today. Quite simply, I was over it. I had to be.

"Scottie is still in bed?" I asked.

"Yeah. Shh..." Josh placed his index finger over his lips. "He doesn't usually sleep this late, but I'm sure as hell not gonna wake him."

When my coffee had brewed, I carried my mug over to where he was sitting. "Look, do me a favor, Josh?"

"What?"

"Just drop the whole thing about yesterday, okay? Whatever irked me is over. I'm not in that weird mood anymore."

"Done." He bit into his bagel. "The subject is officially dropped." His next comment caught me off guard, though. "Why don't you go out and do something for yourself today?"

"Where did that come from?"

"It's just overdue. Aside from that one hair and nail appointment, you haven't taken any time for yourself. Go shopping or something."

I grabbed the other half of his gluten-free bagel and stole a bite. "You gonna give me money for this shopping spree, big guy?"

"Yeah, actually." He reached into his wallet and grabbed a wad of cash. "Here..."

"Whoa." I held up my palm. "Oh my God, Josh. I was kidding. Are you crazy? I'm not taking your damn money!"

"Take it. You're not working much right now."

"That doesn't mean you owe me money."

"I know that. But, Carly, the only reason I'm able to work as smoothly as I do, without interruption, is because you look after Scottie during the day. If I were the only one here, like I'd originally planned, there's no way I could've continued to do my job. So look at it as payback for helping me stay employed through all this. Take the money and buy yourself something nice. Get a massage. Or put some claws back on your fingers. Seriously. Just have some fun." He held out the money. "I'm not taking no for an answer."

"Well, damn. I don't have to be told twice, Sugar Daddy." I took the cash and placed it in my bra. "Thank you."

"You can thank me by picking up some pistachio ice cream on the way back."

"You got it."

The afternoon was blissful. Once out, I realized this was much more needed than I'd imagined. I did exactly as Josh suggested. I went to the mall and had a girl's day for one. I started by treating myself to coffee and a coconut donut in the food court, which I enjoyed in peace as I scrolled on my phone. Then I visited a few of the department stores and tried on various outfits. I needed a new swimsuit that was a bit more modest than my bikini, since I planned to start taking Scottie to the YMCA so he could swim in their indoor pool.

I'd decided to multitask by talking to my friend Christina on the phone in the dressing room while trying on various swimsuits. I'd just filled her in about the latest happenings on the home front—including the night Josh and I had shared the bed.

She had an interesting theory. "He paid you off because he feels guilty about calling you out on your true feelings last night."

"He should feel guilty. He knew I'd never swear on that dog's life." I sighed. "I thought him insisting I get out today was nice, though. I'm not gonna read into it too much."

"Can I ask you something?" she asked.

"Okay..." I slipped out of my pants.

"If he were to try something sexual, would you be receptive?"

My body tingled just thinking about it. Pulling my shirt over my head, I said, "I'm not gonna be the one to initiate anything."

"That's not what I asked. My question was, if *he* were to make the first move, would you stop it?"

No, I wouldn't. But I wasn't ready to admit it. "I don't know."

"That's a yes." She paused. "Wow. I never thought you'd go there."

Her reaction immediately made me second-guess my character. "Are you judging me?"

"No, that's not how I meant it. I'm happy that you'd allow yourself to let go of the guilt."

"Nothing is going to happen anyway," I informed her, a bit too loudly for a dressing room. "Because Josh doesn't see me that way. He knows I think he's attractive, which continues to be embarrassing for me. But he's never once implied that he finds *me* sexually attractive or has feelings beyond this bond we have because of Scottie. So I'm not gonna speculate about a situation that's imaginary."

"I wouldn't call sleeping in the same bed imaginary, though. That actually happened, and I think—"

"Let's drop it, okay?" I unhooked my bra. "Listen... I'm gonna hang up and try on some of these bathing suits. I'll text you photos to get your opinion."

"Okay. What are you going for?"

"Modest. I'm looking at one-pieces because I'm gonna start taking Scottie swimming at the Y. I don't need to impress anyone over there. I only have a bikini here with me, which I've used to shower with Scottie. Don't ask."

She laughed. "Not gonna touch that one."

"Okay. Stay by the phone."

I hung up and put on the first one, a black suit with a sheer strip at the top.

I propped the phone up in a way that allowed me to see my full torso in the viewfinder. I set the timer to snap a photo and sent it to Christina.

Christina: Who knew there was a swimsuit fit for a funeral?

Carly: So you don't like it?

Christina: Maybe buy that one and stash it away until you're 80. But I'm not letting you wear it out.

Carly: I told you I wanted a conservative look.

Christina: That one's just depressing. At least pick a vibrant color if you're going with an old-lady one-piece. The actual old ladies at the pool dress hotter than that.

Carly: Okay. Point taken. Stand by for the next one.

I got out of the black suit and slipped on a bright red one. While the color was more exciting, I didn't love the way this one fit. It was comfortable, but had no padding at the chest. I wasn't super small on top, but I always appreciated a little boost.

I set the timer to take a photo again and sent it with a message:

Carly: Does this one make me look flat?

About a minute later, my phone finally dinged.

Josh: Define flat.

My first inclination was to wonder why she didn't understand my question, but I soon realized that was the least of my problems.

I'd freaking sent Josh the photo of me in the red swimsuit! I'd missed a text from him about picking up sour cream on the way home, so when I clicked on the most recent text to send the photo, it had been his, not Christina's.

I couldn't type fast enough.

Carly: OMG. That wasn't meant for you.

Josh: Damn. Really?

Carly: Christina is advising me on bathing suits. I just clicked the wrong thread.

Josh: So you don't want my opinion?

Carly: No. Didn't you think it was out of character for me to send you a photo of me in a bathing suit?

Josh: I don't know. I thought it was kind of cool... like maybe you valued my opinion on such things.

Carly: I'd rather be caught dead than send you an unflattering shot of myself in a bathing suit!

Josh: You think you look bad?

Carly: Yes.

Josh: What other options do we have?

Carly: There is no WE in this process.

Josh: That's no fun.

I sighed and typed.

Carly: There's a black one but Christina said it looked like a funeral bathing suit.

Josh: What happened to your bikini?

Carly: I want something more modest to wear when I take Scottie to the Y.

Josh: I used to work there in high school. If you take Scottie in the afternoon, it's all senior citizens. But I suppose you might give them heart attacks in your bikini, so maybe you're on the right track. Anyway, I'm here if you want my opinion.

Carly: Thanks.

Josh: And in answer to your question, that red bathing suit did make you look flat.

Is he serious? Just when I thought we were getting along, he had to go and ruin it. *Why does he always do that?*

Then my phone chimed again.

Josh: F.L.A.T.
Funny
Left-handed
Authentic
Tough

I smiled from ear to ear.

Carly: You're so goofy, Josh. I didn't realize you knew I was a lefty.

Josh: You eat with your right and write with your left. Technically, you're ambidextrous. Damn, I should've used that for A.

Carly: And you're observant.

Josh: Evil, goofy, and observant. I'm sure you can think of a few more adjectives for me. Not sure I wanna know them, though.

Carly: LOL

Josh: You were gonna come home and kick me in the balls when you thought I was calling you flat, weren't you?

Carly: I wouldn't have kicked you in the balls. But I might have put a little extra pepper in your pasta tonight.

Josh: Speaking of dinner, I've got it.

Carly: You cook, Mathers?

Josh: I realize you think I'm only good for pounding chicken, but there's one other thing I'm an expert at making.

Carly: Well, this I gotta see.

I tried on at least ten more bathing suits before I finally picked one.

When I walked into the house that evening, I couldn't believe my eyes. The carpet in the living room had fresh vacuuming track marks on it, and Scottie was sitting calmly on the couch with wet hair, which meant they'd already showered. The aroma of something absolutely delicious filled the air.

"Something smells good," I said as I entered the kitchen, setting the groceries I'd picked up on the counter. "What are you making?"

Josh had a dishtowel over his shoulder as he rinsed a few things in the sink. "It's in the oven. You're not allowed to peek until it's done. Scottie already ate his chicken. I gave him an early dinner so we could eat in peace."

"I don't know what I did to deserve all this," I said.

"Well, I'm sort of making it up to you in advance."

"What do you mean?"

He shut off the faucet and turned to face me. "After you left this morning, I found out I have to meet with a client back in Chicago this week. So, think of this as prepayment for you having to hold down the fort alone for a few days."

Dread filled me. I hated when he was away. But it would only be a few days. I could do this. "Oh, okay. That's fine." I smiled and tried not to let my disappointment show.

"Did you end up getting a swimsuit?"

"I did." I grinned.

Josh's brow lifted. "Well?"

"After trying on many, I decided on the red one... because it makes me look flat."

"Nice." He winked.

I got goose bumps whenever Josh winked at me, once again a sign that I needed to get laid—by someone other than Josh. It didn't help that he was getting more handsome by the day, his hair growing out as he rocked the unshaven, woodsy-caveman look. I dug it, and that continued to be a problem.

Josh's mystery dinner was chicken enchiladas, and they were quite tasty. It was nice to sit down to a homemade meal prepared by someone else, especially when Scottie was already showered, fed, and content on the couch.

After eating, Josh and I joined Scottie in the living room. I looked over Scottie's shoulder as he scrolled through the photos in his iPad library, many of which were distorted images of his own face, courtesy of a face-changing app. But then came a photo of a giant dick.

It wasn't Scottie's—I'd seen his. And the small bit of tanned, ripped torso that had also made it into the shot was a dead giveaway as to *whose* dick it was. "Whomever" it belonged to was quite hung.

Oh my. I fumbled over my words as I looked at Josh. "Um..."

He narrowed his eyes. "What?"

"Are you...aware that there's a picture of you stark naked on Scottie's iPad?"

"Come again?"

Taken from a crooked angle, the photo of Josh's dick could have been accidentally snapped. Scottie always had one of his devices with him—even in the bathroom—so he must've hit the camera button during one of their manshowers.

"Scottie, give that to me for a second." I took the device. "I'll give it back. Don't worry."

Surprisingly, Scottie let it go without a fight, and I handed it to Josh.

He stared at it with a blank look on his face. I couldn't read his expression as he clicked on it.

"Are you embarrassed?" I asked, unsure what to say.

After a moment, he handed the device back to Scottie. The photo was gone. *Not that I was hoping for a second look...*

"I don't know. Do I have something to be embarrassed about?" he asked, his ears turning red.

I gulped. "Not at all." *Certainly* not.

"I kind of like to control when I send dick pics out into the world. How the hell did I not know he'd taken a photo of my junk?"

"He's very stealthy."

Josh blew out a breath. "At least we found it before someone else noticed—like the social-services people."

"Oh God." I covered my mouth. "I hadn't even thought about that. Could you imagine?"

Josh stood up and nudged Scottie. "I think you did enough damage for one day, dude. Let's get you to bed. It's past your bedtime anyway."

It was late, but I wasn't anywhere near ready to go to sleep. Especially since Josh would be leaving me alone with Scottie for a few days.

He returned to the living room and rubbed his hard stomach. "You have room for dessert?"

"There's always room for pistachio."

Josh retreated to the kitchen and returned with two bowls, handing one to me. We'd started a tradition each night of watching one of Wayne's DVDs, most of the time while eating ice cream. There were so many DVDs that it would take us several more weeks to get through them all. It reminded me of an Advent calendar; we never knew what surprise we'd be getting. One night it would be a DVD of the boys when they were younger. Another night it was just Wayne taking random videos of deer in the woods. A young Josh had also made appearances in some of them.

I'd just settled into the couch with my bowl of ice cream, ready for our next surprise when I got a rude awakening. Instead of beautiful, blond Longo boys, animals, or idyllic family scenes, a set of big, flopping tits bounced up and down on the screen. We'd popped in a porno.

Josh looked over at me. "Well, I guess we know how Wayne liked to unwind some nights."

My spoon clinked as I put my ice cream down. "Was that not labeled?"

He shook his head. "Most of them aren't." He pressed stop on the DVD and ejected the disc from the player. He then took a closer look at it. "Oh, wait. He's got a P written in Sharpie on this one. Who the fuck knew it stood for porn?"

"I guess we need to be on the lookout for those."

"I'll definitely..." He coughed with a wink. "...keep them in good hands."

"I'm sure you will." I picked up my bowl again and scooped a big bite into my mouth. "Boy, this house is just full of surprises tonight."

Josh cackled. "This evening is brought to you by the letter P: penis pics and porn."

I nearly spit out my ice cream. I needed that laugh.

If Christina was right, and Josh had sent me out of the house earlier while he cleaned and cooked to distract us from the very real tension that had built since we'd shared the bed the other night—then the universe was messing with us. Instead of a distraction, Josh had accidentally showed me his dick and popped in a porno to end the evening.

When I'd emptied my bowl, I stood. "You know how you just know when it's your cue to go to sleep? Pretty sure Wayne's porno was it for me." I went to the kitchen and put my dish in the sink. "'Night," I called.

"Have big, bouncy-tit dreams, Carly," Josh replied from the couch.

I lifted my index finger. "*She* was definitely not flat."

He chuckled. "That she wasn't. I guess Wayne was a tit man."

I shook my head and laughed.

As I settled into bed, I could hear Josh pumping air into his mattress. Despite my better mood today, I hadn't exactly stopped analyzing why he'd chosen not to sleep next to me again. I missed that weight on the other side of the mattress right now. But I appreciated the boundary he'd set, especially because I found myself hornier than ever tonight. Because, well...penis pics and porn.

EIGHTEEN

Josh

I MIGHT'VE VOLUNTEERED for this Chicago trip to meet a client. With the recent tension rising on the Woodsboro home front, I'd thought some separation between Carly and me might be necessary to clear my head.

But as I sat here, alone in my apartment after a long day at work, I regretted my decision.

The silence in this place was deafening. I no longer appreciated living alone the way I had before. I missed having someone to share a tub of ice cream with—or even someone to shower with. *Thanks, Scottie.* I'd never realized until my time back in Woodsboro just how freaking lonely my life had been. Bringing a woman home for sex and nothing more like I used to was a far cry from actually developing a connection with someone that went far beyond sex. Or in the case of Carly, *stopped short* of sex. We had a connection that was undeniable. Whether it was born from our similar struggle after the loss of Brad or something else, I couldn't be sure. But I really missed being home right now. *Home.* I'd thought Chicago was my home, but it felt nothing like it at the moment. This was the first time in my life that I'd actually longed to be back in Woodsboro.

I took out the note Carly had left me before I came out here. She'd put it on the counter next to a slice of pumpkin bread for me to eat on the way to the airport.

> ***A Thank You from The Trappist Monks of St. Francis:***
> *Penis pics, porn…and pumpkin! Have a safe flight.*

Unable to resist any longer, I took out my phone and texted her.

> **Josh: How are things going over there?**
>
> **Carly: It's been a tough day.**
>
> **Josh: Why didn't you text me?**
>
> **Carly: I didn't want to bug you with my venting when you're busy with work.**

My pulse raced.

> **Josh: What happened?**
>
> **Carly: I took Scottie to the pool. But he had a meltdown while we were waiting for the senior swim to end. He couldn't understand why we had to wait.**

I immediately called her.

She picked up after one ring. "Hey." She sounded down.

"Figured it would be easier to talk. Tell me what happened."

"Yeah..." She sighed. "I couldn't get him off the ground. He was kicking and screaming. By the time the senior swim was over, I didn't want to reward his behavior by letting him get in. So we just came home."

"Man, that sucks. I'm sorry it happened. But that was a good call to teach him a lesson. Otherwise, he'd keep pulling that to get his way."

"I'm gonna try again tomorrow."

I lay back. "You're a trooper."

"Well, looking after him is my full-time job right now. I can't just give up when the going gets tough."

"That's not true. You always have that choice. A lot of people wouldn't go back to the pool after that. That's why you're a trooper."

She let out a long exhale that felt like it penetrated me. I could feel her tension from here. *I should've been there today.*

"Anyway, how's Chicago?" she asked.

"Really freaking quiet."

"No one randomly snapping photos of your junk?"

"Not yet, no. But the night is young."

She giggled. "You're lucky he didn't use the Andy Warhol filter on your dick and duplicate it a hundred times."

I cackled. Scottie did love to use that filter. "You've just given me a great idea for Christmas cards."

She laughed. "I bet you're gonna sleep like a baby tonight, huh?"

"I plan on it. After the day you had, you probably will too."

"I don't know. I haven't been sleeping all that great, as exhausting as the days have been."

"I thought you slept well in general," I said.

"Not lately..." There was a long pause. "I slept best the night you were lying next to me, actually."

I shut my eyes, trying to resist the satisfaction I wanted to allow myself to feel. "I slept really well that night too," I admitted.

"I understand why you felt guilty, Josh. But is that the only reason you decided not to repeat it?"

The physical distance between us made me more confident in opening up.

"No, that wasn't the only reason." I exhaled. "I'm just trying to protect you, Carly."

"From what?"

"From me," I snapped back.

"You're not that dangerous," she insisted.

"I think you know where sleeping in the same bed every night would eventually lead. You think I have that much willpower? I'm a horny fucking testosterone-fueled dude who hasn't gotten laid in a long time. I don't trust myself with you."

Her silence made me regret what I'd just admitted. I'd made it sound like I would've been tempted with anyone. But that wasn't it at all. It was *her*. She made me feel that way. *She* tempted me.

"What if I told you I didn't care about consequences?" she said.

"I wouldn't believe you."

"I get the dilemma—why you and I can't ever be together. And I'm certainly not looking to recreate what I had with Brad or start something new right now. In fact, I can't envision my future at all anymore. I don't expect to find what he and I had again. But lately, I've just..."

"What?" I prodded greedily.

"I've been craving physical contact. It's been a long time. I don't even mean sex. Just contact. And the night you slept near me was the closest I've come to having that back."

I'd been craving the same damn thing and a lot more. But I needed to draw the line on my openness now. I refused to admit how much I'd loved lying next to her. It was better if she assumed this was *only* about sex.

She spoke again before I could conjure a response. "I'm sorry if this is too much right now."

"Too much how? You're being honest. Which is a fuck of a lot more than I've been. I'm the one making you feel inappropriate because I've been giving you the impression that I'm unaffected lately, and you're the only one feeling this way. That's not the case." As my walls started to crumble, I tugged on my hair. "I wanted to do more than just lie next to you. You have no freaking clue how beautiful you are."

"Really? Because I thought you hated my face."

I froze.

After a second, she laughed. "I'm sorry. I couldn't resist. Totally kidding."

"I fucking deserved that." I sighed in relief. "But you want the truth?"

"Yeah..."

"I've always thought you were beautiful, even when I texted Brad that stupid comment. Never once did I think you weren't beautiful. And spending this time with you—getting to see that your beauty is so much more than what's on the outside—it's been an experience I don't feel I deserve." I paused, contemplating whether to continue. "I wouldn't *ever* be able to take his place, Carly. And even though you said that's not what you're looking for, I'm not sure I believe you. Maybe that's how you feel today. But I don't see you feeling that way forever. You deserve more than cheap sex with some dude who doesn't have his shit together. You deserve a partner."

"You're right. I do deserve more. I just don't know that I want it. My soul was sucked out of me the day he died, Josh. I haven't found it since. I don't want to feel anything. I want to feel *nothing*."

Fuck. Her words mirrored everything I'd experienced for the past two years—trying hard to feel nothing. Except I *had* been feeling something lately. For the first time in a long time...because of her.

"I'll let you go," she said abruptly. "It's late, and I know you have to work tomorrow."

I didn't want to hang up, but I knew the longer I stayed on the phone, the more dangerous it would be. I was probably on the verge of saying things I'd regret. If we were physically together, I might've *done* something I'd regret.

"Okay. Goodnight, Carly."

"'Night, Josh," she said as the line clicked silent.

After that, as much as I'd looked forward to my bed tonight, sleep evaded me. I couldn't believe I'd admitted all that to her.

Instead of fighting the insomnia, I sat up, took out my phone, and sent an impulsive text.

Josh: Are you around tomorrow night? I'm back in town for a couple of days.

She responded right away.

Naomi: Sure am. Would LOVE to see you. It's been too long.

NINETEEN

Josh

TWO DAYS LATER, I landed back in New Hampshire. While I was supposed to have gotten home around dinnertime, my flight was delayed due to inclement weather, and I'd told Carly not to expect me for dinner or wait up for me. However, then I was able to catch a flight on a different airline, which finally got me home around eleven.

I knew Carly wouldn't be expecting me this early, but I didn't want to startle her if she was already asleep. So, I listened carefully as I used my key to open the door. The house was quiet, so I assumed she and Scottie were both in bed. I gently wheeled my suitcase to a corner of the living room before peeking my head into Scottie's room. His back rose and fell as he slept soundly, and his noise machine was on. I really wanted to see Carly, so I decided to peek into her room, too, fully expecting to see her sound asleep like Scottie.

That wasn't what I found.

When I peered through the crack of her slightly open door, I jolted back at the sight before me. With her legs spread, she writhed as she expelled short and ragged breaths. It didn't take a genius to figure out what was happening.

Holy shit.

I'd been so damn horny the entire day, and coming home to this was pure torture. She was so into what she was doing that she hadn't even heard me come in. I stood there, equal parts shocked and aroused—not shocked that she was getting herself off, but shocked that I'd had the good fortune to witness it.

Her restless legs rustled against the sheets, and my dick swelled. Watching and hearing Carly pleasure herself was the most beautiful thing I'd experienced in a long while. Beautiful and so damn arousing.

Too arousing to resist.

I desperately wanted to join. For the first time in a very long time, I decided to throw caution to the wind and allow myself access to the depths of my desire. Even if for just one night, I needed this. And she clearly needed it, too.

"Carly..."

She flinched at the sound of my voice and drew her knees together.

"It's okay. It's just me. Don't stop," I said.

She leaned up on her forearms, but didn't speak.

"Please don't stop, Carly. It was beautiful."

Her chest rose and fell as she looked at me, her eyes hazy despite her stunned expression.

"Keep doing what you were doing," I repeated, my own chest heaving, unable to contain the desire growing within me.

Carly didn't move as I walked toward the bed.

She was wearing a T-shirt, but now I could see more clearly that she had no panties on.

"Open your legs again."

To my pleasant surprise, Carly played along, slowly spreading her legs and displaying her beautiful, glistening pussy. I noticed she had a thin landing strip. My mouth watered, so tempted to lower my face and taste her.

Kneeling before her on the mattress, I lifted my shirt over my head. "Is this okay?"

She nodded.

"Lie back again," I demanded. "Relax."

Carly did as I said, resting against the headboard, her pillow behind her. She continued to look up at me.

My voice was throaty. "Were you thinking about me?"

She stared at me blankly, then nodded and licked her lips.

"Good." I ran my hand down my torso. "I've been thinking about you all damn day, too."

Carly swallowed, still looking up at me, but not saying a word.

"I want to watch you make yourself come. But I want you to look at me while you're doing it. Okay?"

She nodded again.

"Go back to what you were doing when I walked in."

Carly hesitated before slipping her hand back between her legs. She moved her fingers in a circular motion over her clit. As she gazed up at me, I could hear the sound of her wetness. My cock was rock hard as I imagined what it would feel like to slip inside that beautiful, wet pussy right now.

"That's it. Don't take your eyes off me, Carly."

She didn't, and it was the hottest experience of my life. A look of lust filled her eyes, and I was becoming addicted to the want I could see in them. The only thing hotter than giving in might have been denying her.

"Do you want my mouth on you?" I rasped.

She closed her eyes and nodded.

"I want to taste you so freaking badly, but I also want to savor this feeling, make you want it even more. Keep your eyes on me, Carly," I hissed. "Look at me."

She opened her eyes again as she circled her clit faster.

"I bet you can come just by looking at me, can't you? That's how freaking aroused you are. I love it."

I hovered over her, lowering myself until my mouth was just inches from hers. When her lips parted, it took everything in me not to take her mouth with mine. But I refrained, afraid of what that most intimate act would lead to. Instead, I fucking drooled inadvertently, some of my saliva landing in her mouth. She stuck her tongue out to receive it and swallowed. My dick ached as I imagined her doing the same thing with my cum.

I moved back and placed my hand on my belt buckle. "Do you want to see the rest of me?"

"Yes," she panted.

That was the first word she'd managed to utter this entire time.

As her breathing quickened, I whipped my belt off, tossing it aside, and unzipped my jeans before pulling my engorged cock out through the opening.

My tip was wet as I began to stroke myself. It was a miracle I hadn't already come in my pants.

Carly's eyes fixed firmly on my cock as she massaged her clit.

"No touching me tonight. I want you to want it even more next time," I said through my teeth as I pumped my cock in my hand.

"You're cruel," she breathed.

"You have no idea." I smirked. "You thought you hated me before. Just wait."

She moaned. "Prick."

"You like my prick though, don't you?"

She rubbed herself faster and nodded.

I jerked myself over her body. "You want this inside of you?"

Carly bit down on her bottom lip and nodded.

"Say it."

"I want you inside of me," she muttered.

"What do you want inside of you?"

"I want your cock inside of me." She laughed a little. "Your big fucking dick."

"That's so damn sexy coming from your sweet mouth, Pumpkin." I swiped my tongue over my bottom lip. "Just for that, I should let you ride my face till you come." I tugged on myself harder. "Would you like that?"

"Yes."

"Next time."

"You're evil..." She panted as she continued to rub.

"Evil pig..." I smiled down at her devilishly.

"This is torture," she breathed.

She had it wrong—*I* was the one being tortured here. There was nothing I wanted more than to taste her, but jerking off to how bad she wanted me was uniquely intense. The look in her eyes made me feel like she'd do *anything* for more. And while I was getting off on this, playing this game was also my excuse not to cross the line.

"You're a dick," she said as she looked up at me and moved her fingers along her clit.

"Keep talking like that if you want to get fucked tonight," I groaned.

"You're the biggest asshole."

"You want me in your asshole?" I stroked myself harder. "Is that what you said? You'd let me, wouldn't you? You'd let me fuck your asshole, if I wanted to..."

She bit her bottom lip and nodded. "Maybe."

I nearly came, so I stopped jerking myself for a moment to find my composure.

She bucked her hips as she inserted two fingers into her pussy, pumping them in and out. That nearly did me in again. I had to close my eyes to keep from coming, tightening my entire body to prevent myself from losing it.

"It's been so long for you. I bet your pussy is almost as tight as your asshole. Where do you want me first?"

She pointed between her legs with her unoccupied hand. "Here."

"You want my mouth or my dick there?"

"Both," she muttered.

"Carly..." Her name escaped my mouth almost unintelligibly...desperately.

"Josh..." She sighed, shutting her eyes.

"Look at me, Carly. I want you to come for me. Don't take your eyes off me. I want to watch you make yourself come."

Her eyes seared into mine. In all my years of sexual adventures, I'd never played this game before. There was something incredibly erotic about this slow torture. I'd never wanted anything more in my life than to come deep inside of Carly right now. But I wouldn't. Instead, I'd enjoy every second as she hit her sweet spot while looking into my eyes, neither of us touching each other.

"Come on, baby," I muttered. "Come for me."

Her body began to shake as she let out a silent scream, her eyes rolling back.

When I knew her hand had finished its job, I reached for it as I jerked myself off harder. Taking her fingers in my mouth, I licked them clean, her taste pushing me over the edge as I came in long, hot spurts onto the sheet below. My chest moved up and down as I tried to catch my breath.

When I snapped out of the trance I'd been in, I finally looked down. She was still staring up at me with glassy eyes. And shit... I'd made a mess.

"Where are the spare sheets?" I asked, still panting.

She pointed to the left. "In the closet right there."

I stepped off the bed and turned on the light inside the closet to grab a new top sheet. Rolling the dirty sheet into a ball, I tossed it in the corner of the room before tucking myself back into my pants and slipping my shirt over my head.

Carly continued to lie there, limp and sated, waiting for my next move.

I sat at the edge of the bed and leaned over to kiss the top of her head softly. “Get some sleep.”

TWENTY

Carly

WHAT THE HELL *was that last night?*

That was all I could think as I lay in bed the next morning. What would I even say to him? *"Thank you for NOT fucking me in the best way?"*

When I could hear that Josh had gotten Scottie up, I took that as my ticket to sleep in. Although I wasn't really sleeping. I was obsessing. I had no idea how last night would change our dynamic moving forward.

I finally garnered the courage to get dressed and make an appearance in the kitchen.

"Morning..." I said as I grabbed a mug from the cabinet. Josh was in the living room, watching TV next to Scottie. I wasn't even sure he'd heard me, since he didn't respond.

But as I waited for the coffee to brew, I suddenly felt the heat of his body behind me. A chill ran down my spine, a combination of nerves and arousal. I was clearly still sensitized from what we'd done together last night—and the idea of what we *didn't* do.

"Did you have coffee yet?" I asked.

"No."

"You want one?"

"Yeah, that'd be great," he said in a gravelly voice.

I reached for another mug, but it slipped from my hands, shattering on the ground.

"Shit!" I bent to clean up the pieces.

"It's okay. I got it, Carly."

"No, let me," I cried. "It's my fault." I ran in search of a broom and dustpan, and I wouldn't look at him as I cleaned the pieces of ceramic off the ground.

Josh knelt and grabbed my wrist. "Stop."

"What?"

"You're acting like you're in a race against time."

"I don't want Scottie to step on it."

"That's why you're acting like this?"

"Maybe not," I admitted, slowly standing up.

He stood and placed his hand on my chin. "We don't have to talk about it, Carly."

"We don't?"

"No, we don't. It doesn't have to mean anything."

That was probably the right attitude to take, but it didn't sit well with me. No matter what I told myself, it *had* meant something to me. It meant a lot. I wished it didn't.

Still, I played along. "You know what? You're right. It doesn't have to mean anything. I guess I've just been nervous about what you might say to me this morning. Or what I should say to you."

"How about we don't say anything? It happened. We were both horny. We experimented, but we didn't cross the line. There doesn't have to be a narrative around it. It was an experience we shared. And it's over."

Wow. While there was something very mature about that attitude, it still felt *cold.* Then I remembered this was Josh Mathers I was dealing with. This kind of thing wasn't a big deal to him. Sex—or whatever the hell we did or didn't do—wasn't a big deal to him. He'd had many partners and many sexual experiences. And we hadn't actually touched each other, so it was even less significant.

Before we had a chance to discuss it any further, the doorbell rang.

"I'll get it," he said, seeming eager for the reprieve.

When Josh opened the door, Lauren was standing there, and I had to say, the exchange between them was even more awkward than the one I'd had with Josh this morning. I'd nearly forgotten that she would be coming to work this week after he apparently blew her off after their date. It was the first time they'd scheduled her here since then. Maybe she'd taken time off intentionally. I supposed that made two of us in the house now who'd been blown off by Josh. Or at least that's how it had felt when he suggested we forget about last night.

Lauren greeted Scottie and took him into his room. Josh and I were once again left alone. It didn't help that he looked so damn good this morning. His hair was a sexy, tousled mess. And every time I looked at his mouth, I saw the image of him licking the arousal off my fingers after I orgasmed. I had to clench the muscles between my legs to stop myself from getting turned on again. My biggest problem was perhaps that last night hadn't been enough for me; I needed more, and I doubted it would happen. Not only had Josh been meticulous about not touching me, but his declaration this morning pretty much sealed the deal.

I didn't think he was going to bring up the subject again, but a little while later he leaned against the counter next to me. "I'm sorry, Carly. Not talking about it is the easiest way out, because I don't know how to handle it otherwise."

"I know," I murmured. "I don't either."

"I feel so goddamn guilty, and we didn't even fuck. I still took things too far with you last night."

"I feel guilty, too." That was the truth. I did feel guilty, but I felt a lot of things besides just that. I felt guilt for not feeling *more* guilty. I was developing real feelings for Josh, not just sexual, and I didn't know what to do about them, especially since I was pretty sure they were one-sided.

"I went on a date while I was out in Chicago," he announced.

My stomach sank.

"Well, it wasn't really a date," he continued. "It was more like a botched hookup. I went to the apartment of this girl I saw off and on before I came to Woodsboro."

I wanted to throw up. He'd fucked someone right before he came back? Right before he messed around with me? *Or messed around with my head.* "I don't want to hear any more," I told him, feeling nauseous.

"I'm sorry, but I need to get this out," he insisted.

I nodded reluctantly.

"After I got off the phone with you the other night, I texted Naomi to make plans. I needed a distraction after our conversation. It felt like we were crossing the line." He exhaled. "But when I got to her place, I had no interest. After a couple of drinks, we kissed. She wanted to go to her room and I just...didn't want to. I couldn't fucking stop thinking about you—everything you'd said to me on the phone. And I realized I was using her in an attempt to forget about it all. So I left her apartment. I told myself when I got back to Woodsboro I'd make it clear to you again that nothing could happen between us. But obviously, when I walked in on you...I lost control." He paused. "Even with the guilt, I don't regret it. But I'm not gonna let it happen again."

"I figured you'd feel that way." I looked down at the ground.

His hand found my chin and brought my eyes up to meet his. "Talk to me. Do you not agree?"

"I don't know how to feel, Josh," I said, too dejected to explain myself. There was no point in opening up if he'd ruled out anything more. It would just make me look like a fool.

"If you were *anyone* else, this wouldn't be a big deal," he said. "We could be friends with benefits while we're here or whatever, right? But you're *not* just anyone. You were the love of Brad's life. How could I, in good conscience, continue to mess around with you like that? Mess around with your heart? I've grown to care about you." He paused. "I know you think you're broken and say you don't want a future with anyone other than Brad, but you're not the type of girl to mean that—to be okay with just sex. I want you to have it all. I want you to be happy with someone again someday. It just can't be me. It can never be me." His eyes glistened. "Having sex with you...would most definitely *mean* something to me. And I have no right to feel any of that. Because I'm not him. If we cross that line, we can't ever go back. And I don't want you to have regrets when we leave here."

The look in his eyes was sincere. He was looking out for me. And maybe he did have feelings for me that were beyond sexual. It just sucked that despite him making a lot of sense, I still felt rejected. I wished I could see things more logically, but I couldn't.

He pulled on his hair. "Carly, I just..."

"What?"

"I'm so fucked up."

"What are you talking about?"

"Even aside from you being Brad's ex, I'm not right for you." He hesitated. "I'm pretty sure I have major trauma from what happened with my mother. I've had trust issues with women because of what she did to my dad. I think that's part of why I was the way I was, playing the field like that, never letting anyone get close to me."

I didn't dare say a word that might stop him from continuing.

"The fact that she left my dad for his brother? That my uncle did that to my father? I never could forgive him. So how the hell could I forgive myself for going after *my* brother's girl? Because Brad *was* my brother in every way that mattered. I'm telling you this because I need you to understand that *I'm* the issue here, okay? This has nothing to do with you. I feel like a part of you thinks it does." He shook his head. "You're fucking amazing, Carly, and the man who gets you someday is going to be one lucky bastard."

I held out my hand, and he took it. I needed to respect how he felt. I didn't want to add to his trauma. I was supposed to be here helping in what felt like an impossible situation with Scottie, not creating another impossible situation for Josh.

In that moment, with our fingers intertwined, I vowed to do whatever it took to focus on the task at hand, which was getting Scottie into a home and returning to California unscathed.

TWENTY-ONE

Carly

FOR THE NEXT couple of weeks, Josh and I seemed to put what had happened that night in my room behind us. Even though I still fantasized about it, I tried to tuck the vivid memory further and further away.

So, things were on stable ground again. We were making progress with Scottie's situation, too, as we'd finally been able to visit the second group home and found it at least as nice as the first one—maybe nicer. Scottie was now on two waiting lists, which meant the waiting game had officially begun.

The cold winter was in full swing now in New Hampshire. One Tuesday in December, we were expecting our first big snowstorm of the season. We'd run out of pellets for the wood stove that partially heated the house, and everyone in the area seemed to have had the same problem because no store in the vicinity had pellets available. Josh finally found a place out in western Massachusetts that had them, but that was a few hours away.

He set out early, but the snow started earlier than forecasted, and I was terrified about him driving back in it. The last I'd heard from him, he'd successfully loaded the pellets into the trunk and backseat of my car and was heading back to New Hampshire. But that had been several hours ago. He should've been home by now.

Then, on top of worrying about whether Josh was okay on the road, my biggest nightmare occurred. We lost power, which meant Scottie had no access to the Internet. He always threw a tantrum when he couldn't access his streaming sites. Thankfully, I remembered my stash of jar candles. I had proactively placed some matches next to them under the sink. I used the flashlight on my phone as I lit the three of them, placing one in the kitchen and one on either side of the living room.

With no Internet, Scottie began to pace. I tried to call Josh again, but his phone went straight to voicemail. Had he lost his signal or had something bad happened? It was hard not to imagine the worst. After all, Brad had been killed driving home from Lake Tahoe in the snow. His car had skidded into an oncoming truck. I still had PTSD about the way he died and couldn't get the horrible thoughts out of my mind even on days when I wasn't triggered. But Josh being out in this snowstorm was my biggest trigger yet.

Scottie was on his way to full-on panic mode, jumping up and down with so much force that the house was shaking.

"Buddy, I'm so sorry. I promise we'll get power back. I just don't know when."

I knew he likely couldn't understand my explanation. Still, I tried my best to reason with him, just in case.

"Play with your apps. Please? Play with your apps for now. I promise we'll get the Internet back." I kept pointing to the icons for the downloaded games on his device. But of course, he had no interest in anything but getting onto the Internet right now.

Tears streamed down my face as he began to kick and scream. I'd never felt so helpless. "I'm sorry, Scottie. I hate this, too."

I could've given him my phone, but it was about to die, and that would've only made him mad all over again. Plus, I needed every last bit of battery juice in case Josh tried to reach us. If anything happened to Josh, I wasn't sure I could survive it.

Maybe I shouldn't have been so quick with the fatalistic thinking, but the whiteout conditions outside weren't helping my cause. To make matters worse, Abe and his wife next door weren't even home. They were in Florida for two weeks. Otherwise, I could've at least gone over there with Scottie, so I didn't have to be alone when he dropped to the ground, kicking and screaming, and I couldn't get him up. But I was truly on my own. Lorraine wouldn't want to drive over here in this weather. It wasn't like she could do all that much to help me, anyway. Scottie was going to continue to go ballistic until the power came back on. All I could do was pray. And I prayed hard. For Josh's safety. For Scottie's sanity. For *my* sanity.

At least one of my prayers was answered when Scottie finally stopped protesting and got interested in one of his apps. He sat down on the couch and started playing with it, as if his tantrum had a magic off button, and I'd somehow hit it.

The house was growing colder by the minute. I grabbed my coat and threw it over my shoulders before taking the blanket Josh slept with and draping it over Scottie. I curled up next to him on the couch and began to pray again for Josh's safe return. My hands trembled as I tried his phone for what seemed like the umpteenth time.

"Please, God. Bring him home safely," I whispered.

I wasn't a religious person and felt like a bit of a fraud asking God for help when I didn't acknowledge Him on a daily basis. But in times of trouble, I seemed to gravitate toward praying—which must have meant I knew someone up there was listening.

When the door suddenly opened, a rush of adrenaline hit. It was so dark that I couldn't immediately make out who it was.

"Carly?"

I shot up from the couch. "Josh!" My voice cracked.

He wrapped his arms around me, enveloping my body.

"Oh my God. Are you okay?" he asked.

I broke into tears. "I was so worried about you."

"Me? I was freaking out about *you* being home alone with Scottie and no electricity. My phone died, but I heard on the radio that half of New Hampshire is out."

"I was so scared that you'd gotten into an accident."

He pulled back to look at me, his hands wrapping around my face. I could barely make out his expression in the candlelight. Josh pressed his forehead gently against mine, and we just breathed together for a few moments. I suspected he understood why I'd freaked out so badly.

"Oh, man," he whispered. "I'm sorry you were scared."

With his face so close to mine, I ached for him to kiss me.

"I didn't realize you would think something had happened to me," he said, brushing his thumb along my cheek. "I couldn't call you, and I was taking it slow. That's why it took so long."

"Josh..."

"What, baby?"

The sound of *baby* rolling off his tongue gave me butterflies.

"I'm just so glad you're home."

He spoke into my hair. "Me, too."

I'd spent the last few weeks trying to deny my feelings for him, but everything came barreling to the surface tonight.

He finally let go of me and turned to Scottie, still sitting calmly on the couch. "How is he so quiet?"

"We had a good ninety minutes of major outbursts before he wiped himself out and decided to just play with his apps."

Josh rubbed Scottie's back. "That must have been so hard."

"It was...but I handled it. I was more worried about you than anything else."

Josh reached for my hand, and I sat down next to him, our fingers threaded together. It was a simple gesture, but felt very intimate.

"I'm sorry I scared you. I can only imagine how much it reminded you of the night Brad..." His voice trailed off.

"It did. That's probably why I overreacted. But it wasn't just about my trauma... I didn't know what I would do if something happened to you."

His eyes flickered in the candlelight. "When Scottie eventually gets a placement, and we go our separate ways, I want you to know, I won't regret a second of this experience, Carly. It's hard to believe I was ever dreading it."

I squeezed his hand. "I couldn't have done it without you."

"Likewise, Pumpkin."

A sudden burst of light broke us out of our private moment.

The electricity is back!

He looked around. "Holy shit!"

"Maybe the magic word was *pumpkin* all along! The second you said it, the lights came on."

Scottie began to laugh hysterically and bounce up and down on the couch. He was so freaking happy and immediately logged on to YouTube.

Josh clapped his hands together. "I think we need to celebrate with some backwards Elton John and a bottle of wine. What do you say, Carly?"

"That sounds absolutely divine."

Josh went outside to unload the pellets from my car. He refilled the stove and started a fresh fire.

As I reveled in the peace of knowing all was well again, I thought about how unexpected life can be. I'd always yearned for a sense of family. Having come from a broken home and being an only child, I'd always felt alone, despite my mother's best efforts. The only real exception had been my time with Brad. But here, with this makeshift family, I felt far from alone. At least for the time being.

That night, before I went to sleep, I found a note from Josh by my bedside.

A Thank You from The Trappist Monks of St. Francis:

Not all heroes wear capes. Some are blonde with lemon pits. I don't know if I could've handled Scottie with no electricity for ninety minutes. I would've wanted to blow my brains out. You were amazing holding down the fort tonight, Pumpkin.

TWENTY-TWO

Carly

A WEEK LATER, the mountainous piles of snow left behind from that storm were finally starting to melt in Woodsboro.

We'd had a reprieve from the inclement weather, but here inside the cabin, there was no reprieve from the feelings I'd developed for my roommate.

Josh was working out in the living room one afternoon while Scottie played on his iPad. I decided to sneak in a call to my friend Christina.

With my voice low, I sat on my bed and told Christina about a new guy I'd met a few nights ago while out with my local friend. Lisa had arrived with Rob, the guy she'd met the first time we were out together. Rob was now Lisa's boyfriend, and he'd brought his friend, Mitch. (I'd made sure to confirm that Mitch was not, in fact, related to Josh.) Mitch had ended the night by asking me out, and I'd left things open for the possibility.

Yesterday he'd texted to ask if I wanted to go back to The Bar for an official double date with Rob and Lisa.

"I'm thinking about it," I told her.

"What's your hesitation?"

I was *looking* at my hesitation. It had currently come to do pullups on the threshold of the doorway to my bedroom. My hesitation had a perfect thin line of hair leading down to his V and was still very much forbidden to me. My hesitation was hot as hell.

I'd not told Christina about the mutual-masturbation session Josh and I had engaged in that one night. She would've eaten up that spicy tidbit, but I was keeping those details close to my chest. However, she did know he and I had discussed our attraction to one another, and that Josh had closed the door on anything happening.

I decided I needed a bit more privacy to vent today. "Hang on," I said, grabbing my coat. "Josh, I'm going to the store to get some groceries."

He stepped aside and wiped sweat from his forehead. "Get some more ice cream, and we're all out of eggs."

"Okay."

As I entered my car, Christina giggled in my ear. "You two are so...domestic."

"That's one word for it." I chuckled. "Da-fucked-up is more like it."

"I could tell you didn't want to talk in front of him. What's up?"

"Yeah. Can't really talk about Josh in front of Josh. I just wish I could rid myself of these feelings for him. I know that's what's holding me back from going on this date."

"It sucks, but you need to give this Mitch guy a chance. You don't know how long you're gonna be in Woodsboro. It could be years before Scottie gets into a home. You can't be celibate that long. If Josh has made it clear there's no future for the two of you, you need to move on. But you know that already."

"Yeah, I do." I turned the car on and took off down the long and winding road that led out of the wooded area we lived in.

"Josh must be seeing someone, isn't he?" she asked.

"Well, that's the weird thing. Not that I know of. He's usually either home working or out running errands for us. And he stays home every night. I pretty much know where he is at any given moment. There's no time I can pinpoint when he might be meeting up with someone."

"That must be tough—a virile man like him not having regular sex?"

Something was wrong with me, because as soon as she said that, my mind went to Josh on top of me, and I felt myself getting wet. My body had become sensitized to even the thought of something sexual with him.

"You're right. I need to force myself to move on. The last time I dared go out on a date was a complete disaster, though, with it ending up being Josh's brother and all."

"Oh, that's right." She cracked up. "What are the chances of that?"

"Very high in Woodsboro!"

"That's probably true."

We chatted for a few more minutes until I arrived at my destination.

I sighed. "I'm at the grocery store. I'm gonna let you go."

"Go get your man ice cream."

"Clearly, I don't have a man. Otherwise, I wouldn't feel so damn frustrated right now."

• • •

After I went to the store yesterday, I'd texted Mitch and agreed to the double date. We'd decided on tonight, and Josh was going to look after Scottie, although I'd yet to tell him exactly *who* I was going out with.

But when he asked me a direct question, I could no longer deny my plans.

Josh grabbed a seltzer from the fridge and cracked it open. "So, you're meeting Lisa and her boyfriend?"

"Yeah." I paused. "And one of his friends."

Josh stopped mid-sip. "Oh...so, it's a date."

"Yeah. A casual one."

He nodded and picked some lint off his shirt. "Well, that's good."

Things were quiet after that. Josh went to a corner of the living room, took his shirt off, and started working out—hard. As usual, I couldn't help watching his glistening body in action. Although, never again would I *stare*.

The subject of my date tonight didn't come up again until Josh and I were cleaning up after Scottie's dinner.

"What do you know about this guy you're meeting?" Josh asked as he wiped a dish.

"Just that he's Rob's friend, and he was really nice the last time I had dinner with them. He just happened to be there last time. He's a biology teacher."

"Oh, so you've met him before."

"Yes."

"What's his name?"

"Mitch Ramos. Do you know him?"

Josh shook his head. "Name doesn't sound familiar. Is he from here?"

"I'm actually not sure."

"You don't know where he's from?"

"I guess I never asked him. Where he's from doesn't particularly matter to me, but I'll ask him tonight. Anyway, I feel pretty safe, since I'll be with Lisa and Rob."

He grunted. "Hmm..."

I tilted my head. "Any more questions?"

"No." His jaw tensed. "Guess not."

He turned away and immersed himself in cleaning the kitchen.

"Are you okay?" I asked.

"Yeah." He exhaled. "I'm good. Why do you ask?"

"You're acting a little weird."

He wiped the counter vigorously. "Must be your imagination."

I nodded, feeling dumb for wishing he would admit he was jealous. I quickly changed the subject, blurting out the first thing that came to mind as I watched him clean. "Your hair has grown out so much, Josh. Your scruff, too. It looks good though."

"It goes along with being stuck in the woods."

"Is your job weird about facial hair?"

"They don't give a fuck as long as I bring them business."

"Good. That's the way it should be."

He finally stopped wiping and turned to me. "I meant to ask you... Are you going home for Christmas?"

"To Oregon?"

"Either that or California?"

"I wasn't planning on it."

"You can, if you want. I have no problem manning the ship here with Scottie if you want to see your mom."

I had no desire to be anywhere else but Woodsboro for Christmas. The two Christmases Brad and I had been together, we'd separated to see our families, so I hadn't ever spent the holiday here.

"I was kind of looking forward to experiencing a Christmas here," I told him. "I have no guarantees that I'll be in Woodsboro next year. I mean, we might, but..."

"Okay." He nodded. "Well, my brother Michael usually has our family over there on Christmas Eve. You should come. Scottie, too, of course."

"I would love that."

"I'm sure Neil would love to see you." He winked.

I cringed. "I hadn't thought of that. Will it be awkward if I'm there?"

"No, he's cool. There are no hard feelings."

"Good."

It touched me that Josh had invited me to his family's Christmas gathering. Granted, he probably felt like he had no choice, but I was still moved that he was thinking ahead about it and not wanting me to feel left out.

"I'd love to meet your dad, too," I said.

"He's a trip. He's been through a lot, but he still has a good sense of humor. He's had his ups and downs over the years, but he's in a good place now."

"Does everyone exchange gifts there or..."

"Actually, Michael's wife, Vanessa, assigns us all one person to buy for. I'll let her know you guys are coming, so she can add you to the list."

"Oh, I love that idea. That makes it so much easier."

Josh nodded. "Before this year, Christmas was about the only time I'd come home. But I made sure never to miss one."

"Brad, too," I said. "He loved coming home to Woodsboro for Christmas."

"Yup." After a moment, Josh added, "We should get a tree."

"Yeah?" I smiled, surprised at his suggestion. "Where are we gonna put it?"

"We'll just get a small one. My dad's friend owns a tree place. We should go one night this week. Take Scottie. They sell hot cocoa at the concession stand."

"That sounds like a Hallmark movie."

"I don't know what you're talking about." He gave me a look.

"Have you ever watched one of the Christmas ones?"

"If I had, I wouldn't admit it."

I laughed. I already knew I was looking forward to that tree outing with Josh far more than I was looking forward to my date tonight. *Sigh*.

Just then the doorbell rang. Scottie hopped up and down in his seat, excited by the flashing lights of a delivery truck outside. Josh went out to fetch the package. I could see icicles hanging from the threshold of our front door.

When he came back in, he ripped the white, padded envelope open, then froze. "Shit."

"What?"

"I ordered something online and assumed this was it. But it's yours. I'm sorry for opening it."

Why is he apologizing? After he handed it to me, I figured that out.

It was a bright pink dildo.

I shook my head. "I didn't order this."

"Well, someone did. It has your name on it."

I closed my eyes. Christina had asked for my address the other day. I'd assumed she was gonna send me an early birthday gift or something for the house. Certainly not this. There was a note inside, which Josh thankfully hadn't seen. *A temporary solution to your little problem.*

"It's from my friend, Christina."

"You don't have to lie. It's nothing to be ashamed of."

"I know that. And I wouldn't be ashamed. But I didn't order this for myself."

Josh wriggled his brows. "Well, we should *all* have more friends like Christina, then."

I managed a smile. "She's nuts, but I love her." I waved the package around. "I'll just...put this away."

"Is there any reason she felt the need to send that?" Josh asked as I headed for my room.

"No." I swallowed. "It's just a gag gift."

"Did you tell her about our…slip up?"

A rush of heat traveled through me. "No, I didn't."

"You don't tell her everything?"

"Not everything." I tilted my head. "Did you tell your brothers?"

"No."

"Are you ashamed?" I asked. "Is that why?"

"No. It's just no one's business."

"Exactly."

I looked down and could have sworn the bulge in Josh's pants was a bit bigger than normal. *Is he aroused?* Or did I just want to believe he was?

"Well, I'm going to take a shower and get ready."

"Yeah." He stared at me. "You do that."

As the water rained down on me, I resisted touching myself. I knew if I did, I'd imagine Josh, and I didn't want to go into this date tonight thinking about another man—even if the orgasm would have calmed me down.

When I exited the bathroom, I could hear Josh talking in Scottie's bedroom. It sounded like he was reading him a book. That squeezed my heart. Scottie was technically an adult, but he had a lot of children's books on a shelf that we would occasionally read to him when he wasn't glued to his devices. He seemed to appreciate the vibrant colors and the simplicity of the stories.

I ventured to my room to start getting dressed. After putting on my bra and panties, I wrapped a silk robe over my body while I worked on my hair and makeup.

A few minutes later, there was a light knock on the door. "Are you decent?" I heard Josh ask.

I stopped curling my hair for a moment and put the iron down. "Yeah. Come in."

"Hey." He slipped his hands into his pockets as he entered.

"I heard you reading to Scottie. I love that."

"He likes to turn the pages—sometimes before I'm done reading." He smiled. "I can't take a hint, apparently."

"What's he doing now?" I asked.

"He's just chilling with his iPad." Josh's eyes lingered on mine. "Anyway...I wanted to apologize if I made you uncomfortable earlier with the whole dildo thing."

"You didn't do anything wrong. You accidentally opened it. It begged to be talked about."

His brown hair fell messily over his forehead, and the light in my room made his hazel eyes glow. God, he looked so handsome. My nipples hardened. There was something different about the mood tonight.

There was always sexual tension between Josh and me, but it had felt magnified all day. He wouldn't dare admit it, but I sensed he didn't want me to go out tonight.

I lifted my hair iron and began to use it again.

"It's fascinating what women feel like they have to go through," he noted.

"No one's forcing me. I like curling my hair."

"It doesn't matter what you fucking wear, Carly, or how you do your hair. What I mean is, you're gonna look beautiful either way. This guy is gonna be salivating and ready to pounce. So be careful."

I turned to him. "Are you flirting with me, Mathers?"

"No," he said. "I was just warning you."

My eyebrows rose. "Swear on Bubba-Hank."

He muttered something under his breath, but notably did not swear on our precious former goldendoodle.

Josh continued watching me as I finished my hair and moved to peruse the outfits in the closet. I hadn't brought a ton of nice clothes with me, so there were just a few items that would work for a night out.

"You need help deciding?" he asked.

I blew a breath up into my hair. "Yeah, actually."

Josh came over and ran his big, masculine fingers along the stuff hanging in the closet. I envied those clothes, because I wanted nothing more than to be touched by that hand. He lifted one of the hangers, selecting a slinky black sweater dress.

He held it up to me. "I like you in this."

"You've seen me in that?"

"Yeah. You wore it the day we went to visit the second group home. It looks really damn good on you."

I tried not to show my surprise at his excellent memory. "Well, if you like it, I'll wear it," I said, a hint of seductiveness in my tone. I hadn't meant to come across as flirtatious, but that's the vibe this whole exchange gave me. I was just playing along.

Josh laid the outfit on my bed. Then he returned to the spot in front of me, a distinct look of wanting in his eyes—the same look I was sure I had right now.

I cleared my throat. "I should get dressed." When he didn't move, I added, "Are you gonna stand there and watch me or something?"

Josh didn't answer. But he didn't move from his spot, either, his gaze glued to mine.

Feeling a bit out of control, I slowly opened my robe and let it fall to the floor, leaving me in nothing but a bra and panties. Josh's eyes turned glassy as they traced my body.

He swallowed hard.

While I would've given anything for him to touch me, I knew he wouldn't. Josh was the king of tease and restraint. With every second that passed, I grew wetter as he continued to stare, his pupils dilated. My body begged silently for his touch. I'd take anything he'd give me.

He moved toward me until he was just inches away, his breath teasing my face. He wrapped his hand around my neck, and for a second, I forgot how to breathe.

My eyelashes fluttered. "You're not being very polite right now, Mathers."

"I'm not feeling polite." He ran his thumb along the skin of my neck. "How do you *politely* tell someone you want to fuck them until it hurts?"

My knees nearly buckled.

"Fuck." He shook his head and released his hold on my neck as if he'd just woken from a daze. "I'm sorry. That was..."

Josh stepped back and left the room, leaving me a pile of aroused mush.

He wants to fuck me.

Until it hurts.

Now I'd have to change my damn panties when I'd just put this pair on.

Josh's resolve had finally cracked. Yet he still refused to let go, refused to actually *go there* with me. I wasn't going to entice him further because I didn't want to be his biggest regret. But the way he'd been looking at me, like he could eat me with his eyes, and then those words that would surely replay in my head all night. He had pushed me over the edge. I *needed* relief.

Grabbing the package Christina had sent me, I ripped it open. On the off-chance Josh came back in, I snuck into the closet and picked a spot on the ground before spreading my legs. This wouldn't take long at all.

Except nothing happened. I looked at the package again. *Batteries not included.*

Yep. I was currently the *only* thing turned on in here.

TWENTY-THREE

Josh

AFTER CARLY LEFT for her date, I felt completely stir crazy. I couldn't believe what I'd said to her, but that little striptease had made me lose my damn mind. What the hell was I thinking, hanging around her room while she was getting ready just so I could ogle her and get my damn fix before she left? *Left for a date with another man*, I reminded myself.

I wanted her in the worst way, and evidently, I wasn't even trying to hide it anymore. Also, what was up with my inability to lie for a second and swear on the dog's life when she called me out for flirting? You learn something new about yourself every day.

Tonight I'd learned I was a superstitious pussy.

I was driving myself nuts. I needed to talk to someone, so I dialed my brother Michael.

He picked up on the third ring. "Hey, dude."

"Hey."

It sounded like he was in a crowded restaurant. "What's wrong? You never call me, Josh."

"I think you were right," I told him. "About Carly and me." I tugged on my hair.

"What about Carly?"

"My inability to keep my dick in my pants. I'm a ticking time bomb. I fucked up royally tonight—crossed the line and said some shit I shouldn't have. The longer we're here in Woodsboro, the harder this is going to be."

"What did you say to her?"

Exactly what I'd been thinking in the heat of the moment. "You don't want to know."

"I think that means it's *definitely* something I'd want to know."

"It doesn't matter what I said. Just know that I'm losing it."

"Hang on," I heard him say to someone. Then the noise seemed to fade away. "Sorry. I stepped outside so I can hear you better." He sighed. "Anyway, I know you have this self-imposed rule about not being able to cross the line with Brad's girl, but you need to think about it from a different perspective. There's no one around to hurt anymore."

The reality of Brad being gone forever always hit in waves. A part of me still hadn't truly grasped that. Michael had just cut to the chase, and it felt like a knife.

"This isn't just about what Brad might think," I said when I could take a full breath again. "It's about my own guilt, regardless of how he'd feel."

"I get it. And I can't take that away, but—"

"She's out on a date tonight," I blurted.

"Well, that's fucking stupid. You let her go?"

"What do you mean *let* her? I don't own her. We're not together." I sighed. "Where are you anyway?"

"The Bar. Vanessa and I are having date night."

"Shit."

"Why?"

"That's where she is."

Carly had never met Michael, so she would have no idea who he was.

"You're kidding. Hang on. I'll go back in and scope out the place. What does she look like again?"

"I don't want you spying on her..."

He ignored me. "Long blonde hair?"

"Yeah..." I paced and chewed my lip, waiting for him to say something.

"Holy crap. I think I see her. She's wearing a black dress, right? And she's with a dude and another couple. There's only one pretty blonde in the place. Has to be her."

There was no sense in denying it. "Yeah, that's her."

"Hang on," he said.

I could hear the muffled sound of him talking to his wife.

"Sorry, I wanted to fill Vanessa in."

"Please don't go up to Carly."

"Of course not. It's better if she doesn't know I'm here. But I can text you updates about what I'm seeing."

"I don't need updates. It's none of my business what she's doing."

"So, you don't care that she's sitting on some guy's lap right now kissing him?"

My stomach sank. I didn't even have the words to respond.

"You still there?"

"Are you fucking with me, Michael?"

"Wow, man." He laughed.

"What?"

"You went radio silent." He chuckled. "I was only messing with you."

"Shithead." I couldn't believe I fell for that, even for a second. I'd thought maybe I'd gotten her so revved up she was taking it out on that dude instead.

"She's sitting across from him, just talking. He's pretty good-looking. Not as hot as you, though. And certainly not as hot as me."

It felt wrong spying on her. That was more than I needed to know. "Don't watch her anymore," I told him. "Leave her alone. She deserves her privacy. I'm gonna let you go."

I hung up before he could say anything else.

I ventured into Scottie's room and sat down on the edge of his mattress. He was fully immersed in three different videos on three different tablets. And he was taking photos and videos of all three tablets with a fourth iPad. That's how Scottie rolled. Wayne must have gone broke buying him electronic devices. I knew why though: Scottie went ballistic whenever the battery on one of his devices ran out. You always had to have an extra on hand while the other was charging. Better safe than sorry.

"Man, I wish you could understand me right now because I could really use someone to talk to."

He looked up for a fleeting moment before returning his attention to the iPad.

I laughed. "Heck, maybe you can understand, and I just don't know it. Maybe you think I'm the biggest idiot, too." Letting out a deep sigh, I rubbed his back. "Have you ever wanted something you know you shouldn't have, Scottie? But in the end, you just can't stop wanting it? I'm trying to think of something you can relate to." I snapped my fingers. "Like you and the Internet. Too much of it's not good for you, right? It's constant stimulation and bad for your eyes. But you do it anyway. You're on that shit all the time, and there's nothing any of us can do to make you not want it." I gazed up at his ceiling. "That's sort of how it's been with Carly lately. The more I tell myself I can't have her, the more I want her. It's messed up." I shook him playfully. "You got any advice for me, big guy? You're probably the only person I trust with any of this, you know?"

Rather than respond, Scottie opened his music app and blasted some Elton John in reverse, nearly blowing my eardrums out. After a minute, I deciphered that it was "Crocodile Rock."

I fell into a trance as I listened to him playing various songs for a while, and eventually I dozed off next to him on the mattress.

When I woke up sometime later, he was fast asleep. I took his devices and connected them all to the chargers in the corner of the room before turning his light off.

I looked at the time on my phone. It was past midnight. Carly had to have been having a good time if she'd stayed out this late.

I then noticed a text from Michael.

Michael: I know you said you didn't want updates, but I'm gonna give you my overall assessment. Her body language told me she wasn't that into him. She kept checking her phone. I'd be willing to bet she was looking to see if you'd texted her. When we left, they were still there, but I got the impression she was bored.

When I clicked out of his message, I noticed another text—from Carly.

Carly: I'm trying to enjoy this date, but I can't stop thinking about you—what you said, and the way you were looking at me tonight.

Fuck. She'd sent that a couple of hours ago, and she still wasn't home yet.

I'd messed with her head earlier. I'd *wanted* to ruin her date, hadn't I?

I sat in the living room, unsure how to explain myself when she got home. But I also felt damn satisfied that she'd been thinking about me tonight. And that was fucked up.

When the door opened, I stood but said nothing.

"Hey," she finally said. Her face was flushed, and I couldn't tell if it was from the cold or because she was upset.

"I didn't get your text until a little while ago," I explained. "I fell asleep hanging out with Scottie in his room."

"Oh..." She met my gaze. "I just assumed you didn't know how to respond." She shook her head. "I shouldn't have sent it."

"Never apologize for being honest with me."

I took a few steps toward her, still unsure how to handle myself or what I even wanted to do. But once I was only inches away, my brain could no longer form coherent sentences. My body felt like it was on fire, and I knew the primal desire inside of me had reached the point of no return.

Second by second, I inched closer until our mouths were practically touching. The heat of her quick breaths on my face caused my dick to go rigid.

"Tell me to stop, Carly," I whispered over her lips, savoring her smell as I grew harder.

"No." She panted. "I don't want you to."

"I didn't want you to go out tonight," I admitted. "I wanted you home with me."

Carly nodded, digging her nails into my chest. "I know."

"I don't want to feel this way," I muttered over her mouth. "Like I want to own you. I don't own you. You're not mine. You never will be."

"Tell that to my body." Her breathing quickened. "Josh, I need you to let go." She gripped my shirt. "I need *you*."

That undid all of my resolve. There was no longer a space between us as I took her mouth into mine, noticing a hint of something sweet on her tongue. Was that just the way she tasted or something she'd eaten? I didn't give a shit; I just needed to consume it all. I couldn't devour her fast enough.

She needs me.

And damn, I needed her.

I unbuttoned her coat and slid it down her arms before tossing it aside and pressing my chest against hers. I could feel her heart beating against mine, which was racing even faster. The guilt was still inside me somewhere, but it wasn't strong enough to overpower the intensity of my heartbeat, the intensity of my desire for her in this moment. As if she somehow knew my guilt was trying to creep in and ruin this, Carly gripped my hair and pulled me close, a silent plea not to change my mind. She didn't realize there was no chance of turning back now. My body was ready to explode.

I lifted Carly off the ground as she wrapped her legs around me. She felt light as a feather as I carried her into the bedroom, never taking my lips off hers. Kissing her was like a damn drug, impossible to stop, my tongue exploring her faster with each second. This was why I'd never kissed her before—I'd somehow known it would be like this. That I'd be too addicted to think straight.

There was no lock on the door, but I closed it behind us and prayed that Scottie slept as soundly as he usually did. That was the beauty of that static sound machine he had in his room.

Carly tumbled back onto the bed as I landed on top of her. We broke our kiss as she looked up at me with hazy eyes, which were once again begging me not to stop.

"I'm not gonna stop, Carly. Okay?" I kissed down her neck. "We're about to fuck, and you're gonna hate me tomorrow. But I plan to make it worth every second of your time."

She nodded as I helped her slip out of her black dress. She unclasped her bra from the front and tossed it aside. I lowered my mouth and took her nipple between my teeth before sucking hard and groaning into her skin as she squirmed beneath me.

Carly raked her hands through my hair. "That feels so good."

Licking her nipple in circles, I teased, "I think I found the booby prize."

Her body shook with laughter as I continued to devour her gorgeous tit.

"I love your mouth on me," she moaned.

"You're about to feel it everywhere." I spoke over her soft skin.

My cock was so hard it ached as I grinded against her mound through my pants. I switched over to her other breast to give it equal love before reaching my capacity to resist going lower.

I ran my tongue along my bottom lip. "I need to taste you."

She nodded, and I lowered her panties, slipping them down her legs and tossing them in the air.

My mouth trembled with need as I pressed my tongue against her clit, lapping up the delicious wetness of her arousal. It tasted exactly the way her fingers had that first night I'd lost control. Except this was a hundred times sweeter and more addicting. *Forbidden fruit.* Carly continued to pull on my hair—which I fucking loved—as I ate her out, circling my tongue around her clit while I sank my fingers inside her. I stopped for a moment to witness the look of ecstasy on her face, her head bent back and her eyes closed. As I moved my fingers in and out, I murmured, "You want me inside you like this?"

"Uh-huh," she muttered. "Yes."

I had to ask. "Do you want me to wear a condom?"

She stilled. "No. I'm on the pill. Unless you're not—"

"I'm safe, Carly. I got my last tests before I came out here and haven't been with anyone."

She nodded as she looked up at me. "Same."

The thought of fucking her raw was almost enough to make me come on the spot. I lifted myself off of her to undo my jeans and pull them down. When I lowered my boxer briefs and took my rock-hard cock out, Carly scooted up, crawling toward me so her mouth was at my crown. Without hesitation, she took me in and down her throat.

I felt like I'd been transported to another dimension. I bent my head back and enjoyed what felt like the most selfish thing I'd ever allowed to happen. If I stopped for even a second to truly acknowledge that this was Brad's woman sucking me off, it would have ruined it. So I didn't let my mind go there. After the longest drought of my life, I needed this release like I needed my next breath. I'd deal with the consequences later.

When it felt like I was about to come, I pulled my dick out from between her lips, enjoying the popping sound that followed a little too much. I nearly came again when she licked across her lips, swallowing the bit of precum staining them.

"How do I taste?" I rasped.

"Delicious," she breathed.

"I need to be inside you now, Carly," I said, doubting whether I could last long enough to give her an orgasm. I'd never been this damn aroused by a woman in my life.

Carly lay back, spread her legs wide, and I eased myself inside of her. I intended to be gentle since it had been a while for her. But as soon as her hot wetness enveloped my cock, I lost all ability to take it slow. Within a few seconds, I'd thrust so hard I was balls deep, moving in and out rhythmically and not so gently anymore.

"Is this okay?" I mumbled.

"Yes. You feel so good. Keep doing it like that."

I pulled all the way out and pounded into her again, bottoming out. "Your pussy wrapped around my cock is the best thing I've ever felt, Carly," I whispered in her ear. "So damn good."

My thrusts grew so hard that the bed was shaking, the headboard banging against the wall. It would be a damn miracle if Scottie didn't wake up, but even the threat of that wasn't enough to make me stop. I just couldn't fuck her any other way right now—it had to be like this as weeks of pent-up frustration came barreling out of me.

Then she began to pulse her pussy—squeezing hard and letting go.

I nearly lost my shit. "Are you fucking trying to kill me?" I groaned, kissing her harder.

She laughed over my lips.

"Stop it, or I'm gonna come inside you right now."

"Do it," she taunted.

"Fuck, no. I'm not ready for this to end."

She kissed me harder and thankfully stopped her muscle tightening, buying me some time. But I knew it would be short-lived when Carly grabbed my ass to guide my movements. Her breathing became even more intense, and I knew she had to be close. That was a good thing because my balls were about to explode.

A few seconds later, I felt her pussy pulsing around me as she made an unintelligible sound. That's when I finally lost it, speeding up my thrusts to capture every last moment of her climax while I emptied what felt like endless streams of cum inside of her. There was no going back now. Carly was forever stained by me. I couldn't take it back, and I didn't want to. In fact, I wanted to do it all over again already.

Eventually the synchronous movements of our bodies slowed to a gentle rocking, though we stayed locked together. Showering her with kisses, I enjoyed the feel of moving my cum deeper and deeper inside of her—claiming her, even if for just one night.

TWENTY-FOUR

Carly

I OPENED MY eyes and immediately had a thought. *Did last night really happen?*

Sex with Josh was everything I'd imagined it to be. Actually, it was more—worth every second of the slow torture leading up to it. The way he'd taken control of my body was unlike anything I'd ever experienced. But as amazing as last night had been, a cloud of reality hung over me today.

Josh had gotten up early with Scottie. I suspected he might have volunteered himself for that task to avoid having to talk about what we'd done. That seemed to be his MO. I hoped he didn't think I had any expectations. I was smart enough not to allow my heart to go there. Our bodies simply hadn't been able to resist anymore. It was nothing more than mind-blowing, primal sex. I'd accepted that, bittersweet as it was. *Just sex.* At least that's what I needed to continue convincing myself as a survival mechanism.

Somehow, I needed to assure Josh that last night didn't change anything. If he felt pressured—or worse, riddled with guilt—it was going to be very difficult to get through the rest of our time here. We needed each other and couldn't afford to feel awkward twenty-four-seven.

Even though Josh and Scottie bathed at night more often than not, I could hear the water running in the bathroom. Maybe Josh felt dirty after last night.

I dragged myself up, figuring I had a little time alone before I had to face him.

Scottie emerged from the bathroom first. His hair was damp, and he smelled like some kind of aftershave. "Morning, buddy," I called from the kitchen. Per usual, he ignored me.

I was going to need a shower soon myself. Josh and I had sex three times last night before we finally passed out. I probably got four hours' sleep.

"Morning," Josh said from behind me.

My hand stilled on the coffee machine before I turned around to face him. Just the sound of his deep voice made me quiver.

God, I loved every second of last night.

He wore nothing but jeans. My eyes fell to his shirtless chest, his body another reminder of all the ways he'd entered me. *Another* reminder because the biggest was the fact that I was sore between my legs. I already wanted him again, and that was going to be a recurring problem now that I knew what it was like to have him.

"Good morning." I cleared my throat. "You decided to shower early, I see?"

"Actually, Scottie was super sweaty when he got up. I think he might have a fever, so I gave him a shower to try to cool him off."

I walked over to the couch to feel Scottie's forehead. "Jeez. You're right. He does feel warm."

"I looked for a thermometer, but I couldn't find one," Josh said.

"There's one in the cupboard next to Wayne's old vitamins." I went to fetch it.

Thankfully, it was the kind you just swipe over the forehead because I didn't think Scottie would let us put anything in his mouth. The thermometer beeped when it finished, and he did have a slight fever.

"Poor guy," I said, facing the number toward Josh.

"I'll go get some medicine for him." Josh threw a shirt over his head and found his coat.

It seemed he couldn't wait to escape. Scottie did need to take something for his fever, but I got the impression Josh needed some air before we faced the inevitable discussion about what last night meant—or didn't mean.

"How can we get him to swallow ibuprofen?" I asked.

Josh scratched his head. "I remember Wayne used to get him the liquid kind and sneak it into juice. You know, the kind made for kids. It's better than nothing."

"Okay."

"You need anything while I'm out?"

You not to act weird? "No, I'm good." I smiled.

"Okay... Be back."

Later, when Josh returned with Scottie's cherry-flavored medicine and some Gatorade to hide it in, we worked together to figure out the right dosage. Josh's close presence wasn't lost on me as he leaned over my shoulder to read the small-print directions. I tried hard to control my physical reaction, which was worse than ever after last night. I'd never had orgasms so intense. I'd never been so lost in someone.

And yes, that realization certainly made me feel even more guilty. Brad was the love of my life, and that experience should have been his. It wasn't, though—it belonged to Josh. And if I were truly honest, as much as I tried to convince myself otherwise, my heart was also starting to belong to Josh. Or at least whatever part of my heart hadn't been buried with Brad.

But I knew what Josh could handle, and it didn't include me falling for him that way. He had too much unresolved guilt when it came to his best friend. I wouldn't be responsible for making that worse.

It was just sex. That would be my mantra.

After we put the medicine in the Gatorade, Josh walked it over to Scottie and sat next to him. I got goose bumps as Scottie leaned his head against Josh's shoulder, and Josh spoke to him gently to get him to drink the concoction. Josh would make an amazing father someday. My heart clenched. I wondered if he and I would keep in touch after we left Woodsboro. I couldn't imagine a life where we didn't at least speak from time to time. Ironically, he was all I had left of Brad. Maybe that sounded screwed up after last night. But it was the truth.

After about twenty minutes, Josh finally got up from the couch. He waved the empty cup. "Got it all down."

"You're seriously my hero for that," I said.

"Hopefully he'll start to feel better." He went to the kitchen to rinse out the cup. "It's strange how the fever makes him calm. Did you notice he wasn't stimming at all this morning?"

Stimming was the term we used for the self-stimulatory behaviors Scottie constantly exhibited, things like hand-flapping and humming.

"Yeah," I said. "It's fascinating. They should research that, how fevers affect people with autism."

Josh nodded. "Did you have coffee this morning?"

"No." I rubbed my temple. "I got distracted and never made it. It's no wonder my damn head is aching."

"I'll make us some," he said.

"Thanks."

As I watched him fumble with the coffee pods, I realized how tense he was. I obviously knew why. And I couldn't take the silence anymore.

"I guess we should talk about last night, or is it better if we don't?"

Josh froze—literally stopped everything he was doing and leaned against the counter.

He finally turned to me. "I've been trying to figure that out. I don't want you to think I'm blowing it off—just the opposite. I can't think about anything else. I'm sorry if I've been quiet."

"I know." I nodded. "I get it. Last night was..."

"Fucking incredible," he said. "But I haven't figured out how to handle it."

"I don't know how to handle it, either. Maybe we just *don't* handle it and don't put any pressure on each other to find the right words or make it make sense." I shrugged. "What happened, happened. It was just sex."

There it was. One of the biggest lies I'd ever told.

He stared into space for a moment. "I don't think we should do it again."

That declaration came as no surprise. It was the same thing he'd said the first time we'd messed around.

"I agree," I said, though it was the last thing I wanted. No way would I push for something he wasn't ready for. Maybe it was better if we took a step back, now that we'd gotten it out of our system.

We quietly watched the coffee drip out of the machine. Then my cell phone rang. When I saw that it was Scottie's social services agency, I put the call on speaker so Josh could listen, too.

"Hello?"

"Hi, is this Carly Garber?"

"Yes?"

"This is Maxine Gerard from The Johnson Pruitt Center."

"Yes..."

"I can't believe I'm saying this, but it seems we have an opening at the group home you've applied for. The one on Jones Avenue."

Josh and I looked at each other.

His eyes widened.

My jaw dropped.

"How is that possible?" I asked. "They told us it could take months, or even years, potentially."

"Well, as it happens sometimes, family members decide that a different place may be a better fit. There was one resident who seemed to be very agitated by another in this particular house, so one of the families put in for a transfer to another home across the state. And they were approved."

"When would this spot be available?" I asked.

"Well, the transition won't happen until after the new year. With Christmas only a week away, everything will slow down for a bit. The current resident's official moving date is January third, and then we'll need a few days to get the space ready for Scottie, if you choose to take this opening."

"How long do we have to decide?" Josh asked.

"I can give you until the end of tomorrow. Honestly, Scottie wasn't the first one on the waiting list, but we think he would be a better fit for this particular home, because he's fairly calm. Not every home is a good fit for everyone. But we really can't give you much more than a day to decide since we have to get going on all of the transition paperwork and give the opportunity to someone else if you're not going to take it. And since Lorraine Longo is officially Scottie's next of kin, she'll need to be the one who signs off on everything, though I know she instructed us to communicate with you first."

"Okay... Well, Josh and I will discuss it and keep Lorraine apprised, too. We'll get back to you by tomorrow." I placed my hand on my chest to try to contain my racing heart. "Should I call you back at this number?"

"Yes, that will be absolutely fine."

Josh spoke over my shoulder. "Thanks for calling, Maxine."

After I hung up, I stared into the living room in a daze.

Scottie sat there, mellow and red-faced, oblivious to this major turning point in his life.

"Holy shit," Josh muttered.

I held on to my stomach as if I were ready to hurl. "I know."

"I wasn't expecting it to happen this fast. You?"

I shook my head. "Not at all."

Josh's face looked sunken. "I don't feel ready..."

"Would we *ever* feel ready, Josh?"

He frowned. "Probably not."

"It's like...be careful what you wish for, right?" I sighed. "This is what we've been working toward from the beginning, but now that it's happening, it's scary. I also keep wondering if this is what they'd really want..."

He arched his forehead. "You mean Wayne and Brad?"

"Yeah." I nodded. "Would they be okay with this, or would they want us to stay?"

Josh looked away. "I don't think they would ever expect us to stay."

"Not what they'd expect, but what would they want? Would they want us to stay if we were willing?" I shook my head. "I guess it doesn't matter. Obviously, it's not feasible. I keep telling myself that the group home has more resources for him than we would."

"We need to move on with our lives, and so does Scottie," he said. "It'll take some adjusting for all of us, but the group-home situation is for the best."

The sad look on his face told me he was trying to convince himself as much as me.

"Yeah." I rubbed his arm. "This is a good thing. But we still have until tomorrow to decide. Although, I'm not sure what would deter us."

"There's nothing that would deter me...you?" He looked into my eyes.

Every reason deterring me would be selfish. I didn't want to leave Josh, and a part of me had become really attached to Scottie, despite how much work it was taking care of him. But in the end, Scottie needed round-the-clock care, and I needed to get back to my life in California. I knew in my heart that as much as Brad loved his brother, he would never be okay with me giving up my freedom to care for Scottie full time.

"There's nothing that would deter me, no," I finally answered.

"Then I think it's settled." He let out a long breath.

"We'll just call them tomorrow with Lorraine and tell them we accept."

Josh seemed lost in thought as he murmured, "Yup."

A somber mood followed us the rest of that day. The only good thing was that Scottie's medicine seemed to be working, and his fever stayed down. We tried to get him to eat, but he had no appetite, which was understandable. And the ibuprofen or the illness made him drowsy, so he went to bed earlier than normal that night.

Josh sat with him in his room until Scottie was totally out, and I was in our tiny laundry room unloading the washer when he finally emerged. I felt him come up behind me.

When he wrapped his arm around my waist, I shut my eyes. How quickly my body fell right back into a place of complete surrender. His touch made me feel weak in the knees.

"I told myself I wouldn't touch you again," he said, tightening his grip on my waist.

"How's that going for you?" I breathed, bending my head back to meet the heat of his breath on my neck.

"Not well..." The rumble of his gentle laughter shook against my back. Then I felt the warm caress of his lips on my neck, the scratch of his chin scruff.

"I'm fucking starving, Carly." He spoke over my skin, his erection pressing into me. "Did you notice all the marks I left on you last night?"

"Mmm-hmm."

"I kept looking at them all day, wanting to make more." He sucked on my neck. "I can't stop thinking about fucking you, my cum inside you. I've gotten hard every time you've so much as walked by me today. I feel like I'm going crazy."

"I thought you said we should stop." The words rolled off my tongue lazily as I bent my head back again.

"I know what I said," he whispered. "Just one more time. We can stop cold turkey tomorrow."

I was so turned on that I couldn't even respond with words. I simply nodded as erratic breaths escaped me. This was a no-brainer, considering I'd wanted him again from the second I got out of bed this morning. There was nothing I wouldn't risk to have Josh inside of me one more time.

The heat of his hard bulge pressed against my ass. My panties were already soaked. Josh lowered his hand and slid down my yoga pants. Stopping short of removing my panties, he slid them to the side.

"I've always wanted to fuck you against this thing. So many times I've walked by while you were doing laundry, and I got hard thinking about what I wanted to do to you."

I pushed my ass against him. Then I heard his zipper, and the next thing I knew he'd entered me in one hard thrust that felt like pure nirvana.

He groaned. "Fuck...you're so wet already."

His name rolled off my tongue in a gasp. "Josh..."

"Don't say my name. You'll make me come."

I spread my legs as I leaned my hands against the washing machine.

"That's it, open wider for me, baby."

Josh thrust harder, pumping in and out of me so fast that I could hear the slick sound of my arousal. There was something so hot about being screwed by someone you used to hate. It only added fuel to the fire.

"Josh..."

"What did I say about saying my name?"

"Josh..." I teased again.

He fucked me harder, gripping my hair and pulling it. I decided to do that thing that made him crazy. I tightened my muscles then let go.

Josh's breath hitched. "You must want me to lose it right now."

Panting, I breathed, "I do."

"I can't wait to fill you with my cum again."

That totally undid me. My climax rising to the surface, I slowed the movement of my hips and lowered my hand to my clit to finish myself off. Josh pounded into me harder as he let his own release go, the warm feeling of his cum making the last of my release even sweeter.

That was the fastest anyone had ever brought me to orgasm. It was supposed to be laundry room sex—rough, quick, and nothing more. But as his warmth filled me this time, my heart felt ready to burst. I *was* going to get my heart broken—by the last man on Earth I'd ever imagined would end up with that power.

As he moved in and out of me, Josh spoke into the crook of my neck. "That was amazing, beautiful."

When he pulled out, I turned to face him. His eyes were still hooded, drunk with lingering desire. The weight on my chest became too much to bear—especially with the news we'd received this morning. I had to tell him.

I wrapped my hands around his face and blurted, "I haven't been honest with you."

"What are you talking about?"

"My feelings are stronger than I've let on." I placed his hand on my heart so he could feel how it beat for him. "I don't feel dead inside anymore, Josh. You did that. But I think it's a good idea if we really do stop now. I'm starting to feel *too much*. Soon we're not gonna be together, and it's better if we stop before we do more damage."

He shut his eyes. "I'm sorry. This is all my fault." He moved closer, resting his forehead against mine. "I'm so fucking weak."

"You're not the only one," I said. I could feel his cum dripping down my thigh.

I already wanted him again, mere seconds after I'd told him we needed to stop. The problem, though? Not only did I want him inside of me, I wanted him in my bed tonight—holding me. I was starting to want *everything* with Josh—things he likely wasn't willing to give me. That was precisely why we needed a step back.

TWENTY-FIVE

Josh

THE FOLLOWING MORNING, I met my brother Michael for breakfast. My plan was to continue denying that anything sexual had happened between Carly and me. Unfortunately, my brother could always see through me.

"Carly and Scottie are coming with me to your house on Christmas," I told him. "Hope that's okay..."

"Are you kidding?" he said with a mouth full of pancake. "The more the merrier. I'll let Vanessa know. She'll be excited."

"Yeah, and can you have Vanessa add Carly and Scottie to the Secret Santa assignments?"

"You know it. She'll be thrilled."

"Thanks." I grabbed a packet of sugar and emptied it into my cup, flicking it repeatedly.

"So...what happened the other night, after Carly got home from her date?" he asked. "You never told me, nor did you respond to my text."

I didn't say anything as I stirred my coffee, but he apparently saw something on my face. Or maybe it was the fact that I wouldn't look up at him.

"You slept with her, didn't you..."

Shit. There was no point in denying it. Tapping my spoon against the mug, I finally met his eyes. "It just... happened. I was fucking jealous. And you were right. She was texting me from there. But whatever happened with us that night, it's over."

"Wait, so you actually slept with her *that* night after she got back?"

I nodded, muttering, "The first time, at least..."

"And wait..." he said. "What do you mean by *it's over*? Didn't it just start? That was only two nights ago."

"We decided—" I stopped myself. "Well, actually *she* decided most recently that we have to stop. And she's right. We won't be here in Woodsboro much longer."

"What do you mean?"

"That's one of the things I wanted to tell you." I forced a smile. "Scottie got into a home."

"No way. I thought it was supposed to take a year or more."

"We did, too. But they have an opening for him. He's moving after the new year."

"Wow." My brother gazed out the window. "I have to say... I'm a little bummed. I was kind of hoping you'd stick around longer."

Yeah. Me too. "Everything happens for a reason. I can't take back what I did with Carly. And honestly, I wouldn't want to. But sex and love are two different things. If we were to get any more involved...that wouldn't be good. It's bad enough that I had sex with her, but anything else doesn't belong to me. That will always belong to Brad. I have no right trying to pick up with her where he left off." I rubbed my temples. "God, this is so fucked up."

"You're only human, Josh. It's perfectly natural to have the feelings you do for each other. Especially since you've both been through the same loss. I know that's the ironic part, but it's probably what bonds you the most."

My insides twisted at the thought of Brad being the tie that bound Carly and me. I changed the subject. "Anyway, we're going to Pete's Christmas Tree Farm today. Gonna try to bring Scottie. See how that goes."

Michael smiled. "I'm sure he'll like the hot cocoa stand."

"Not sure if he'll even drink that stuff. He's weird about food choices. But I remember he used to like the lights on Wayne's Christmas tree. Seeing as though this will be his last Christmas in that house, I couldn't not get a tree for him." I felt my eyes start to water. "What the fuck? That almost made me cry just now when I thought of him never going back."

My brother shook his head. "Okay, now you're gonna make me cry. Two grown men crying into their damn pancakes in the middle of a diner. Not a good look."

• • •

Carly was all set to go when I returned to the house that afternoon. I'd texted her to tell her to be ready.

She looked like a freaking snow princess, wearing a white coat with a matching white hat and a candy-cane-striped scarf.

"You look adorable," I told her. I couldn't stop myself.

She spun around. "I figured I'd get into the whole Christmas-spirit thing."

Not even a minute home, and I wished I could wrap her legs around me and have my way with her against the wall. Getting through these last days without touching her was going to be excruciating.

Instead of acting on the impulse to kiss the Christmas right out of her, I picked up Scottie's coat. "You ready to go, buddy? We're gonna get a Christmas tree!"

He seemed to understand because he didn't give us any trouble getting his coat on. More often than not, he resisted when you tried to take him out of the house, but thankfully not today.

On the way to Pete's Christmas Tree Farm, I turned on the radio station that played holiday music. It mixed with the sounds of Scottie's iPad coming from the backseat.

When we arrived, the place was packed—no surprise since it was getting pretty close to Christmas. But they had plenty of merchandise left. There were rows of trees in every size and width imaginable lining the open field, putting the smell of the season in the air. Light snowflakes started to fly, which added to the perfect holiday ambience. Nostalgia washed over me. I'd come here since I was a little kid, often with the Longos—and Brad. Then a wave of guilt hit me.

Since I suspected Scottie wouldn't want to be here all that long, I led him and Carly over to an area where there were several smaller trees.

I pointed to one of them. "What about this? It looks pretty even all around."

"I think it's perfect." Carly turned to Scottie. "Do you like this tree?"

He uttered something unintelligible and hopped up and down.

"Scottie seems to like it, so I guess this is the one." I smiled, clipping the ticket off the tree, which we were supposed to take to a cashier. "Why don't I stand in line to pay with him? Do you mind getting in line for the cocoa so we're not wasting time? I can already see he's getting fidgety."

"Not at all. That sounds like a good plan."

The line to pay moved at a snail's pace. A burst of wind blew my cash away, so I rushed to grab the bills before they were gone forever. I took my eyes off Scottie for no more than three seconds. But that was all it took.

"Hey! Stop! Mine!" I heard a kid scream behind me. "That man just tried to take my iPad!"

The next thing I knew, the kid's father had Scottie in a chokehold.

My heart nearly stopped.

"Please! Let him go!" I begged, prying Scottie away from the man. "He doesn't know what he did!" I yelled.

"What the fuck is wrong with him, taking my kid's iPad?" the man raged.

"He has autism," I said, panting. "He doesn't know right from wrong. He loves iPads, so he thought..."

The guy's eyes moved back and forth in confusion. "Well, keep a better eye on him, then." He then carted his snotty-nosed kid away.

Carly ran over to us, looking frazzled. "What happened, Josh? I saw the commotion, so I left the concession line."

"I turned around for literally three seconds, and Scottie grabbed some kid's iPad. The dad thought he was a thief. He almost hurt him." My voice cracked.

"Oh no." She covered her mouth.

"I shouldn't have taken my eyes off him."

She rubbed my arm. "It's not your fault, Josh."

"It is. I turned my back. Anything could've happened."

"That could've happened to either of us. It's not easy taking him out. You had no way of knowing he would do that. He's so erratic sometimes."

She held Scottie's hand and used her other hand to run her fingers softly through my hair. "It's okay. You've done so much for him...for both of us these past few months. Give yourself grace, okay? He's fine. We're all fine."

We're all fine.

Except I felt hollow inside that our time together was ending. And poor Scottie didn't realize what was coming.

We're all fine.

Closing my eyes, I relished the feel of Carly's touch, which brought me so much comfort. *So undeserving.*

I shook my head to snap out of this haze. "Okay. It's over. Let's get the tree and get home."

The rest of our time there went fairly smoothly. I tied the tree to the top of Carly's car, and after Scottie was safely in the backseat, watching his iPad, I left him with Carly and went back over to the concession stand to get us all some hot cocoa for the ride home. I told them to put extra milk in Scottie's so it wasn't too hot. He seemed to like it.

The Carpenters' "Have Yourself a Merry Little Christmas" came on the radio as we drove back. The soothing sound of the singer's voice calmed me a bit. I vowed not to let what happened this afternoon ruin the rest of our night.

Back home, as Carly and I set up the Christmas tree, Scottie bounced around, playing some reverse Elton John. Normally, he'd sit or escape to his room, so it seemed like he was intentionally hanging out with us tonight. He knew the lights were coming, and it was cute to see him so excited—especially about something that wasn't an electronic device. Inhaling a deep whiff of the fresh pine smell, I let it take me back for a moment to the many Christmases I'd spent in this house.

Carly went to her bedroom for a moment and came back holding a large red box. "I have a surprise."

I stopped messing with the tangled lights. "What is it?"

"A while back, I found this box of Christmas decorations. I know we bought some ornaments at Walmart, but we can add some of the Longos', too."

"Holy shit, Carly. That's awesome."

We opened the box together. The bulbs were wrapped in tissue paper, and we carefully unwrapped each one. Some looked to be many years old. One had Brad's name written in glitter on it.

At one point, Carly lifted another out and said, "Josh, look..."

Wow. There it is.

"It's yours." She smiled.

I still recalled the day Brad and I had sat at the kitchen table and made these with Yvonne. I'd always loved seeing my name on their tree each year. Christmas here had felt like a true holiday, unlike the depressing scene back at Dad's. After my mother left, he never put up a Christmas tree.

"We made one for Scottie, too, that day," I recalled. "It has to be in there somewhere."

We eventually found Scottie's ornament, along with so many other sentimental ones I remembered. We hung each and every one of them and didn't need many of the ones from Walmart at all. There wasn't any room.

Then I got an idea. "Be right back," I said as I disappeared into Scottie's room.

I knew he had some glitter that Lauren had brought to make arts and crafts with him. I found some glue, too. I returned to the living room and grabbed one of the ornaments from Walmart, carefully using the glue to write out CARLY before sprinkling sparkles over it. The glitter ended up all over the floor, but no one seemed to care.

"You're part of this extended family now. You deserve a spot on the tree," I told her. "We just need to let it dry."

Carly smiled down at my messy creation. "Thank you, Mathers."

"I think after Christmas, I'll take all these decorations and keep them at Dad's so they don't get lost. Lorraine will probably just throw everything out if we don't take what we want before she sells this place."

Carly frowned. "I can't even think about that. It makes me so sad to think that once Scottie goes into the group home, he won't ever get to come back here. But you're right. She's already mentioned that she needs the cash."

I put my arm around Carly for a side hug. "The whole thing sucks, Pumpkin."

We looked over at Scottie, who had his face practically buried in the lights of the Christmas tree.

"Look at him," she said. "He's so happy right now."

I chuckled. "I would've put those lights up a lot earlier if I'd realized how stoked he'd be."

"He's really not that hard to please. He just needs a safe place to live, electricity, and his chicken. And now lights." Carly turned to smile at me and caught me staring at her. "What?"

"Nothing."

I wanted to kiss her so badly. That's what I'd been thinking. I wished I could kiss her all night long and end the night inside her. I knew my feelings for her were far more than sexual, though. This was unlike anything I'd felt before. I had a deep desire to escape into her, hold her, and fall asleep with her in my arms. Become one with her. The way she'd comforted me at the Christmas tree farm—all she'd had to do was touch me, and everything seemed better. She always made everything better. She made my life better. She made *me* better. And that scared me. Because we were about to walk away from each other for good. *Because we had to.*

TWENTY-SIX

Carly

THREE DIFFERENT TYPES of fruit cake. Candy cane martinis. Roasted chestnuts. Josh's sister-in-law, Vanessa, had put out quite the spread on Christmas Eve. It was so nice of her and Michael to have invited me here with open arms.

But the festive tone of the night was bittersweet. Josh and I were getting closer to the end of our time in Woodsboro. In less than two weeks, Scottie would move into the group home, and Josh and I would be on our way back to where we'd come from. I'd never wanted to pause time more.

I'd dressed up in my holiday best, a bright red cocktail dress, but the vibe was casual at Vanessa and Michael's house. In fact, Vanessa wore buffalo-plaid pajamas. So I might have been a little overdressed. *Oh well.* Scottie had already planted himself next to the Christmas tree with his iPad, and Josh was hanging out in a corner of the living room with his nephew, Max, helping him assemble a new toy. His niece, Maya, was with her mother in the kitchen while Michael watched TV with their dad. That left me and Neil at the buffet, about to make uncomfortable conversation.

"I just wanted to say hello," he said. "Get the awkwardness out of the way." He grabbed an olive and popped it into his mouth.

I tucked a piece of hair behind my ear. "Thank you. I'm sure you'd rather just enjoy your family's Christmas without your botched date showing up."

"Are you kidding, Carly? I'm glad you and Scottie are here."

"Thank you, Neil."

"And there truly are no hard feelings whatsoever." He took one of the candy cane martinis. "I know now that it never could've worked between us."

"Why is that?" I was almost afraid to ask.

"You don't know?" He took a sip of his drink and looked around. "Can I tell you something, between you and me?"

"Sure..." I needed a martini, too, right now, so I took one.

"I've never seen my brother look at anyone the way he looks at you. I know there are reasons hearing that may be bittersweet. But just an observation. I also noticed the way you spoke about him on our date. Maybe you're both in denial. But I can see that you're very fond of each other."

I took a long sip of my drink. "You're right about that. But as I'm sure you realize, it's a complicated situation."

"Oh, I know." He set his drink down. "But...I think Josh sometimes complicates things when he doesn't need to. Life is messy, you know?" He sighed. "But I also understand the dilemma in this case. I guess my point is, no matter what happens between you and Josh, I wish you both the best after you leave Woodsboro. I really commend you guys for taking on the responsibility of looking after Scottie."

I smiled. "I couldn't have done it without Josh."

"I know he says the same about you."

"What, are you trying to shoot your shot again?" Josh chided as he entered the room, interrupting our conversation.

"What if I am?" Neil teased, winking at me. "Actually, Carly just informed me that she thinks I'm the better-looking brother."

"Well, now I know she's had too much to drink." Josh smiled over at me, and it gave me chills.

"Nice chatting, Carly." Neil picked up his drink. "I'm gonna go see if Vanessa needs any help."

I felt myself blushing.

"You okay?" Josh asked.

"Yeah. Neil is so nice. Your entire family is awesome."

Josh looked really handsome tonight in a fitted maroon sweater. I wanted to dig my fingernails into it. I was the one who'd created this no-further-sex rule, but it'd been tough to stick to it. I wanted Josh every second of every day, and tonight was no exception.

His eyes fell to my cleavage. My little red dress might've left too little to the imagination for a family affair. I'd caught Josh checking me out numerous times tonight, and each time, it gave me a thrill. Though I'd vowed not to let anything happen between us, I still craved his attention and any confirmation of his desire. It was my one consolation prize.

He cleared his throat as he once again pried his eyes upward. "Vanessa wanted me to let you know we're about to exchange gifts."

"Oh, cool."

I took my drink and followed Josh into the living room, sitting next to him on the smaller of the two sofas. The heat of his thigh warmed my skin as he sat close to me, and I felt it right between my legs. Taking a long sip of my martini, I hoped to numb the torturous feeling.

Vanessa sat on the ground in the middle of the room with a giant bag full of all of the Secret Santa gifts. A few of them had been wrapped in buffalo-plaid paper that matched her pajamas.

She reached inside the bag. "Okay, I'm gonna pass these gifts out, and then we're gonna go around the room and take turns opening."

Josh's dad, Tom, was first up. He was the person I'd been assigned. Josh had told me his dad was an avid fisherman, so I'd bought him some gear from Bass Pro Shops. I got goose bumps as I watched him open his present, really hoping he wasn't disappointed.

After Mr. Mathers realized the items were from me, he stood and gave me a hug. "Carly, I couldn't have picked a better present myself. Thank you, darling. How did you know what I like?"

"A little bird told me." I glanced over at Josh, who was grinning at us.

His dad seemed like a sweet guy, and it angered me that his wife had done him and their sons so wrong. I'd grown up without a dad around, so I appreciated what a good father Josh and his brothers had.

Vanessa was next to open her gift: a basket of Starbucks coffee and various mugs. "My husband knows me so well." She got up to give Michael a kiss. "The nearest Starbucks is forty minutes away," she explained to me. "So it's like a field trip whenever I get to go."

Next, Scottie opened his present from Vanessa: a brand-new Kindle Fire tablet. As if he needed another device. But apparently, she knew that was the quickest way to his heart. He could never have enough electronics.

"Just in case all of the others run out of batteries at once, Scottie." She grinned.

He had several others with him tonight, but Scottie examined the new device with great interest. She'd already loaded it with many of his favorite apps. Josh must've helped her with that.

Next, the kids opened their gifts. They'd been assigned each other. Max had bought Maya clothes from Hollister, and she'd gotten him a gift card to a gaming store and some candy.

When it was my turn, there were only a few possibilities left for my Secret Santa. When I opened the card atop my box, I was giddy to find that it said: *To Carly from Josh.* A warm and fuzzy feeling came over me. I wondered if the dice had landed this way, or if Josh had pulled some strings.

I'd thought my heart was full a second ago, but when I opened the small box, I wondered if it might burst. Inside was a silver bracelet with a number of charms. I looked at each of them closely—a little house, a dog, ice cream...and a lemon. Many of our "things." But what touched me the most was the charm of three people holding hands: a girl between two guys. My first instinct was to think Josh, Brad, and me, crazy as that was. But that didn't make sense. It was Scottie, Josh, and me. Our makeshift family that was about to be disbanded.

"Josh, this is..." I couldn't find the words to express how sweet this was.

"I figured I'd immortalize this crazy time since it's about to come to an end."

"It's beautiful. Thank you." My eyes began to water. "Truly, the best thing I could've received."

"You're welcome." His eyes found mine. "I'm so happy you love it."

All eyes in the room seemed to be on us as I reached for him, wrapping my arms around his neck. I wondered if my struggle to fend off my feelings was as obvious to others as it felt to me.

Then Josh opened the clasp and put the bracelet on me. Even the contact of his hand over my wrist gave me butterflies.

As the last of the presents were opened, I kept staring down at the bracelet and thinking about our time coming to an end. Once Josh and I returned to our respective cities, this time would be only a memory. At least I'd have this bracelet to remember it by.

After everyone had received their present, we sat down to dinner. We'd brought Scottie's chicken with us, and I took it into the kitchen and heated it in their toaster oven.

As we ate, Josh and I chatted with various family members at the dinner table, but from time to time, I'd catch him sneaking glances at me. His eyes silently told me he was struggling with the same longing I was tonight.

After dinner, I went back into the kitchen to take my plate to the sink. A few seconds later, Josh entered, and for a moment, the two of us were alone. The hairs on my neck stiffened as he came up behind me as I stood at the sink. The last time he'd been so close, we'd ended up screwing against the washing machine.

When I turned, his face was just inches from mine. "It wasn't just sex, Pumpkin. That's the problem." He leaned in, ever so slightly.

My lips parted, desperate to connect with his.

A second later, Josh's niece skipped into the room. He retreated immediately.

"Uncle Josh, come see my new skateboard!"

She dragged him away, leaving me alone with my palpitating heart.

TWENTY-SEVEN

Josh

THE DAYS FOLLOWING Christmas went way too fast. I'd managed to keep my vow, and therefore, my dick in my pants. I deserved a freaking award for that. A booby prize, at least. I'd nearly slipped up several times, but in the end, I knew I needed to respect Carly's wishes and my own promise not to let what she and I had started escalate into something we couldn't come back from.

It was like I blinked, and all of a sudden here we were, ushering Scottie into his new home. Moving day felt surreal, even though we'd done everything we could to prepare for it. Carly and I had taken turns going to his new home over the last few days, slowly bringing Scottie's stuff. It was our goal to make his room here as similar to his bedroom at home as possible. But we couldn't take everything. There was simply no space. Carly had framed a picture of the three of us and left it on his bedside table. My sister-in-law had taken it at the Christmas Eve party. I could only hope that whenever Scottie looked at it, he didn't hate us for leaving him.

Carly and I now sat on either side of his new bed, not wanting to go home yet. We were supposed to have gone by now.

"This doesn't feel right," I said.

Carly looked over at Scottie, who was playing on his iPad. He didn't seem to understand the magnitude of this day, or at least he wasn't showing it.

"I kind of wish we could stay the night with him or something," she said.

"We can't. That would make it even worse and harder for us to leave him here."

"Yeah." She picked at some lint on his bedspread. "I guess this is one of those situations where you have to rip the Band-Aid off."

That sort of reminded me of what I would have to do with my feelings for her—walk away from everything all at once. Not only did we have to say goodbye to Scottie today, but we'd say goodbye to each other tomorrow.

"I've already confirmed with Lorraine that she's going to bring his chicken by on Friday," Carly said. "The batch I just made should last until then."

"I hope she follows through with that." I looked out the window; it was starting to drizzle.

Carly held on to the bedpost. "I wonder how long it'll take before he jumps on this bed and breaks it."

"I give it two days." I chuckled. "I'm certain the next time one of us visits, there will be a mattress on the floor. They'll learn their lesson."

Someone came to the door. "We're going to be having dinner soon. You're welcome to stay, but it might be better if you leave so Scottie can get acclimated to the usual routine."

I could take a hint.

Did I mention this really sucked?

"Thank you." I nodded. "We'll be leaving shortly."

Without further ado, I reached out to hug him. "I love you, bud. I promise to come home to Woodsboro more often. And when I do, you're gonna be my first stop."

Carly had tears in her eyes as she wrapped her arms around him. "I'm sorry we have to leave, Scottie. I know this will work out for the best in the end, though. I hope you grow to love it here. I really do."

The whole thing felt so damn unnatural. But I forced myself up because I knew I'd never want to leave. Carly and I had started down the hall when we noticed footsteps behind us.

I turned.

It was Scottie.

He'd grabbed his jacket and his iPad.

He thought he was supposed to be leaving with us. He didn't get it.

My fucking heart was about to break.

"No, Scottie. You're staying," Carly said. She turned to me with a helpless look in her eyes. "What do we do?" she whispered.

"I don't know." I scratched my head and muttered, "I don't fucking know."

Holding his arm, I led him back inside his room. "Scottie, you stay here, okay?" I couldn't even say we'd be back...because that wasn't the truth. "This is where you're gonna live now."

By some miracle, when we walked out the second time, he didn't follow us. But I couldn't look behind me, fearing this would be one of those rare times he'd look me in the eyes. That would've made it impossible to walk away.

On our way out the main door, Carly and I said goodbye to the staff, who assured us Scottie was in good hands.

When we got outside, Carly broke down. I took her into my arms and spoke into her hair. "It'll be okay, Pumpkin. We both know this is best for him in the long run, even if it's hard today."

"I don't think he gets it—that we're not coming back to take him home ever again."

Even though it was killing me inside, I needed to be strong for her. "Eventually it won't matter as much. He'll start to look at this place as his home. It'll just take some time."

"I hope it gets easier for me, too." She sniffled. "Because right now this feels unbearable."

"Let's pick up some pistachio ice cream and wine on the way home. We should try to relax. We both have to get up early tomorrow."

There was something I'd yet to tell her. I couldn't wait, to be honest. I knew I wasn't going to lift her mood all that much, but I hoped it would help. I just wanted to wait until we were back at the house.

• • •

When we opened the front door at home, the silence was deafening. No sounds of Scottie's iPad or his humming or Elton John being played backwards. It was the first time we'd experienced this kind of silence. I'd wished for a moment of peace and quiet so many times while taking care of him, and now it was the very last thing I wanted. I would've given anything to look over and see my guy there on the couch with his device at his ear while he rocked back and forth, the smell of his fried chicken heating in the oven.

Carly walked over to his room. There was still a lot left behind.

"I don't think Lorraine is going to be able to handle cleaning out this place to get it ready for sale."

"She won't have to," I said, straightening my posture, so amped up to let it out.

Carly blinked in confusion. "You're coming back to help?"

"No, Carly." I took a couple of steps toward her. "This house...it's not going anywhere."

Her eyes widened. "What do you mean?"

"I bought it," I said, bursting with pride.

Her expression filled with hope. "What?"

"I bought it from Lorraine."

Carly placed her hand on her heart. "You're moving here?"

"No. I mean, I don't know that I'll ever live in it permanently. But I'm keeping it. I was thinking I could fly home on holidays—pick Scottie up and bring him back here for a visit, so he knows things don't always go away forever. Sometimes they come back."

Her eyes were watery, her voice barely audible. "Oh, Josh..." Carly leapt into my arms. "This is the best news ever."

My dick came alive at the feel of her breasts pressed against me. I took a whiff of her hair and willed my dick to calm down.

"I don't plan to change anything, either," I said, forcing myself to move back. "So no need to spend the last night we're here cleaning shit out. We can leave everything as is and just relax."

She wiped her eyes. "I can't believe you did this." She smiled. "I don't feel as sad anymore about leaving him, knowing this will still be his home."

"Good. Because I don't want you to have any guilt, Carly. You went above and beyond what anyone else in your shoes would have done. You did Brad proud. And you deserve all the happiness in the world."

"You, too, Josh." She sniffled, wiping her nose with her sleeve. "I mean that."

If I'd had one wish, it would've been that I could make love to this woman tonight without undoing whatever progress we'd made since stopping. But making a move when we were leaving tomorrow seemed like the dumbest decision ever. So I refrained from leaning into all the things my body begged me for.

Instead, we watched some of Wayne's DVDs, ate ice cream, and reflected on our time with Scottie. It took everything in me not to blow my resolve, but somehow I managed to get through the night without fucking up.

• • •

The following morning, Carly made us coffee and breakfast, but I had very little appetite. When we exchanged addresses, the fact that we were leaving each other started to feel all too real. I dreaded going back to my life in Chicago, which felt so empty after the past few months here.

The plan was for Carly to drop me off at the airport and continue on her long road trip back to California.

Last night's struggle had continued into this morning. Every second I had to restrain myself from pulling her close, dragging her into the bedroom one last time, and showing her how badly I still wanted her—a proper goodbye. I'd never wanted Carly more. But if last night was bad timing to lose control, this morning would've been even worse. Now I had a flight to catch, and there was no turning back. She deserved to return to her life without me complicating everything in the eleventh hour. Carly deserved so much more than to be strung along by me. I just wished my heart wasn't aching with the knowledge that whatever we'd had was officially ending the moment she dropped me at the airport.

The drive to the airport in Manchester was over an hour, but somehow it seemed to take minutes. Almost the entire ride, I debated changing my mind and offering to accompany her on the road trip to California. The idea of her traveling so far alone didn't sit well with me. I was worried about her, tempted to change my flight and fly from L.A. back to Chicago.

But I wouldn't be able to trust myself; a change of plans would just be an excuse to spend more time with her and risk giving in to temptation.

Carly parked her car at the airport drop-off area. Everything in me wanted to lean in and kiss her, but instead I reached over and threaded my fingers in her hair.

"Please be careful driving," I said.

"I will."

The sadness in her eyes was palpable. She looked exactly the way I felt. Neither of us seemed to want to leave, yet here we were, about to say goodbye.

"Josh..." she finally said.

Unable to help it, I brought her hand to my mouth and gently kissed it. "Yeah, baby?"

"Do you think it would be too much for you if I also came back to Woodsboro next Christmas? You know, to see Scottie?"

"Too much for me why?"

"I don't know..."

I played dumb, but I knew what she meant. Anything could happen in a year. She and I seeing each other again would mean inevitable awkwardness if one of us had moved on. I needed to be mature about this because I didn't want to lose touch with her. I needed to know she was happy, and I needed to believe I'd see her again, even if that might be painful.

"Of course, I would love that. So would Scottie."

"I'd really like to make it happen," she said.

The potential of seeing her again next Christmas both terrified me and gave me something to look forward to all at once. I'd either be dreading it or counting every damn day until then. "I'd better go..." I said, forcing myself to let go of her hand.

She followed me out of the car and stood across from me on the curb. "Have a safe flight."

When I took her into my arms for the last time, I realized just how badly I'd been lying to myself. Not only did my heart come alive, but all the feelings I'd been harboring flooded to the surface. My heart hadn't gotten the message that whatever we had was over. It was still very much in the middle of falling in love with someone it could never have. I wrapped my hands around her face and gave her a firm but chaste kiss, not allowing my tongue to taste her for even a second.

Carly was the first to pull back. I watched as she returned to the driver's seat of her car. I waved and blew her a kiss. Then I forced myself to turn around and make my way through the sliding glass doors. I turned back one last time to find her still waiting for me to disappear from sight. I blew her another kiss and vowed not to look back again.

Even with all of the sadness in my chest, as I walked toward the escalator to check in, I had no regrets. I wouldn't have changed a thing about our time together and what I'd learned about my capacity to open my heart. I'd thought I was dead inside, but Carly Garber had brought me back to life, and for that I'd always be grateful.

TWENTY-EIGHT

Carly

I ALWAYS CARRIED the last note Josh left me. From time to time, I'd reach into my purse and look at it again.

> ***A Thank You from The Trappist Monks of St. Francis:***
> *Thank you for the best three months of my life.*
> *P.S. I'll probably regret not giving in one last time for as long as I live.*

Josh had stuck that piece of paper in my bag sometime before we'd left Woodsboro a month ago. But I hadn't found it until I'd gotten back to California and unpacked my bags.

I'd just finished my last makeup client of the day and was about to head home when I grabbed my phone, scrolled down to his name, and typed: **I miss you.**

But instead of sending, I immediately erased it. I'd typed those three words too many times to count recently. And not once had I had the courage to send the message to him. Because what was the point of saying it? It wouldn't change anything.

Four weeks had passed since I'd returned to California. Getting back into the groove hadn't been easy. My apartment felt cold and sterile. Even though I was lucky enough to have had a few makeup jobs lined up when I returned, I wished work was more of a distraction. There was simply way too much time to think while applying foundation and lining eyes because I knew how to apply makeup in my sleep. My thoughts constantly drifted to Josh—wondering what he was doing, whether he'd gone on any dates yet. I'd daydream about the house in Woodsboro, imagining sitting by the pellet stove next to Josh and Scottie, just hanging out. And I'd especially get lost replaying our sexual encounters.

I didn't know what was worse, the fact that I couldn't stop thinking about Josh, or the fact that it used to be Brad my mind would wander to. My obsession with Josh had taken some of the attention away from the sadness of losing Brad. Not sure if that was a blessing or a sin.

Once I arrived home from work, I was preparing to make myself some dinner when a text came in.

Josh: Is it even possible to see one of these ever again and not think of your lemon pits?

It was followed by a photo of him at the supermarket in Chicago, holding up a lemon. Just the sight of his big hand holding the lemon gave me shivers. I stared at his calloused thumb. My body missed him in the worst way. *I* missed him in the worst way. What were we now? Friends?

Another message came through.

Josh: Okay, maybe I think of you even when I'm not staring at lemons. I hope you're having a good day. xo

Once again, I typed out: **I miss you.** Then I erased it, instead typing out a less-emotional response.

Carly: I am. Long day at work but happy it's over.

I wanted to tell him so much more—that the feelings of loneliness and depression had come back in full force when I returned to California. That the last time I was happy, I was with him.

Josh: I'm sorry you had a long day.

About an hour later, a delivery man knocked on my apartment door. I knew I hadn't ordered anything, but he insisted it was the right address. When I opened the bag, there was a carton of pistachio ice cream inside. There was no note, but it wasn't necessary.

• • •

The following day, the bright California sun streamed through my apartment window. The small palm tree outside blew gently in the breeze.

"Oh my heart. That's the sweetest thing I've ever heard." Christina sighed.

I'd just finished telling her how Josh had purchased the Longos' home. She and I hadn't had a chance to catch up since I'd returned to L.A. because she'd been visiting her grandmother in Portugal. But she'd finally stopped by my apartment for tea today to catch up.

"How is Scottie adjusting to his new place?"

"Lorraine says he seems okay when she's popped in there to drop off his food. I need to visit him eventually. I promised I would. I don't even care whether he understood me. I just need to see him again for myself, to know he's doing okay. So I'm thinking maybe next Christmas."

"You need to see Scottie...not Josh?" She looked at me skeptically.

I stared down into my teacup. "I want to see him again, too. I just have a hard time picturing what that would be like in a year's time."

She crossed her legs as she made herself comfortable on my couch. "You think it will be awkward—like, if one of you has moved on?"

"Right. Like, I wouldn't want to stay at the house with him if he were with someone."

She chuckled. "I could see how that might suck."

"That would probably be what I deserve, though."

She arched a brow. "You mean because of Brad?"

Running my finger along the side of my cup, I shrugged. "I'll never not feel guilty about it. The guilt wasn't enough to stop me, though—clearly."

Christina reached for a cookie. "What if Brad orchestrated the whole thing?" She took a bite. "You ever think of that?"

I squinted. "What do you mean? Like, from up above?"

"Yeah." She spoke with her mouth full. "How do you know he didn't have something to do with you and Josh getting together? Anything is possible."

"Why wouldn't Brad have sent me anyone in the world besides his best friend?"

"Because maybe he knew no one else could understand what you went through like Josh could. I don't know." She took another bite. "You can't rule it out."

"Or, he could be rolling in his grave that I had unprotected sex multiple times with his best friend. My money is on *that* scenario."

"Speaking of which..." She took a sip. "I never asked you about the sex. You've been very aloof about it. But I'm sure it was amazing."

I blushed. "It was."

"Like I've said before, one look at that guy, and you just know he knows how to fuck." Christina paused, then grinned. "Okay, I can tell you don't want to give me details."

"You're right. I don't." My cheeks burned.

I also stopped short of admitting that I'd thought of little else besides Josh since getting back here. Or that I'd nearly texted him to say I missed him upwards of a hundred times.

"Well, you can't sit around and wait until next Christmas to get laid. You're going to try to move on now that you're back, right? Put yourself out there?"

The thought of that made my stomach churn. "I have no choice."

"You seem like you could use a little help."

I reached for a cookie and bit into it. "I might."

• • •

Christina took the whole "helping" thing a bit too seriously.

On Friday night the following week, I went to a party she'd invited me to—something for a client of hers down in Newport Beach. It took me two hours to get there in traffic. I was exhausted after a long day, but I couldn't continue to just hang out in my apartment alone most nights.

When I got into the country club, it became pretty apparent that this was more than just a party. Christina introduced me to a guy she'd apparently been on a date with already and—surprise—he had a friend who'd just happened to come with him to the event.

This was a setup. She'd said she was going to help me get back out there, and apparently, she'd meant it.

Todd Marino was a charming and charismatic realtor in Orange County. Although he was a bit older than I typically dated—probably in his late thirties—he was tall, handsome, and smelled great. He seemed very interested in hearing about my career as a makeup artist and the charity work I'd soon be starting again for a local homeless shelter, giving free makeovers to women looking to rejoin the workforce.

Todd was attentive, good-looking, successful—all the things you could want, right? But alas, I wasn't feeling it. And having to be "on" for minutes on end was exhausting. It made me realize I wasn't ready to date anyone yet.

When Christina and I escaped to the bathroom, she gave me the third degree.

She ran her hand through her long, black, curly hair as she looked in the mirror. "So...what do you think of him?"

"First of all, you didn't tell me *anything* about tonight being a double date."

"Would you have come if I had?"

"Probably not."

"There you go." She laughed.

"He's a great guy. I just don't feel ready to give him the attention he deserves."

"Translation: I still haven't gotten over Josh."

Not even trying to deny it, I held my hands up. "What do you want me to do? I can't help how I feel..."

She blotted her lips and turned to me. "Pining for a guy who's made it clear that you and he don't have a future together because he feels too damn guilty to do anything more than fuck you is not a good use of your time, Carly."

Her words were harsh. They literally hurt my chest.

"I'm aware of that." I swallowed. "But you do know that feelings aren't always based on logic."

She sighed and shook her head. "Alright...I'm sorry. It's a little too soon for tough love. I'm gonna head back out there. How about I tell the guys you're not feeling great and needed to head home?"

"You're gonna make fun of me for days if I do that."

"Aside from my ball busting, what do you want to do right now?"

"I'd like to leave."

"Okay, girl. Then go. I got you."

"Thank you," I said, feeling immense relief.

I hugged her before exiting the bathroom and slipping out a side door.

But I didn't end up going straight home after all. Instead, I took a long walk down a nearby pier. As the sun set, there were so many happy people wandering about, readying to enjoy a Friday night on their party boats.

Listening to the sound of the waves crashing, I sat down on a large rock and took out my phone. Once again, I scrolled down to his name and typed: **I miss you.**

But this time, I actually sent it.

TWENTY-NINE

Josh

I LOOKED AROUND the restaurant, anywhere but at her. There was nothing wrong with Sydney, and she held the distinction of being the first woman I'd gone out with since being back in Chicago. I'd forced myself to return to the dating app because it was the only way I stood a chance at moving on. Based on my lack of interest from almost the moment we sat down, though, it would seem that decision might have been a bit premature.

Sydney had done most of the talking this evening. She told me her divorce was recently finalized, and she'd just reentered the dating scene.

"This is my first time out, actually," she explained.

Great. First time out, and it was wasted on a man who wasn't that into her. Now I really felt bad for the poor woman. "I didn't realize that. You mean like the first date since your husband?"

"Yes."

"You said you were new to the dating scene. I didn't actually think this was your first date."

"It is. And I feel like I won the jackpot." She batted her lashes. "You're adorable."

"Well, thank you." I swirled my drink. "This is my first time out in a while as well...since I've been back."

"Back?" She tilted her head. "Where did you go?"

"I went home to Woodsboro, New Hampshire, to take care of a family issue."

"Oh." She placed her napkin on her lap. "Is all well now?"

"Yeah." I lifted my hand to order another drink. Even the mention of Woodsboro made me feel like I was gonna need it. An ache grew in my chest as I waited for the waitress to deliver it, and that ache was only made worse by Sydney's next question.

"When was your last relationship, Josh?"

Without thinking it through, I answered, "I don't really do relationships. I haven't had a girlfriend since high school."

Wow. That was the canned response that had always been at the tip of my tongue. But it felt wrong saying it this time. It *was* wrong. Sydney had opened up to me about her divorce, and in return, I'd just lied to her face. Carly and I might not have been officially "boyfriend and girlfriend," but to identify what we'd had as anything less than a relationship was a lie. Even the word *relationship* didn't quite seem strong enough. It was a true partnership, even if only for a few months. And even though it was over now, it felt unnatural to pretend like it never happened.

"Actually, that's not really true." I shook my head and stared down into my empty glass. "I'm sorry."

Sydney blinked in confusion. "Oh?"

The waitress placed my new drink in front of me, and I took a long sip before slamming the glass down harder than intended. "I was in a relationship recently. Back in New Hampshire. It ended about a month ago."

Her eyes narrowed. "Why did you lie?"

"I wasn't sure I wanted to talk about it. I'm sorry."

Sydney nodded sympathetically. "The wounds are still fresh, then."

My chest felt tight. "You could say that."

"Can I ask what happened?"

"It was a mutual decision. Like me, she was only in New Hampshire temporarily. We live on separate sides of the country." I swallowed.

Another lie. That wasn't the reason we weren't together at all. I'd have gone anywhere for Carly, if things were simpler.

"Actually...that's not entirely true, either." I took another long sip of my drink. "Admitting what I did is a little difficult."

"You're not a very good liar, Josh." She laughed. "You confess the truth within seconds."

"Fuck. I know." I rubbed my temples. "I'm genuinely sorry, Sydney. I really am. You aren't getting the best version of me tonight, I'm afraid. I've been out of sorts ever since I came back."

She flicked her red hair, leaning in curiously. "What did you do that was so bad?"

I took a deep breath, bracing for judgment. "Carly was engaged to my best friend in the world before he died. Brad was killed in a car accident a few years ago."

"You moved in on his fiancée?"

A knot formed in my stomach. "It's not as simple as that. It wasn't like I decided to go after her because he wasn't around. In fact, I never liked her much when they were together." I chuckled. "You could even say we hated each other."

"Why did you not like each other?"

"Misunderstandings. Preconceived notions that weren't true. Dumb decisions on my part. Take your pick. We don't really know anyone until we spend time with them."

She tilted her head. "So how did you end up dating her, then?"

At that point, I explained the whole situation with Scottie and everything that had happened over those few months back in Woodsboro.

"So you were just two people thrown into the same situation at the same time. I guess I can see how that could happen."

Maybe that was how it started. But here I was, far away from Carly now and still thinking about her every day, my body still craving her. So this was not exactly situational for me. My feelings for her had crossed over to my normal, everyday life now, too. I guess that's what happens when someone makes their way inside your heart. It doesn't matter where you are; they're there with you.

"Pretty sure I fell in love with her." Surprised at my own candor, I paused to reflect on that. "Pretty sure I still am."

"Then why are you here with me?"

Grade F for my performance on this date. "I don't know." I shook my head. "I'm sorry."

"Me too." She flashed a sad smile.

Then the next thing I knew, Sydney had tears in her eyes.

"Shit. Why are you crying?"

She grabbed a napkin to wipe her eyes. "Because hearing you talk about her reminds me of how I still feel about my ex-husband. I'm out with a gorgeous man tonight, yet all I've been able to think about is Ray."

Leaning back in my chair, I crossed my arms. "Well, aren't we a dream team..."

Remarkably, once Sydney and I decided we were a lost cause, we were able to enjoy a meal together. All the pressure of the situation evaporated.

She told me more about her ex, and I recalled stories from Woodsboro. I even told her about the silicone breast insert chicken incident. She cackled so hard I'd thought she was gonna piss her pants.

When we'd finished dinner, Sydney and I wished each other well before we parted ways. I doubted I'd ever see her again, and that was okay. Our meeting had served a purpose; through each other, we'd learned things about ourselves tonight.

I stayed at the table to pay after she left, scrolling on my phone. I noticed I'd somehow missed a text from Carly.

Carly: I miss you.

I rubbed my thumb over the screen, as if to caress

those words. Carly must have been thinking about me as intensely as I'd been thinking of her.

Josh: I'm sorry I didn't see this come in. But how did you know I was thinking about you tonight?

The little dots moved as she typed.

Carly: Can you talk?

Josh: Yeah, give me a few. I'm in a noisy restaurant at the moment.

Newly motivated, I paid the bill and headed out to my car. As soon as I started the engine, I dialed Carly and put her on speaker.

"Hey," I said.

"Did I interrupt your night?" she asked.

"There was nothing to interrupt."

"Were you alone when you texted me?"

"I was."

"You went to a restaurant by yourself?"

"Well, I'd met a woman there earlier."

After a brief pause, she murmured, "Oh."

"Can we talk about this kind of stuff?" I asked.

"I don't really want to, but I also don't want you to lie to me. So, yeah. Tell me." She let out a long breath into the phone.

"It was the first time I'd attempted to meet someone new since I came back. And it was an epic fail. I wasn't feeling it."

"What was wrong?"

She wasn't you, I wanted to say. "Just no chemistry. And I didn't quite feel ready for the whole dating thing, to be honest."

"I have a confession..." Carly said. "I just got home from a sort of ambush date that Christina arranged."

Jealousy immediately set in, but I tried not to let it show. "Christina? Dildo Girl?"

"Yup." She chuckled.

"How did it go?"

"Well, considering I left early and made up a story that I wasn't feeling well...not great."

"Wow, look at us, huh?"

"Yeah." She sighed.

"For the record, I miss you, too, Carly."

After a short pause, she said, "It's so good to hear your voice. That's really all I wanted."

We talked for several minutes as I pulled up to my apartment.

As I entered my place, she said, "It doesn't sound like you're driving anymore."

"I just got home." I threw my keys down.

"Do you need to go?"

"Nope. Let's stay on the phone, unless you have somewhere else to be?"

"I don't," she said.

We continued talking as I got out of my clothes and climbed into bed, wishing desperately that she were here with me.

"I went to visit my father in Arizona," Carly told me.

I straightened against my headboard. "When?"

"Last weekend."

"You hadn't seen him in years, right?"

"At least seven years, yeah."

"What made you do it?"

"I think when I saw your dad at Christmastime, it made me miss mine—or at least miss the *idea* of him. I decided maybe I'd regret it if I didn't try to make amends with him."

"How did it go?"

"He was really happy to see me. He said he's felt like I hated him, and that had deterred him from contacting me, said he didn't want to upset me. I know that's bullshit in a sense, because if you love your kid, you reach out to them no matter what. But I realized over the course of the trip that he has a certain immaturity about him that affects the way he handles things. I don't think he's a bad person, nor do I think he means to hurt me. But I also don't think he loves me the way I wish he would."

It broke my heart to hear her say that.

"Pretty sure I lost the one man who ever truly loved me when Brad died."

"*No, you didn't,*" I wanted to scream. But I knew there would be no turning back if I did. More than that, I wasn't going to overshadow a statement about Brad's genuine love for her by unleashing an inappropriate revelation of my own, with impeccable timing. Nor did I want to give her false hope when we were supposed to have ended things.

I shut my eyes, then opened them, relaying only a fraction of what I really wanted to say. "The best is yet to come for you, Carly. I just know it. Please don't give up on the idea of love. There's always hope, as long as we're alive. Don't let your shitty dad impact your outlook on life."

"I think you should take some of your own advice, Josh."

In many ways, with Carly, it felt like I'd found the female version of myself. Which was ironic, considering how much we'd disliked each other at one point.

"We do have a lot in common," I told her. "More than just Brad. I've never been able to reconcile how my mother could just leave. And it's impacted my sense of self-worth. I understand why your dad makes you feel the way you do, but we can't define our value by the poor actions or decisions of people who probably need mental help. I'm trying to get myself to believe that. And listening to you talk, knowing how strongly I feel that you've been misled to believe certain things because of your dad's actions, makes me understand that I could be wrong about myself. I've taken my mother's actions personally, too. It's enlightening to see your situation from the outside."

"Well, I'm glad my fucked-upness can help you, Josh."

"We're both a little fucked up, Pumpkin. But that's okay."

"Can I confess something else tonight?" she said.

"Of course."

"I miss having sex with you."

Tightening my muscles, I hissed. "We did that very well, didn't we?"

"I know it's done. But...I think about it a lot," she admitted. "It was the best sex of my life."

Whoa.

That was quite the proclamation.

Better than Brad?

I shunned that thought because it was sick.

"It was different with you," she added. "Maybe *best* wasn't the right word or fair to say...but I experienced things with you that I hadn't before. That's what I meant." She hesitated. "I don't compare you to him. You know that, right? Whatever you and I had is totally separate."

She'd hit a nerve—the idea that no matter how much I felt for her, I could never measure up to him, that I'd always only have her because he wasn't here anymore. And if somehow he miraculously came back, she'd choose him.

It felt like the most selfish thing in the world to compare myself to someone who didn't have the privilege of life anymore. So I forced those thoughts out of my mind. At the same time, I didn't want to accept the satisfaction that came from knowing I'd apparently taken her to places sexually that no one had before. What kind of a person would that make me, to take pride in such a thing?

Carly and I stayed on the phone until I could sense her nodding off. Going into this night, I'd hoped I'd finally be able to date again. Turned out the date I'd ended up with was the only one I really wanted.

THIRTY

Carly

IT STARTED OUT like a normal workday. I was on a made-for-TV movie set, getting ready for a client at 6 AM when I noticed a New Hampshire number calling my phone.

That's odd.

I immediately picked up. "Hello?"

"Carly, it's Lorraine. I don't know what to do. I'm freaking out."

"What happened?"

"I just got a call from the group home. Scottie escaped this morning. He's missing."

My heart dropped. "What?"

Her voice trembled. "There was a new staff person, I guess, working at the house, and they didn't lock the back door."

The room felt like it was spinning. "Did this just happen?"

"They called me ten minutes ago. The police are already onsite in the area. I'm driving over there now. I just felt like I needed to let you know."

My heart was going a mile a minute. "Does Josh know?"

"Not yet. I called you first."

"Okay. I'm gonna call him right now." I began packing up my things as fast as possible. "Lorraine, everything is going to be okay. They'll find him." Mindlessly tossing various tubes into my carrier, I said, "I'm getting on the next flight out there."

"Thank you, Carly. I'm shaking right now. I don't know what to think or expect."

I slammed my large makeup trunk closed. "Please call me right back if anything changes."

"I will."

I turned to my client. "I'm so sorry. I've had a family emergency. I have to get on a plane to New England."

Her eyes widened, and she nodded. "Oh no. We'll find someone to cover for you. No worries."

As I ran out of the building, I dialed Josh. We hadn't spoken since our long phone call a week ago, and I hated that this was going to devastate him.

"Carly? Everything okay?" he asked as he picked up.

"Oh, Josh..." I started to cry.

"Carly, what's wrong? Are you crying?"

"Lorraine just called." I sniffled. "Scottie escaped from the group home. The police are searching for him."

"What?" he shrieked. "Oh my God. How the fuck could that happen? That place was like Fort Knox."

"A new staff member neglected to lock a back door, and that was apparently all it took."

"Fuck. I'm getting on the next flight."

"Me too. I'm in my car now headed to the airport. I'm gonna call to book myself on the next flight out as soon as we hang up."

"Carly..." His breaths were erratic. "I'll never forgive myself if anything happens to him."

"Don't go there, Josh." I started my car and raced down the road. "We can't go there."

• • •

Thank God, after I landed in New Hampshire, I was able to get a rental car fairly quickly. Another blessing? There was nearly no traffic between Manchester and Woodsboro.

When I arrived at Wayne's house, I used my key to open the door.

Lorraine was standing in the middle of the living room, looking lost.

"Anything?" I begged.

"No. I'm so scared." She rushed over and threw her arms around me.

I pulled back. "Did Josh get here yet?"

"Yes." She nodded. "He's already out with the search team."

"Okay." I took a deep breath. "I'm gonna use the bathroom and then I'll meet up with him."

Just as quickly as I'd entered the house, I was in my car again, headed back down the road. Though I shouldn't have been using my phone and driving, I voice-texted Josh to find out his exact location.

When I got to a street around the block from the group home, I saw him standing on the corner. After finding the nearest parking spot, I rushed out of the car.

Josh's eyes looked sunken, yet wild at the same time. He was completely distraught, and he hadn't noticed me yet.

"Josh," I called to get his attention.

He turned, the pain in his eyes easing ever so slightly. "Hey."

We fell into each other's arms for a moment.

When he released me, he said, "The police told me not to get involved, but there's no way I'm sitting around doing nothing while he's out there somewhere. I've been searching the area on foot, but I think we should drive around now."

"Let's go," I urged.

We jumped into Josh's rental car and drove through the neighborhood. I held his hand the entire time, as if holding onto him was holding us both together. Scottie *had* to be okay. But really, anything could have happened by now. Scottie had never even crossed the street by himself. I had to push the what-if thoughts from my mind.

I'd never seen Josh like this, so laser focused. As we drove slowly in silence, he balanced paying attention to the road with scouring the area for clues.

He suddenly pulled over. "I think we should park here and walk for a while."

"Should we go in separate directions?"

Josh pondered that for a moment before he nodded. "That's probably a good idea. Best use of time." He exhaled. "But please be careful, Carly."

He'd been smart and grabbed two flashlights from the house, since it was dark out now. We each took one and went in opposite directions, vowing to keep in contact via text.

After an hour of looking, the situation started to feel grim. I didn't feel entirely safe wandering the dark rural roads alone, but I would've stayed out here all night if it meant finding Scottie.

I texted Josh.

Carly: Anything?

Josh: No. I can take you back to the house for the night, but I'm going to stay out.

Carly: I don't want to go back. I want to keep looking.

Josh: Okay. Meet me back at the car?

Josh was holding a bag when I returned to the car.

"I bought some water and snacks," he said, handing it to me. He leaned against the car with his head in his hands. "Do you pray, Carly?"

"Not enough, but I sure as hell have been today—under my breath pretty much constantly."

He turned to me, his eyes red. "If he took a device with him, it's gotta be running out of battery power by now." He shook his head. "What the fuck? This wasn't supposed to be the way things turned out. I'll never forgive myself if anything happens to him."

"I know," I muttered, rubbing his back. "We can't lose him."

After some tears and a quick moment of hysteria, we managed to pull ourselves together again. We continued combing the streets on foot with our flashlights until sunrise. My eyes felt so heavy, and Josh had bags under his. We must have looked like zombies.

Since we knew Scottie better than anyone, the cops had asked us to meet them at Wayne's house this morning. They had a list of questions they wanted to ask.

An officer was waiting for us at the house when we arrived. We invited him in and set our phones to charge before sitting down with him.

"I take it you didn't sleep last night?" he said to Josh.

"No, sir."

"Well, I want to assure you we still have a full team out searching for Mr. Longo. But we hoped to get some information from you that can help us."

We spent the next half hour telling them all about Scottie's favorite things—his chicken, his apps, his reverse Elton John music. I wasn't entirely sure how any of that was going to help them find him, especially since he wouldn't have any of those things at this point. The thought of even one cop here at the house and not out there looking for him made me uneasy.

After the officer left, I tugged on Josh's jacket. "Let's go back out."

"You sure you don't need to sleep?"

"Positive. I just need to pee."

We quickly used the bathroom and then returned to the car, this time heading to another area a couple of miles from the neighborhood where the group home was located. No particular reason, but we needed to branch out.

Once we'd parked, Josh and I again split up and headed in different directions. I silently prayed every step of the way, feeling like I was wishing for a miracle. The more time that passed, the less likely we would find Scottie unharmed.

We each walked miles, passing out fliers the authorities had made with Scottie's face on them. God, did he ever look like Brad in that photo. In the end, though, it turned out to be another long day of no leads.

As darkness fell again, I felt myself coming unraveled, and I could tell Josh was reaching the same point. By now every corner of Woodsboro had been surveyed. Josh and I hadn't eaten, aside from the snacks he'd picked up at a convenience store last night. Even though neither of us felt hungry right now, I knew we'd need the sustenance for another night of searching. And at some point, I knew my body was going to shut down.

We decided to stop at the house to use the bathroom and scarf down some fast food we'd picked up on the way. I'd done the best I could to find something workable. My gluten-free diet didn't matter in times like this.

Lorraine had called to tell us that she'd left Wayne's house to shower back at her place and get a few hours of sleep, so the house was empty when we returned. Things were so quiet it was almost eerie as Josh and I sat across from each other at the kitchen table and wolfed down our food. At one point, our eyes locked. Josh's expression was as hopeless as I imagined mine was right now.

I started to speak a few times, but nothing came out. I wished I could tell Josh everything was going to be okay, but I wouldn't say it unless I believed it in my heart. The idea of getting a phone call terrified me, though I was also desperate for news. My nerves were shot as I braced for the worst. I needed to be prepared, just in case.

Just as we were about to leave again, Josh's cell phone rang. We'd given his number to the police, and my heart sank deeper than I'd realized it could go.

THIRTY-ONE

Carly

"HELLO?" JOSH'S HAND trembled as he lifted the phone to his ear.

His chest rose and fell as his eyes moved from side to side.

There's news. I just didn't know what. My heart beat like crazy. He kept nodding, and suddenly his lips began to quiver.

He looked at me. "He's alive. They found him. He's alive! He's okay."

He's okay.

He's okay.

Oh my God! He's okay!

I burst into tears, a massive amount of air escaping me. My body felt like oxygen had just been returned to it. I'd been a walking shell of myself since arriving here, and I was alive again.

Josh ran his hand through his hair as he paced. "Where is he? Can we go to him?" He kept nodding and turned to me and whispered, "They're bringing him here." He nodded some more. "Okay. Okay. Thank you, officer. Thank you so much."

After he hung up, Josh tossed the phone and collapsed to his knees. He held his head in his hands and wept. I walked over to him and knelt, joining him on the floor. We clung to each other as we both cried tears of joy. Tears of love.

After several minutes, I sniffled and asked, "Where did they find him?"

Josh's eyes glistened. "A guy called the police because he thought there was a bear inside the clubhouse attached to his kids' swing set. Thank God he didn't shoot. When they got there, it wasn't a bear. It was Scottie." Josh wiped his eyes. "He'd holed himself up inside this clubhouse for God knows how long. That's all I know. They said the paramedics are checking him out before they bring him home, but he seemed fine, like maybe he'd gotten a hold of food and water somehow because he didn't seem dehydrated."

After we called Lorraine to tell her the wonderful news, Josh and I could barely stand still as we waited for that car to show up. When it finally did, we ran to meet them outside.

An officer opened the backseat and led Scottie out. His shaggy blond hair was disheveled, and he had some dirt on his shirt, but otherwise, he looked great. Just like our Scottie.

Josh wrapped his hands around Scottie's cheeks and kissed his face. "You scared the hell out of us, buddy."

I rubbed Scottie's arm. "We're so happy you're okay."

With hazy eyes, Scottie seemed a bit disoriented, likely still in shock from the experience of being lost. He still had his iPad in his hand, although the screen was black. It had likely died a long time ago.

He looked at me and pointed to his device.

"Yes. Yes!" I reached out, never happier to charge something for him. "I'll charge it for you. It's the least I can do." I ran into the house to plug it into my phone charger.

Two cops accompanied us inside. Scottie took his spot on the couch, and I handed him my phone while he waited for his tablet to charge. I'd pulled up his favorite streaming site and thankfully, that seemed to do for the moment.

"Where exactly was this house?" Josh asked one of the cops.

"A little over a mile from the group home. It's a miracle that he didn't get hit by a car."

I looked up at the ceiling and thought about Brad. *His brother was watching over him.*

Josh looked over at Scottie. "The owner has no idea how long he was there?"

"No. The guy just noticed him an hour or so ago. He saw a shadow moving inside the clubhouse and assumed it was an animal since he'd had them in his yard before."

"Thank God Scottie's a kid at heart," I said. "He probably saw the swing set, and that's what drew him to that yard. We're lucky he was in a safe place."

"The paramedics checked him out at the scene. They were gonna take him to the emergency room, but his vitals are good, and he doesn't seem to be dehydrated. He somehow had access to food and water. We suspect he might've stolen something from a convenience store because they filed a report about someone matching Mr. Longo's description. They reported that a man walked in and brazenly took a bottle of cranberry juice from the refrigerator and a box of Oreos before walking out. The older woman at the register has a bad leg and didn't want to chase after him, and she said the man just looked at her blankly when she screamed at him. So that's in line with what you report about Scottie's behavior. But that report came in just shortly before we found him, so we hadn't made the connection. Anyway, that might explain why he's in good condition. In any case, we gave him water and a couple of granola bars, but I'm sure he's still hungry."

"Scottie was a bandit on the run." Josh laughed.

The door flew open, and Lorraine walked in.

She charged toward Scottie. "You had us worried sick." Scottie ignored her, continuing to play on my phone.

After she held him for a few seconds, Lorraine joined us where we were standing with the officers.

"I'm Lorraine Longo, technically Scottie's guardian," she said, holding out her hand. "But as you probably know, he lived with Carly and Josh before he moved to the group home."

"Are you planning on taking him back to that residence?" one of the cops asked her.

Lorraine looked toward us for guidance.

"No," Josh said adamantly. "Not anytime soon, at least. We haven't gotten that far, though."

"Okay, well, we let them know that we were bringing him here because that's what Ms. Longo instructed us to do in the event he was found. You'll have to contact the group home and make them aware of your plans."

"Will do, Officer," Josh said. "I can't thank you enough for bringing him home safely."

The officer nodded. "This is what we do, son. It's our pleasure."

The officers turned to walk out the door, and Scottie hopped off the couch. He came over to Josh and began disrobing. His pants were halfway down his legs by the time Josh put a stop to it.

"Does he always do that?" One of the cops chuckled.

"He wants to take a bath," I tried to explain. "He's not very subtle."

"Okay, we'll let you get on with your evening," he said, looking uncomfortable.

After the door shut, Josh lifted his shirt off and threw it. "I've never been happier to get naked in my life." He laughed. "Come on, Scottie! Let's go take a shower!"

"Manshower party!" I laughed.

Josh then realized he hadn't brought a change of clothes, so he went into Wayne's old closet and grabbed a few things for him and Scottie.

After they disappeared into the bathroom, I could hear the music blasting through the door. It was a true celebration in there. All of the emotions from the past couple of days seemed to hit me at once. Lorraine had gone into the kitchen to prepare Scottie's chicken, and I sat down on the couch and sobbed into my hands. We'd been so lucky today. So very lucky.

When Josh and Scottie emerged, they both had wet hair and were wearing Wayne's clothes, which were too tight.

Josh shook my shoulders playfully and teased, "No offense, but lemons aren't gonna cut it after forty-eight hours, Pumpkin. I think you need to shower next."

"Thanks for the advice. And I concur. You're right this time. Let me go see if I can find something to wear, too."

I went into Wayne's room in search of anything I could possibly throw on. When I checked the drawers, I couldn't believe my luck. I'd apparently left behind a single thong the last time I was here. I got one of Wayne's green plaid shirts and a pair of his drawstring shorts, so I'd be okay until I had a chance to go to the store tomorrow, or wash the outfit I'd arrived in.

A hot shower had never felt so good. As the water rained down on me, I spoke to God, formally thanking Him or Her for bringing Scottie back safely today. Then, I spoke to Brad and Wayne and promised them I would do whatever I could to make sure this never happened again. Despite all the emotions, it was probably the best shower of my life, not only for the level of gratitude I held in my heart, but because I couldn't ever remember going two days without taking one.

When I came out, Lorraine was in the kitchen. Scottie was already at the table eating his chicken.

She glanced over at me. "Oh my, don't you look interesting."

I looked down at my checkered plaid shirt. "I think you mean ridiculous." I laughed. "How did you make that chicken so fast?"

"I've been making a lot, freezing it, and taking them over to the group home in batches. I still had some in my freezer, so I brought it with me. I figured he'd be starving."

It was the fastest I'd ever seen Scottie devour his food. And I'd never been happier to witness anyone eating in my life.

"Where's Josh?" I asked.

"He went to get some of Scottie's things at the group home, and to the store to get some spare clothes and other things you and he might need."

Just as Scottie finished his supper, Josh returned, and Lorraine went back to her house.

It was just the three of us again, like no time had passed.

Not only had Josh scooped up the majority of Scottie's belongings, but he'd also gotten takeout for us and some stuff from Walmart.

"What did you get from Walmart?" I asked.

"I bought myself a few items of clothing. I figured you might want to pick out your own stuff tomorrow, but I bought you some spare underwear, some pajamas for tonight, and an outfit that won't make you look like Howdy Doody."

I looked down at Wayne's checkered-plaid shirt again and chuckled. "What are you trying to say?"

He winked. "I also got you some lemons for your pits, some coffee, and stuff for breakfast. You know, the essentials."

"How did you even know my underwear size?"

"There was this woman who looked about your size, so I asked her what size underwear she wore. She thought I was a perv."

"Seriously?"

"No." He laughed.

"I was gonna say, that woman was probably excited that a guy who looked like you was interested in her underwear."

"I ripped open one of the packages and made my best guess. But I've also fondled your underwear in the past, so I kind of knew your size."

I shook my head and laughed.

We took our takeout into the living room so we could sit by Scottie, neither of us willing to leave his side for very long.

"What's the plan?" I asked after we'd finished eating.

Josh turned to me. "I have no idea, Pumpkin." He smiled. "How about sleep? That sounds like a good plan for starters."

I yawned. "That I definitely can't wait to do."

"I know that's not what you were asking, though. Hopefully, I'll have a better idea what to do about Scottie and the living situation once I've got a clear head again. But that won't be until tomorrow at the earliest."

It was late. After Josh led Scottie into his bedroom to get him situated for bed, I went to Wayne's room, hoping Josh wouldn't attempt to sleep on the couch. I'd been hesitant to bring up the subject of where he'd be sleeping because the issue seemed trite compared to everything we'd been through today. I decided to let things play out on their own.

I opened the bag of stuff he'd purchased for me. I took out a cute pair of pink sweatpants and a matching sweatshirt that sort of looked like they'd come from the junior's department. But they'd fit me. He'd also gotten a six-pack of bikini-cut panties that had indeed been ripped open. Then my jaw dropped when I took out the pajamas he'd mentioned. It was an adult, footed onesie!

What the hell?

He appeared at the door to the bedroom. "You like your pajamas?"

"What the heck?"

"I'm sleeping in the bed with you tonight," he explained. "And even though I'm doing nothing but crashing now, when I get up in the morning, I'll need all the help I can get to keep my hands off you."

Feeling like I had nothing to lose after the hell we'd been through, I unbuttoned my Howdy Doody shirt and slipped out of Wayne's clothes right in front of him. Josh swallowed hard as he took in the fleeting view of my bare breasts and thong. He kept his eyes on me every second while I slipped into the footie pajamas, zipping them all the way up.

"Okay..." He let out a shaky breath. "That was cruel, and defeated the purpose, you know."

"Nothing you haven't seen before, Mathers," I teased before climbing into bed.

A few seconds later, I felt the heat of him at my back. Josh wrapped his arms around me and pulled me close. Whatever boundaries we'd set the last time we left each other seemed to have gone out the window after the experience of the past two days. As his body enveloped mine, I closed my eyes and let myself enjoy it. I had no idea what tomorrow would bring, but falling asleep in Josh's arms was everything I needed tonight.

THIRTY-TWO

Carly

THE FOLLOWING MORNING, I opened my eyes to find Josh staring at me.

"Hey..."

"Hi," he said in a deep, morning voice.

"You were watching me sleep?"

He rested his chin on his hand. "I was."

"That's supposed to be my thing."

"I figured I'd beat you to the punch—watch you creepily before you could wake up and watch me." He winked.

"Have you heard Scottie up yet?" I asked.

"No. If I had, I'd be out there and not enjoying the view from here."

"How did you sleep?"

"Like a rock," he said. "You?"

"Like a baby."

"In a onesie." He tugged on my pajamas, sending a bolt of electricity down my side.

"Exactly." I rolled my eyes.

Josh placed his hand on my waist and squeezed, his touch awakening the muscles between my legs. My eyes went to his lips. Needing desperately to touch him, I reached up and threaded my fingers through his lush hair. He closed his eyes and groaned. I shut my own eyes for a moment, and before I could open them, I felt the heat of his lips on mine.

Yes.

Yes.

Yes.

I immediately opened my mouth for him as our tongues became desperately reacquainted. The kiss grew intense as I continued to dig my fingers into his hair, pulling with need. His rock-hard erection pressed against my abdomen through the material of these silly footed pajamas. My leg wrapped around his body. And... That was the moment we heard the door burst open, followed by a thud on the bed.

Scottie.

"What the..." Josh grumbled.

"Scottie!" I laughed.

He moved between us and situated himself as if it were a totally normal thing to do. Leaning against the headboard, he made himself comfortable and pulled up a video on his device. Josh and I smiled. I knew we were both thanking our lucky stars to have Scottie back safe and sound.

"He never used to come in here in the morning," I said. "I wonder if he was checking to make sure we were still here—for obvious reasons."

Josh dragged himself out of bed. "You're the best cockblocker ever, Scottie."

Despite the ambush, Josh was still visibly hard through the gray sweatpants he'd slept in. He disappeared out the door. Who knew how far we would've taken things had Scottie not interrupted.

Since Scottie seemed content in the bed, I got up, leaving him there, and went to find Josh, who was now standing by the coffeemaker in the kitchen.

He lifted a mug. "Coffee?"

"Yes, please." I smiled. "You're looking all sexy in that T-shirt while I look like the Easter Bunny."

He leaned against the counter as he waited for the coffee to drip out of the machine. "Well, my plan to cover you from head to toe, so I couldn't access you easily, didn't work. I still want you right now, even though you're in that getup." He caressed my hair. "We need to talk. But later tonight. Maybe after Scottie goes to bed. Alright?"

I gulped. "Okay..."

Unsure whether he wanted to talk about Scottie or us, I didn't ask him to elaborate; a part of me was scared to find out.

"I just want to enjoy this day without any stressors," he said.

"What are we gonna do?" I asked.

"Nothing. Hang out with him. Watch some of Wayne's movies. Eat ice cream. Fucking decompress from the nightmare of the past two days." His hand found mine.

I linked my fingers with his. "You won't hear me complain about that."

Josh took me into his arms and held me, resting his chin on the top of my head.

A knock at the door caused us to step away from each other.

"Who the hell is that this early?" he asked.

Josh went to answer it, and I followed. My heart sank when I saw a police officer standing there. I knew Scottie was safe in Wayne's bedroom, but my first inclination was to panic. It must have been PTSD.

"Sorry to disturb you folks." The officer looked over at me and chuckled, a reminder of how ridiculous I must've looked in this damn onesie. "The owner of the house where Mr. Longo was found discovered this framed photo on the ground underneath the clubhouse he'd been hiding in. So we figured we'd return it to you. Mr. Longo must've had it with him when he escaped from the group home."

I took the photo from him. It was the one of the three of us taken at Michael and Vanessa's Christmas party.

"Wow." Josh covered his mouth, staring at the photo.

"I gave that to him when we dropped him off at the group home that first day," I explained to the cop. "Thank you so much for returning it."

"It's our pleasure. Glad everything worked out."

"Thanks again, Officer," Josh said as he shut the door. He turned to me with a look of awe. "Scottie took two things with him when he decided to escape—his device and a photo of the three of us together. I'd thought him getting out was sort of accidental, just a result of them leaving the door unlatched. But now I think he might have thought it through." Josh scratched his head. "I think he was..."

"Looking for us," I finished his sentence.

"Yeah," Josh muttered in a daze. "Holy shit, Carly."

My chest felt heavy. "I know."

• • •

We'd spent the day lounging around the house, and it was glorious. Though I did take a quick trip to Walmart to get myself some normal pajamas, a few more items of clothing, and some groceries.

Now, it was almost bedtime, and we were once again hanging out in the living room. Josh and Scottie had showered, and they were now looking at something on the iPad.

"Look at what he's doing." Josh pointed to the screen. "He's using the Andy Warhol filter again on, like, a hundred pictures of his own face."

"Just like old times," I said. "He must like himself."

"That's a good quality." Josh mussed Scottie's hair. "If only we all liked ourselves that much."

Scottie laid his head on Josh's shoulder and continued playing with the photos. *My heart.*

"He's very calm tonight," I said. "You can tell he's happy to be home."

Josh smiled. "Can you blame him?"

"No, I can't."

"I'm happy to be here, too," he said.

"It's crazy that it took Scottie going missing to get us back together like this."

"Not the way I would've chosen for it to happen, that's for damn sure," Josh said.

He looked down at his phone for a moment and placed his hand on Scottie's shoulder. "It's past your bedtime, dude." He led Scottie into his room to get him ready for bed.

It seemed to take forever for him to return to the living room, which figured, since I was nervous about the talk we were going to have.

When Josh came back, he plopped down and rested his head on the couch for a moment. Despite how much we'd relaxed today, Josh still seemed a bit preoccupied and spent. He didn't immediately start talking, but I decided I couldn't wait anymore.

"So..." I cleared my throat. "You said we needed to talk..."

He turned to me and straightened. "Yeah." He bounced his legs. "So..." He paused. "I want to know if you'd be willing to stay out here for a couple of weeks with Scottie while I go back to Chicago."

My eyes widened. That was about the last thing I thought he'd say.

"I'm moving back to Woodsboro, Carly. I pretty much made that decision the moment I landed back here. I promised myself that if Scottie came home safely, I'd never let him out of my sight again. I don't want him going back to the group home. I'm gonna take care of him myself."

"Wow." I nodded. "So you...need me to stay here while you go get your stuff?"

"Basically, yeah. I need to talk to my job to see if they'd be willing to let me work remotely on a permanent basis."

"And if they won't?"

"Then I'll quit and figure something else out. Or I'll work for Neil's construction company in some management capacity and hire part-time help for Scottie here. We tried with the group-home thing, right? But he clearly didn't want to be there. *This* is his home. He deserves to be here, and I want to make that happen for him, even if I have to hire help."

There wasn't anything to think about. I nodded. "Of course, I'll stay."

"It's not permanent," he assured me. "You can go back to California as soon as I get back."

My stomach felt unsettled as I said the first thing that came to mind. "What if I don't want to?"

That seemed to surprise him. Heck, it surprised me.

"You're welcome here for as long as you want to stay," he told me. "You know that. I just assumed you'd *want* to go back to your life."

What I really wanted was for him to *ask* me to stay. But I didn't want to make this conversation about him and me. He'd just made a huge life decision, and throwing in the complicated matter of where we stood wouldn't be fair right now. I didn't think the reasons he felt we couldn't be together had magically disappeared in the time we'd been apart.

Taking a deep breath, I decided to trust the process. Fate had brought us back together again—even if it was temporary. I vowed to not overthink anything, to enjoy my time with him for however long it lasted, and even to appreciate my time alone with Scottie while Josh went back to Chicago to settle things.

Instead of unleashing all my worries onto him, I just nodded. "You're making the right decision, Josh."

He let out a relieved breath. "You think so?"

"Absolutely."

"I'm gonna ask Lorraine to transfer guardianship over to me. You think she'll go for it?"

"I do, actually. We both know she's not capable of taking care of him. And I think it will be a relief to her that you want to officially take over."

"I was worried you might think I was getting in over my head, taking this on permanently."

Moving to sit closer to him, I placed my hand over his. "You've proven yourself, Josh. Over and over again. The truth is, even if you're not perfect at this, no one's gonna love him like you do. You're the closest thing he has to family. And I think Scottie will be the luckiest guy in the world to have you as his guardian."

Ask me to stay. There was nothing I wanted more than for Josh to include me in these plans. But he would have to be the one to suggest it. I'd already hinted that I didn't want to go back to California. The ball was in his court. I sure as hell wasn't going to push for anything. I vowed to wait until he returned from Chicago before I started worrying about what the future held.

Trust the process.

I decided to take a shower before bed. Being around Josh again had made me so damn horny—especially after what we'd started this morning never came to fruition.

Under the water, I slid my hand down and circled my clit. I'd wanted Josh to touch me so badly all day today. I was unsure whether he planned to sleep in the bed with me again tonight, but either way, I was fairly certain I had another night of frustration ahead.

After a few minutes, the bathroom door opened. I jumped, thinking it was Scottie, but when I saw the tall, muscular silhouette with fuck-me hair through the foggy glass door, I realized it was Josh.

My stomach did somersaults as he slid open the shower door and stepped inside, gloriously naked. My eyes moved over his gorgeous body. I hadn't seen him like this in so long, and I'd thought I might never have the opportunity again. His engorged cock glistened with precum at the tip. Feeling embarrassed for staring—still a bit of trauma from the time he'd called me out way back when—I turned away from him, facing the showerhead.

His warm body pressed against my back, his voice vibrating against my skin. "Hi."

"Well, hello," I whispered.

"Is this okay?" he asked.

"Yes," I breathed.

My muscles clenched as he situated his hot, rigid dick against me, gliding it along my ass cheeks.

"I've missed this beautiful ass."

"It missed *you.*" I smiled.

"I've been dying for you all day, Carly." He wrapped an arm around my waist. "I'd wash you with soap, but if I'm being honest, I want you to smell like nothing but me tonight."

My legs quivered.

"From the moment we left each other, I haven't been able to stop fantasizing about fucking you." He spoke into my ear, "I haven't been with anyone else. I don't *want* anyone else. I only want you. And I need to show you how much right now."

"Take me," I begged.

"I want to fuck you hard. Okay?"

Trembling, I nodded. "I want that, too."

"Yeah?" He massaged my clit.

"Yes, please."

"So polite." He chuckled. "Lean your arms against the wall. You're gonna need to hold on."

Shaking with need, I did exactly as he said, planting both hands on the wet tile wall.

His hard dick was still right up against my ass cheeks but not penetrating me yet.

"I can't wait to watch my cock moving in and out of you and come inside you again."

He pushed into me without warning, hot and wet friction, the beautiful burn igniting a fire inside of me.

"I missed this, baby." He groaned as he went balls deep. "So fucking much."

"Me too." I panted as my walls clenched around him.

"I don't want to need you like this, but I do." He pumped into me faster.

"It's okay," I gasped.

"I hate myself, but I fucking *love* this too much." He pulled out and then thrust in harder. "You own me, Carly, but I don't feel like you could ever be mine."

Thrust.

"I am yours," I mumbled. "I missed you so much, Josh."

Thrust.

"I missed you, too, baby. Gonna so go to hell for this, but I don't give a fuck right now. I need you too damn much. I'm done trying to pretend like I don't."

He circled my clit again as he moved in and out of me. "Tell me if I'm hurting you."

"It doesn't hurt. I can take it."

His balls slapped against me as he took my words to heart. It had never been this intense, this beautifully rough.

He bit my shoulder lightly. "Carly..." His body spasmed as a rush of hot cum filled me. "Fuck, I can't stop this. It's too much. I had to come."

My own climax soared through me a few seconds later, pulse after pulse of pure ecstasy shooting through my core until the rhythm of our movements tapered.

He fingered me after we came down from our orgasms. "I love feeling my cum inside of you." Josh gently kissed my back and lingered behind me as I continued to lean against the wall, sated. "Love seeing it drip out of you even more," he rasped.

Out of breath, I murmured, "Josh... I..."

"What, baby?"

"I don't know what to do with you."

"I know what you can do." He turned me around and placed his forehead against mine. "Take me to bed, so we can do this again. Because I'm nowhere near done with you tonight."

THIRTY-THREE

Josh

I'D NEEDED TO stay in Chicago a little over two weeks.

The long drive back to New Hampshire was exhausting, but since I wanted to bring my car, I drove rather than flying. Let's just say, that had given me a hell of a lot of time to think—mainly about the fact that I didn't want Carly to leave. And I needed to let her know that without seeming like a selfish asshole. At the same time, asking her to stay would mean asking her to give up her life in California. It would also mean me committing to her in a way that would disregard my vow not to betray Brad.

In my heart, I knew I couldn't stop the way I felt about her just because I thought I should. I would've given anything to have a real conversation with Brad about this, to truly know where he stood. But I'd never know, despite the fact that I'd prayed for him to send me a clue.

I had about five miles to go before arriving in Woodsboro. As I passed through the neighboring town of Shearborn, I noticed a sign in the distance.

St. Francis Abbey: Home of the Trappist Monks of St. Francis

It was a beautiful compound in the middle of a large, grassy field, set back atop a hill. With multiple buildings attached to one another, there was also a big cathedral off to the side. *Wow*. This was the place Wayne had donated all that money to. How had I never noticed this property in all of the years I'd lived in this area?

In a last-second decision, I stepped on the brakes and turned my car around, ultimately pulling into the parking lot of the monastery. This place had been a mystery to me since I'd found all the notepads at the house. I couldn't understand why it had been so important to Wayne. Maybe it wasn't about the monks, but rather what they could do for him. But he must've had his reasons for giving those donations.

When I rang the doorbell to the main entrance, a series of chimes rang out. A man dressed in a long, black cloak opened the door.

What the heck have I gotten myself into?

His voice was low and gentle. "May I help you?"

I blinked. "I'm not sure."

"Are you in trouble?"

"No, no. I'm sorry." I looked beyond his shoulder at a large religious statue Wayne had probably paid for in the otherwise empty vestibule. "I'm...just curious about this place. It meant a lot to someone who meant a lot to me."

"Would you like to come in?"

I thought for a second. Even though it was getting late, I felt compelled to enter—like this place had been calling to me, and it was somehow not a coincidence that I'd driven by.

"Sure. Thank you."

He brought me into a small sitting room just off the entrance.

"Are you from the area?" he asked.

"I'm actually moving back home to Woodsboro. I'm relocating from Chicago, but I grew up here."

"What brings you back?"

"I'm going to be taking care of an adult family member with special needs." I paused. "You're talking to me. Why did I think monks were silent?"

He chuckled. "We do not keep perpetual silence here. That's rare nowadays. Although we do have moments of silence and certainly avoid idle talk."

I arched a brow. "This isn't considered idle talk?"

"When conversation is necessary to help others, it is encouraged. I get the impression you're in need of some guidance."

You're right. I spent the next several minutes filling him in on the situation with Scottie, without mentioning any names. But ultimately, I couldn't help myself.

"Actually, you may know Scottie's father."

He folded his hands together on his lap. "Oh?"

"Wayne Longo."

The man's eyes widened. "Wayne Longo...yes, I do certainly recognize the name."

"I figured you might. Clearly this place meant a lot to him. I found a bunch of notepads with this monastery's name on them back at Wayne's house. I assume he must have donated a lot of money for those."

The monk nodded. "Indeed, he did."

"Do you have any idea why? I mean, not that anyone needs a reason to give to your fine establishment, but—"

"People donate to the monastery with specific prayer requests. We then add their appeal into our daily benediction."

"Was Wayne on, like, autopay or something?" I joked.

He didn't crack a smile. "Wayne always had the same, single request: that we pray for his son, so that Scott should always be looked after, safe, and cared for in the event that anything happened to Wayne."

I took a moment to let that sink in. "Really..."

"Yes. That was the only thing he asked for."

"Wow."

"So it seems his prayers have been answered."

I looked away, taking in that revelation. "Yeah. I guess so."

"Something else is troubling you..." he said.

This monk had a sixth sense. There was no reason to hold back.

"As I told you, Wayne's older son, Brad, passed away in an accident before Wayne died." I took in some air. "I'm afraid I've fallen in love with Brad's fiancée—the woman he was engaged to before he died. We've been taking care of Scottie together and fell for each other in the process. I don't know how *not* to love her, but I also don't know how to live with myself for betraying my friend."

The man's expression didn't change. He seemed unaffected by what I'd just confessed. "Your friend has a much greater purpose now than to be concerned with such things," he said.

"How do you know that?"

"He is one with God. He knows no jealousy or feelings of betrayal anymore. Beyond this life, it is understood that such things are poisons. They don't exist with God. There is only love and forgiveness."

"Are you saying Brad wouldn't be angry at me for basically living the life he was supposed to have here? He wouldn't think that was unfair?"

"That life he knew here on Earth is over, son. Brad is in a better place. But even if he *were* concerned with such things, I doubt he would want his loved ones to suffer, if what you and she want is to be together. But again, Brad is with God, and your actions now are no longer relevant to him."

His perspective, at the very least, was one I desperately wanted to believe.

I nodded. "I never thought of it that way, I guess—that he's moved on from any of the emotions that might come with things happening here. Most days it's still hard for me to grasp that he's actually gone."

"He's not gone," the man corrected. "He's with God, son. And you are here, taking care of his brother. And mending the broken heart of your dear..." He paused. "What is her name?"

"Carly."

"Carly." He shut his eyes momentarily. "Bless you both."

"Thank you. I greatly appreciate your kind words." I got up from my seat. "While I have to head back, I feel like I was meant to stop in here today. You have no idea how much you've helped me. This seemed to come at the exact moment I needed it."

"That's how it works, son."

The monk escorted me out, and I left there feeling a peace I'd never expected. It felt like a gift—from Brad or Wayne, maybe both.

All throughout my ride today, I'd wished I could speak to Brad. Now I chose to believe he had communicated with me through that Trappist monk. Or maybe I *had* to believe that in order to do what I knew I had to as soon as I got back home.

• • •

Carly put down the laundry she was folding and ran to the door when she spotted me.

"You're back!" She wrapped her arms around me.

"Hey, Carly…" I took a long whiff of her scent.

"I missed you."

"I missed you, too." I squeezed her tighter. "So much, baby."

She pulled back, looking surprised. "Really?"

I leaned in to kiss her forehead. "Really…"

I sat down next to Scottie on the couch, interrupting his internet surfing. "I missed you, too, buddy."

At first, he barely made eye contact with me. Then he finally looked at me before pressing the "take bath" icon on his app.

"Not yet." I laughed, getting up from the sofa. "Soon, though, okay?"

Carly stood across from me. "How was the ride?"

I rubbed my hand over her arm. "Long."

"Did everything go smoothly moving out of your apartment?"

"Thankfully, the landlord is keeping all my furniture. He got it for a steal."

"At least you don't have to deal with moving it."

"Exactly."

"Your boss is okay with everything?"

"For now, yeah. We'll see how it goes. There'll be times I'll have to travel back to Chicago, but I'll get coverage for Scottie when that happens. Hopefully it will all work out."

She looked down. The uncertainty I knew she was grappling with was tangible. That was my fault. I'd left everything in limbo before I went to Chicago. That's because I'd still been hanging on to the guilt that was holding me back. Not anymore.

"Are you okay?" I asked her.

"Yeah." She feigned a smile. "I'm just not sure where things stand. It's sort of been eating at me."

"I had a feeling I knew what you were thinking." I caressed her cheek with the back of my fingers. "Well, *I've* been thinking, too. About us. I was gonna wait to have this conversation until Scottie went to bed, but I see now that it can't wait another second."

She put her hand over her heart, as if bracing herself. That pained me. I understood why she'd assume this was going to hurt. I'd conditioned her to think the worst for so long, pushed her away for too long. Not anymore.

I took her hand in mine. "Carly, I let you go because I thought the worst thing I could do to Brad was love you. So I tried to stop it from happening, as if it were a choice." Squeezing her hand, I looked deeply into her beautiful green eyes. "But I've realized I *can't* stop loving you. And even if I tell myself I shouldn't or can't, it doesn't matter. I still do." I took a deep breath. "I love you, Carly Garber. I love you so much, and I don't want you to leave. Ever. I want you here in this hole in the wall in the woods with us. But only if you want to be. I know it's a lot to ask you to leave your clients out there and—"

"There's nothing more I want, Josh." Tears stained her eyes. "I've never been happier than being here with you two. *Everything* I need is here." She looked over at Scottie and back at me. "I've just been waiting for you to ask." She wrapped her hands around my face. "And, oh my God, I love you, too!"

My body finally relaxed. As our lips locked, all I could think was that I couldn't wait until Scottie was asleep tonight.

I broke our kiss to add something. "I want to emphasize that I want you to stay *not* because I need your help, but because I don't want to be apart from you again. I can't imagine my life without you."

She massaged my hair. "You struggled with feelings of guilt for so long. What changed?"

"I've known I loved you for a while. I knew I needed to tell you how I felt when I got back from this trip, but something happened on the drive home today." I looked up at the ceiling, still in awe of that magical meeting. "It was amazing, and I'll tell you the full story another time. But just know...I believe Brad is okay with us. He sent me that peace today. He loves us. And he wants us to be happy."

"Wow. Okay." She wiped her eyes. "I worried you were going to tell me to go back to California—just like the old days."

"Never again, Pumpkin." I lifted her up and spun her around. "Did you ever think you'd fall in love with an evil pig?"

"Did you ever imagine you'd learn to love my face?" she said as I put her down.

"Not only do I fucking love your face..." I placed my forehead against hers. "I see my future children in it."

Carly looked stunned as she smiled up at me, her eyes glistening. "Wow," she whispered.

As we held each other, I continued to feel at peace. That meeting at the monastery had set me free, in part because I simply *had* to believe it so I could allow myself to be happy.

I turned to Scottie. "Buddy, what do you think about Carly staying with us permanently? The three of us living together again...but for good this time?"

His response was to jump up from his seat, come over to us, and press the bath icon again on his device.

I patted him on the back. "Well played, my man. Your escape plan not only got you back where you belong, but it finally knocked some sense into me. I have to thank you for getting us back here."

I planted a kiss on *my woman's* lips and said, "I know Brad will always be the love of your life... But I hope you have room for a second."

Carly wrapped one arm around me and the other around Scottie. "I have room for three."

EPILOGUE

Carly

One Year Later

AN INTERESTING ENVELOPE had caught my eye when I'd run out to check the mailbox.

It was from The Trappist Monks of St. Francis and addressed to Josh. Too curious, I ripped it open, and sure enough, inside was one of the *A Thank You from the Trappist Monks of St. Francis* notepads.

Huh. Interesting.

Speaking of Josh, he'd been out for a very long time this afternoon, and I was anxious for him to come home. He'd said he had some errands to run, but he'd been gone for a couple of hours.

Scottie and I, on the other hand, were having a lazy day in. I sat next to him on the couch as he scrolled through the photos in the album of his iPad. I covered my mouth when he came to some more candid images of a naked Josh in the bathroom. Not only that, he'd decided to put the Andy Warhol filter over them this time.

I immediately took out my phone.

Carly: Your cock has now been immortalized with the Andy Warhol filter.

Josh: Surprised it took this long.

Carly: Should we sell them? ;-)

Josh: I'm thinking we erase them.

Carly: On it! Are you on your way back?

Josh: I just have a few things to take care of. I should be home soon. Why? Are you needing something?

Carly: I'm always needing something from you. ;-) But no, I'm in no rush.

Josh: I'll be back soon, babe.

"Let me see that for a moment, Scottie." I reached for his device and began erasing all the photos of Josh's Warhol-ed dick before they got into the wrong hands. Thankfully, Scottie just switched over to another tablet.

After the problematic pics were gone, I looked through some of his other photos. Scottie took the most bizarre screenshots and had recorded some strange videos. Many of them were simply videos of other videos on his tablets. His favorite thing by far, though, was to take photos of himself or Josh and place filters over them. Thankfully, most of them were G-rated.

I noticed a batch of videos taken during his bedtime routine with Josh, too. Josh read to him a lot in the evenings, and often they would have funny one-sided conversations, man to man. I would peek in sometimes, and it was the most adorable thing. Josh talked to Scottie as if he were going to get a response. He would open up to him about things that might've been bothering him and ask Scottie questions. Sometimes, Scottie would make brief eye contact with him.

Stealthy as ever, Scottie had apparently recorded some of these conversations. I pressed play on one such video. I could just see the side of Josh's body as he spoke to Scottie. Something he said in the middle of their talk caused me to freeze.

"Can I tell you a secret, Scottie? I have a big surprise for Carly on Saturday. She's not gonna see it coming, and I absolutely can't wait. You can keep secrets, right? What am I saying? You're the best freaking secret keeper in the world. That's one of the things I love about you. I can tell you anything, and I know no one is going to find out."

Pausing it, I looked at the date of the video; it had been recorded three days ago. That meant the Saturday he was referring to was *today*. I immediately closed it without listening to anything else because I didn't want to spoil his surprise. Josh was cooking something up. My mind raced to guess what the surprise might be, trying not to go to the place my heart wanted to.

Is it possible he's going to ask me to marry him?

Josh and I had spoken about getting married over the past year. But we'd also agreed we didn't need that formality to validate our relationship. Josh had never seemed particularly set on it, so we'd never come to a firm conclusion.

But a part of me always sort of hoped he'd ask me anyway, even if I didn't need a piece of paper to feel satisfied. I had everything I needed already. Josh, Scottie, and I had made a true life together here in Woodsboro. Josh continued to work remotely, and he just traveled occasionally to Chicago. And I'd started my own traveling special-event makeup business, servicing most of New Hampshire and other parts of New England. We were also making plans to put an addition on the house so we'd have more space.

Everything was perfect, so why did I need a legal document to legitimize my relationship with Josh? I knew he was it for me regardless, and he knew I wasn't going anywhere, so there was no reason to put pressure on either of us.

Sigh. All that said—a part of me still wanted to be his wife.

The rest of that afternoon, I was on edge. It got worse the longer Josh stayed out. Whatever the surprise was, I wondered if it had gone wrong. He'd told me he would be back fairly soon over an hour ago.

When his car finally pulled up, my heart nearly jumped out of my chest. I was so freaking nervous—for him and for me because I knew I'd likely blown my hopes out of proportion.

I situated myself casually on the couch next to Scottie, as if I hadn't been waiting with bated breath for Josh to walk in. Yet when the door opened, I stood up. So much for remaining nonchalant.

The sound of a dog collar jingled behind him.

And then I saw him—a familiar goldendoodle.

Bubba-Hank?

Tears filled my eyes as I ran to my big, fluffy dog. "What in the world?" I cried as the dog started jumping on me and licking my face. "What is he doing here, Josh?"

"Surprise!" Josh beamed.

"You didn't steal him, did you?"

"Of course not. I'm not a thief like you." He winked.

"Then what is he doing here?"

"He's back, baby."

"What do you mean?"

"The poor woman who owned him passed away."

"Oh no." I looked up at him. "But how the heck did you know that? You stalked her or something?"

He laughed. "No. But I always remembered her name and where they lived. So, I did some digging and contacted her daughter a while ago to check on him. At that time, she told me her mother was ailing but still wanted the dog. I told her Bubba-Hank meant a lot to you, and if anything with the situation were to change, we would love to take him in. I didn't actually think anything was going to happen, but then I got a call from her a couple of weeks ago. She told me her mother had died, and the dog was too much responsibility for her. She wanted to know if we still wanted him."

Hope filled me. "He's not going back?"

"Nope. He's here to stay."

Digging my nose in his orangey-brown fur, I cried, "This is the best surprise you could've given me, Josh. I thought I was happy before, but having Bubba-Hank back? I feel complete now." I stood up and wrapped my arms around Josh as the dog circled us. "What took you so long to get back?"

"Well, the woman's daughter lives in Massachusetts. I had to go pick him up. There was an accident on 93 on the way back, so it took forever." Josh leaned in to kiss me. "I'm so glad it worked out."

Bubba-Hank settled into the spot on the couch next to Scottie as if he'd never left this house. I sat on the other side of him and rubbed between his ears for several minutes. Bubba-Hank's eyes slowly closed. Scottie didn't seem fazed one way or the other by the dog's presence. Josh sat across from us, seeming to derive immense pleasure from watching me get reacquainted with my precious pet.

The pile of mail I'd fetched earlier was sitting on the end table next to him.

"You got a notepad from the monks. You must've donated."

"Oh." He turned and picked up the envelope containing the notepad. He took it out and flipped through it. "Yeah. I figured I'd keep the tradition going."

"Anything in particular you're asking them to pray for?"

"I have a few things." He smiled but didn't elaborate. Then he stood and went to the kitchen. When he returned, he handed me a note as he passed by the couch.

A Thank You from The Trappist Monks of St. Francis:
You're killing me.

"What's this about?" I blinked. "Why am I killing you?"

He sat back down across from me, rubbing his hands together. His face was actually turning red.

What the hell is going on?

He pointed over to the dog. "I think Bubba-Hank wants a neck rub. You know, right under his collar. Why don't you give it to him?"

Squinting skeptically, I began to massage our goldendoodle's neck. The dog closed his eyes, seeming to be in heaven.

Then I got a closer look at the shiny ID tag hanging from his collar. I hadn't noticed what was actually *written* on it. Engraved on the tag was a message: *Will you marry us?*

My mouth fell open as I looked over at Josh. The next thing I knew, he was on his knees in front of me.

My hands shook. "I must be blind."

"I couldn't wait another second, Pumpkin. I walked in the house so damn nervous, and nearly an hour went by, and you still hadn't noticed it." He opened a small, red ring box, his hands shaking. "Carly, I know we talked about marriage and said it wasn't something we had to have, but I *want* you to be my wife. I *want* you to take my last name. Maybe I'm just selfish that way." He removed the ring from the box and held it out, taking a long, deep breath. "I lost my best friend when Brad died. He knew I needed a new best friend. I now believe that's why *he* sent me you. I'm so damn grateful every day for where life has taken me, but especially for what it's brought me." Josh slipped the ring onto my finger. "I hope you say yes."

My mouth hung open. I finally found the words. "Yes!" I wrapped my arms around him. "A million times, yes, Josh Mathers."

He squeezed me tightly, and I could feel his heart beating against mine. *Wow.* He was really nervous. When he let me go, he turned to Scottie. "We're getting married, buddy! Are you excited?"

Scottie stared at him blankly, then pressed the icon on his device. *"I want to take a bath."*

Josh slapped his leg playfully. "Thank you for sharing our joy, man." He turned back to me. "Do you like the ring? I was afraid maybe it was too unconventional."

"I love it," I answered, looking down at the ornate design. I'd never seen anything like it. The center stone was an elongated, hexagon-shaped diamond, flanked by two smaller diamonds of the same cut.

"It's different than the one Brad bought you," he said. "I didn't want to upstage that in any way. He gave you a big, round stone—centered and perfect, just like he was. This ring...well, I guess, it's probably not something you were expecting. More like me. Rough around the edges."

"That's exactly right. Unexpected and nothing I'd ever imagined—something I never knew I needed so badly. That's what you are, Josh. And that's why this ring is perfect." I looked up at him again. "I love it so much. And I love *you*. You've made me the happiest woman alive today."

"You swear on Bubba-Hank?"

I leaned over to hug our goofy dog. "I swear on Bubba-Hank."

Josh stood from his kneeling position, and Bubba-Hank immediately began humping his leg. Josh ignored him, still smiling down at me with a look of pure love in his eyes.

This man was the last person I'd ever dreamed would love me like this. How lucky was I to be loved by *two* great men in my lifetime?

"I thought my life was over when Brad died," I told him, rubbing his stubble. "I never saw you coming."

Josh winked. "Now you get to see me coming for the rest of your life."

I once heard a saying that family is the greatest wealth you will ever possess. Having no sense of family at the time, I didn't understand it. Sure, our family was unconventional. My future husband was once my sworn enemy. Our dog liked to hump him. And our baby weighed two-hundred pounds.

There's no white-picket fence or manicured lawn here. Nothing is perfect, and *everything* is chaotic. But there's a whole lot of love. And if family is the greatest wealth you could ever possess? Well, then I'm rich.

OTHER BOOKS BY *Penelope Ward*

Toe the Line

RoomHate

The Aristocrat

Moody

The Assignment

The Crush

The Anti-Boyfriend

Just One Year

The Day He Came Back

When August Ends

Love Online

Gentleman Nine

Drunk Dial

Mack Daddy

Stepbrother Dearest

Neighbor Dearest

Sins of Sevin

Jake Undone (Jake #1)

My Skylar (Jake #2)

Jake Understood (Jake #3)

Gemini

The Rules of Dating My Best Friend's Sister (Co-written with Vi Keeland)

The Rules of Dating (Co-written with Vi Keeland)

Well Played (Co-written with Vi Keeland)

Not Pretending Anymore (Co-written with Vi Keeland)

Park Avenue Player (Co-written with Vi Keeland)

Stuck-Up Suit (Co-written with Vi Keeland)

Cocky Bastard (Co-written with Vi Keeland)

Happily Letter After (Co-written with Vi Keeland)

My Favorite Souvenir (Co-written with Vi Keeland)

Dirty Letters (Co-written with Vi Keeland)

Hate Notes (Co-written with Vi Keeland)

Rebel Heir (Co-written with Vi Keeland)

Rebel Heart (Co-written with Vi Keeland)

Mister Moneybags (Co-written with Vi Keeland)

British Bedmate (Co-written with Vi Keeland)

Playboy Pilot (Co-written with Vi Keeland)

ACKNOWLEDGEMENTS

I HAVE TO start by thanking my beloved readers all over the world who continue to support and promote my books. Thank you for sticking with me on this journey and for allowing me to have this career. To all of the book bloggers and social media influencers who work tirelessly to support me book after book, please know how much I appreciate you.

To Vi – I'm so grateful that we continue to make magic together nearly a decade later. You're the best friend and partner in crime I could ask for. Here's to the next ten.

To Julie – The epitome of strength and resilience. Ten toes in the sand!

To Luna –Thank you for your love and support, day in and day out. I am grateful that you are always a message away when I need you and that I get to see you once a year.

To Erika – It will always be an E thing. I am so thankful for your love, humor and summer visits. Thank you for always brightening my days with your optimistic spirit.

To Cheri – Thanks for always looking out and for never forgetting a Wednesday. You know which scene in this book was written for you!

To Darlene – The best carrot cake maker in the world and an even better friend. Thank you for being so sweet to me.

To my Facebook reader group, Penelope's Peeps – I adore you all. You are my home and favorite place to be.

To my agent Kimberly Brower –Thank you for working hard to get my books into the hands of readers around the world.

To my editor Jessica Royer Ocken – It's always a pleasure working with you. I look forward to many more experiences to come.

To Elaine of Allusion Publishing – Thank you for being the best proofreader, formatter, and friend a girl could ask for.

To Julia Griffis of The Romance Bibliophile – Your eagle eye is amazing. Thank you for being so wonderful to work with.

To my assistant Brooke – Thank you for hard work in handling all of the things Vi and I can't seem to ever get to. We appreciate you so much!

To Kylie and Jo at Give Me Books – You guys are truly the best out there! Thank you for your tireless promotional work. I would be lost without you.

To Letitia Hasser of RBA Designs – My awesome cover designer. Thank you for always working with me until the finished product exactly perfect.

To my husband – Thank you for always taking on so much more than you should have to so that I am able to write. I love you so much.

To the best parents in the world – I'm so lucky to have you! Thank you for everything you have ever done for me and for always being there.

Last but not least, to my daughter and son – Mommy loves you. You are my motivation and inspiration!

ABOUT THE AUTHOR

PENELOPE WARD is a *New York Times, USA Today* and *#1 Wall Street Journal* bestselling author.

She grew up in Boston with five older brothers and spent most of her twenties as a television news anchor. Penelope resides in Rhode Island with her husband, son and beautiful daughter with autism.

With over two million books sold, she is a 21-time *New York Times* bestseller and the author of over twenty novels.

Penelope's books have been translated into over a dozen languages and can be found in bookstores around the world.

Subscribe to Penelope's newsletter here:
http://bit.ly/1X725rj

Made in the USA
Coppell, TX
25 September 2023